Margery Allingham was born in London in 1904, the daughter of two journalists. She was educated at the Perse School, Cambridge, and her first story, which she wrote at the age of 16, was published soon after she left school. She began her career by writing for pulp magazines and then decided to concentrate on thriller and detective fiction. In 1927 she married a journalist and artist, Philip Youngman Carter, upon whom her fictional character, Albert Campion, is said to be based. They spent much of their time in London and Essex where many of her novels are set and during the war years she became the local billeting officer and an Underground Resistance Liaison Agent. She wrote prolifically throughout this time, and when she died in 1966, she left behind a wealth of superb fiction, including *The Fashion in Shrouds* (1938), *Black Plumes* (1940), *Coroner's Pidgin* (1945) and *The Tiger in the Smoke* (1952).

JESSICA MANN is the author of *Deadlier than the Male* (1981), a study of crime writers, and of ten crime novels including *The Eighth Deadly Sin* (1976), *Funeral Sites* (1981) and *Grave Goods* (1984). She is a regular reviewer and broadcaster, is married to an archaeologist and lives in Cornwall.

ALSO BY MARGERY ALLINGHAM

Margery Allingham

TRAITOR'S PURSE

Introduced by Jessica Mann

J.M. Dent & Sons Ltd
London

First published in Great Britain by William Heinemann Ltd 1941
This paperback edition first published by J. M. Dent & Sons Ltd 1985
Text Copyright Margery Allingham 1941
Introduction © Jessica Mann 1985
Reissued 1992

Printed in Great Britain by
The Guernsey Press Co. Ltd., Guernsey, C.I.
J. M. Dent & Sons Ltd
91 Clapham High Street, London SW4 7TA

British Library Cataloguing in Publication Data is available

INTRODUCTION

Jessica Mann

Four years after the end of the Great War many people were experimenting with spiritualism in the hope of communicating with the dead. A group of girls at the Perse School in Cambridge were in the fashion when they tried out a ouija-board. Margery Allingham introduced her family to it as a game, and they found that, evening after evening, episodes of a dramatic story of smuggling and murder in seventeenth-century Essex were spelled out. The family seemed to believe that Margery was indeed a medium, and she thought so herself, being so frightened by the experience that she refused ever to have anything to do with spiritualism again. Later she accepted that her own adolescent fantasies had been the genesis of the story, and her career as the author of romantic adventure stories owed nothing to the occult; but she had written down that first tale, which was published soon after she left school. Later she was to disown the book, but she always retained the quality of extravagant fancy that had produced it. She created worlds of her own, based on the world her readers knew.

It is often said by those who are on the defensive about their preferred reading matter that light crime fiction will give future historians more evidence of how people in the twentieth century conducted their daily lives than any number of surveys or social histories. Where better to learn the significance of the cigar-cutter, the monogrammed handkerchief or the fragment of tweed found caught in a murder victim's clutch, than in the meticulous enquiries into their provenance made by a provincial police inspector or an amateur sleuth? Those timetables of the suspects' movements, those maps of the scene of the crime (morning room, library, boot cupboard), all full of details that were taken for granted when the books were written, and that almost need footnotes now if we are to understand them, are the truest evidence of what people took for granted in their daily lives, of what was normal and what an acute detective would realise was not. Most of the crime stories of the inter-war years are readable nowadays only by those who enjoy period pieces, but some can still be sold as if they were newly written. Many of the purchasers of paperback editions of Agatha Christie's or Dorothy L. Sayers' novels from station bookstalls must be unaware of the fact that the books were written half a century before. References to manners and mechanisms no longer in use presumably seem no more strange than the futuristic devices in, for example, a James Bond story: neither is part of the reader's daily experience; either is equally credible.

Almost alone among her contemporaries, Margery Allingham wrote books that could have no documentary function, except as evidence of that indefinable attribute, atmosphere. Admittedly, she set her books in her own times and in places she knew well, always writing about London or East Anglia, where she lived herself. Her talent for evoking places was so great that a first-time visitor to Essex who has read her books will feel an almost uncomfortable familiarity, as though recognising a place that has appeared in a dream. Her characters too, like the policemen Luke and Oates, the heroines Valentine Ferris or Gina Brande, the families like the Ivories in *Black Plumes*, remain in the memory like people one has briefly known well, as real as temporary friends made in hospital wards or on ship-board.

It is not lack of realism that prevents Margery Allingham's books from being evidence of life as it was lived; rather it is an abundance of realism, so that each place or person is too individual to be typical. This is not a writer (unlike others in this field) who assembled her cast from a list of characteristics suitable for a vicar, say, or a retired colonel, or who copied her country villages from a picture postcard. Margery Allingham was not interested in archetypes but in originals, and accuracy was always embellished in her work by fantasy.

Margery Allingham began to concentrate on thriller and detective fiction after several years of contributing action melodramas to pulp magazines. Many were original, others the rendering of the plots of silent films into five-thousand-word stories suitable for the printed page. This hard labour on the wilder shores of fiction unfettered her imagination. When she could write to please herself instead of an editor—she expressed the difference as being between right and left-handed writing—she remained interested in simple stories of action. She had once tried writing a 'straight' novel about human relationships but nobody would publish it, much to her own relief in later years. Like many crime novelists she was a very private, secretive person and had no wish to expose her own emotions or personality to her readers. She welcomed the protective covering that the mystery story conferred on its author. No reader would 'write to analyse his twisted ego or to sneer at his unformed philosophy.' The fact was that Margery Allingham believed unfashionably in romance, meaning the adventurous and the picturesque, and in the decade after the First World War when she began to write, romance seemed to have been buried for ever, along with the romantic young men, in the mud of Flanders. The only type of fiction in which the knight errant in modern guise, as Allingham once described the detective hero, was not out of place was the mystery novel.

Albert Campion was exactly that: the modern equivalent of Roland and Lancelot. On his first appearance (in *The Crime at Black Dudley*, 1929) he was a minor crook, described as 'a lunatic . . . quite inoffensive . . . just a silly ass'. In all subsequent appearances, he is 'the deputy adventurer', gradually maturing along with his creator, so that the silly young ass of the early 1930s graduates, twenty years later, into a reliable universal uncle. In marked contrast to that other silly young ass of the period, Lord Peter Wimsey, whose entry in *Who's Who* preceded his adventures, we know very little about Campion. It is implied that he is the younger son (disowned) of a noble, perhaps even royal family. His appearance is immaculate, his manners impeccable, and he wears a habitual expression of contented idiocy. He appealed to Margery Allingham and her contemporaries as 'a private joke figure, the zany or the goon, laughing inanely at danger'. He remains an enigma throughout his career, and it is only in *Traitor's Purse*, in which he is concussed for most of the book, that his thought processes are exposed.

Amanda Fitton, introduced in *Sweet Danger* (1933), reappears in *The Fashion In Shrouds* (1938) as Campion's ally. Margery Allingham explained later: 'The group-hero of the action story is a classic character. Don Quixote and Sancho Panza, Robinson Crusoe and Friday, D'Artagnan and his three friends, and even Holmes and Watson, combine to make single personalities in their tales of action. When Amanda reappeared . . . a sane and practical aspect of the leading character walked in to strengthen the book.' By its end, Campion and Amanda were engaged. But marrying off a series hero is a tricky business. Raymond Chandler, creator of the ultra-romantic Philip Marlowe, went so far as to say that a good detective never gets married. Dorothy L. Sayers and Ngaio Marsh each took several books to get their detectives to the altar, stumbling through long-drawn-out courtships, and Margery Allingham agonised over the problem. Early in the war she met Dorothy L. Sayers in a blacked-out train during an air-raid, and confided that she expected to have to knock Albert Campion on the head before he could be made to co-operate. In *Traitor's Purse* she did just that.

Campion's earliest appearances, without Amanda as lieutenant, had been in Buchanesque adventures, told in an allusive, feminine style. Later he graduates to purer detection, in *Police At The Funeral* (1931). Allingham was dismayed to find that her public did not like the change. Always a highly professional worker, she was irritated that her publishers were reticent about the diminished sales. 'Why will people take it for granted that I am sensitive about my work? I only want to send them what they can sell.' She decided to persevere with the detective form, but using more attractive characters than those in *Police At The Funeral* and with a more romantic atmosphere. That resolution resulted in some of her most successful work which included perceptive, amusing social comment along with the mystery plots. In successive books she gave sparkling pictures of the worlds of art, of publishing, of high fashion and of musical comedy. Campion does not appear in *Black Plumes* (1940) and by the time Allingham wished to write about him again the Second World War had started.

> It occurred to me then that if I was going to continue to escape into fiction from the real life which had so suddenly become a thriller itself I would have to find a new kind of [pattern]. So I hit on a pattern which I called Adult Adventure, which makes good reading for those who lead an active life since it depends on a single compelling idea which, if it comes off at all, has tremendous holding quality. In this sort of story, any killing is almost always incidental, and the mystery concerns the idea, which differs from those in juvenile adventures in that it has to be completely convincing to an adult mind.

The book was called *Traitor's Purse*, published in London in 1941, and two years later in New York as *The Sabotage Murder Mystery*.

It is impossible to write about the book without committing the unforgiveable sin in a critic of revealing the plot. These pages should only be read *after* finishing *Traitor's Purse*; for the main-spring of the plot, that single compelling idea, is one that was thought to be outrageously implausible by reviewers in 1940, but which turned out to be no stranger than real life. It became known after the war that there had been a detailed Nazi plan just as Margery Allingham had described, namely to destroy Britain's economy with artificial inflation engineered by flooding the country with forged bank notes. Later still it turned out that the British too had considered such a plan. Margery Allingham confessed, 'I am by nature an intuitive writer whose intellect trots along behind.' This time her intuition had been inspired.

Allingham knew the limitations of her intuitions. She never tried to portray those scenes in the offices of power that appear in most political thrillers. Whether their authors have personal experience of the affairs of state and describe what they know, like John Buchan, or whether they simply feel better able to invent them is not always clear, but it is noticeable that Margery Allingham did nothing of the kind. Perhaps it was to remedy that omission, to explain her hero's involvement in another way, that she included conventional murder mysteries in what would otherwise be purely political thrillers. It would be possible to analyse *Traitor's Purse* as the account of a murder's detection. It was probably a wise restraint on Margery Allingham's part. Intuition can go only so far, and she would have known nothing whatever about the inner workings of government. She had always lived among people who believed that the only reasonable way to earn a living was with the brush or the pen, and like most women crime writers' her life was protected and peaceful.

Margery Allingham was born in 1904, the daughter of Herbert Allingham, who edited and wrote for weekly newspapers, and of Emily Allingham who had been trained as a milliner but also became a prolific journalist. 'My mother wrote, my father wrote, all the weekend visitors wrote.' Very soon Margery wrote too. Her first published piece appeared in the *Christian Globe*, edited by her grandfather, when she was seven.

The Allinghams lived in Essex, and later in London. Margery went to boarding school in Cambridge, publishing that first book, with its apparently supernatural provenance, when she was eighteen. She then spent a few terms at drama school, but gave up any idea of the stage believing that neither her face nor her figure could compete in the professional theatre. Instead she began to earn her living writing for the pulp magazines, and married Philip Youngman Carter who was a journalist and etcher and, according to his friends, the model for Mr Campion. The Carters lived in London, with a holiday house in Essex, and later made the country their permanent home. They lived a productive and harmonious life about which neither could find much to say in their few autobiographical pieces.

At the beginning of the war the house in Essex was thought to be in the Front Line. It was under the flight path to London, and the area was often bombed. Margery was the billeting officer for refugees from London until Essex was declared a Defence Area and the evacuees moved somewhere safer. When forces were stationed locally to face the expected invasion, Margery Allingham accommodated five officers in her house and two hundred men under canvas on the cricket field. She was designated Underground Resistance Liaison Agent, and her husband became a soldier. Throughout all this she managed to finish *Black Plumes* and to write *Traitor's Purse*. Later in the war she wrote unsuccessful books of social history, but returned to mysteries in 1945. The next three books had ingenious plots, and are vivid evocations of that austere time. *Coroner's Pidgin* (1945) and *More Work for the Undertaker* (1948) are both excellent books, and *The Tiger in The Smoke* (1952) has been nominated by numerous critics as one of the best crime novels ever written. Margery Allingham wrote a book every three years until her death in 1966, when her husband completed the half-written *Cargo of Eagles*, and wrote two more Campion books under his own name. They lack her magic touch, even though he had shared in all her work, listening as she read every word aloud and commenting liberally. Her technique was laborious and perfectionist. 'I write every paragraph four times— once to get my memory down, once to put in everything I have left out, once to take out everything that seems unnecessary, and once to make the whole thing sound as though I had only just thought of it.'

A pastoral, industrious life, then, and one without any personal experience of the themes Margery Allingham chose to write about; it poses the question that applies to all women crime writers—how and why does their creative imagination centre on crime, of which they had no factual knowledge? Margery Allingham seems never to have met a criminal, nor even to have been interested in reading accounts of true crimes. She was in fact an unusually gentle and light-hearted woman, who could be described in print—however hyperbolically—by her widower as 'gay, generous and affectionate, and, I think, as near to being a saint as makes no matter'.

No doubt that was more pious than precise. It is hard to believe that Margery's conversation did not reflect the sardonic observation of oddities that is so marked a feature of her writing, and that makes her books memorable particularly when it is applied to the minor characters. Think, for example, of *Traitor's Purse*, with Mrs Ericson, the devoted woman who is so glad to be useful to Leo Aubrey that she unwittingly organises the greater part of his crime; Sir Henry Bull, 'the great British Public itself incarnate'; and Magersfontein Lugg, Campion's manservant, who understands amnesia and copes with it, but is still sentimentally hurt at not being recognised. This combination of ironic wit with action is what makes this book so satisfactory. It is in a form ideally suited to Allingham's talents. The Second World War changed her from a frivolous young woman who was uninterested in public affairs into a serious older one, who was to study religion, sorcery and witchcraft. She lost her cynicism, realising in 1939 that there were some things she thought worth dying for. *Traitor's Purse*, and the postwar mysteries, are novels in which events are precipitated by the characters of those who partake in them. *Traitor's Purse*, whose theme is the defeat of tyranny at more than one level, marks a turning-point in Allingham's work. Without reference to its predecessors or successors, it is an engaging and exciting thriller.

TRAITOR'S PURSE

I

The muttering was indistinct. It crept down the dark ward, forcing itself upon the man who lay in the patch of light at the far end of the vast room.

It was a pleasant muttering. It made a reassuring undercurrent below the worry, that terrifying anxiety which was thrusting icy fingers deep into his diaphragm.

He tried to concentrate on the muttering. Mercifully it was recognizable. There were two distinct voices and when he could catch them the words meant something. That was good. That was hopeful.

In a little while the words might start connecting and then, please God, he would learn something and this appalling fear would recede.

From where he lay he could just see a wedge of polished floor, a section of a neat empty bed, and a tall shrouded window, fading into complete darkness at the top where the shaded light over his own head was too faint to reach it. All these were entirely unfamiliar. He was not even sure that he was in a hospital. That was part of the whole situation. He knew what a hospital was; that was comforting. They were large grey buildings, made grimly gay by enormous posters announcing scarifying debts. The recollection of those placards cheered him up. He could still read; he was sure of that. Sometimes one couldn't. Sometimes on these occasions one could only recognize spoken words. That was an odd piece of information to remember now. His mind was clear enough as far as it went . . . as far as it went.

He concentrated on the muttering. It was a long way away. They must be just outside the farther door up there in the darkness. The woman was a nurse, of course. The discovery delighted him foolishly. He was getting on. At any moment now other obvious things must occur to him.

He had no idea who the man was, but his rumble was human and friendly. He settled himself to listen.

'I shan't question him myself, you know.' He heard the man's words with mild interest.

'I daresay not.' She sounded acid. 'It's very serious indeed. I wonder they left him alone with only us here. It's not very nice.'

'There's no need to worry about that, Miss.' The rumble was aggrieved. 'I'd like a quid for every one I've handled. He'll be quiet enough, you'll see. Probably he won't even remember what's happened – or he'll say he doesn't until he's seen a lawyer. They're like that nowadays, up to anything.'

The man in bed lay very still. The muttering had ceased to be so comforting. He forgot to be glad that it was coherent. He listened avidly.

'They'll hang him, I suppose?' said the nurse.

'Bound to, Miss.' The man was both apologetic and definite. 'It was one of us, you see, so there's no way of getting out of it. Once a man slugs an officer of police he's for it. It's a necessary precaution for the safety of the public,' he added, not without satisfaction. 'This chap had all that money on him, too. That'll take a bit of explaining on its own.'

'All I can say is it's very unpleasant.' The nurse crackled a little after she had spoken and the man in bed thought she was coming in. He closed his eyes and lay rigid. There were no footsteps, however, and presently she spoke again.

'It seems very strange here without any patients,' she said and laughed a little unnaturally, as if she recognized the ghostliness of the great empty wards. 'We're only a skeleton staff left behind to deal with emergencies like this. We're the one hospital in the town cleared for action in case of anything. All our regulars have been evacuated. I don't know how they're all getting on in the country, I'm sure.'

'My missus and the kids are in the country,' said the policeman unexpectedly. 'It keeps me short and she's lonely. . . .' His voice died away into a murmur of confidence and at the other end of the ward the man in bed opened his eyes again.

Slugging a policeman. He knew what that meant, whatever

condition his mind was in. That was pretty serious. It was so serious that it made him sweat.

He had had nightmares like that and he'd known policemen. Now he came to consider the matter it seemed to him that he had known policemen very well and had liked them.

What on earth had happened to him? The bobby outside had just said that he might not remember anything about it. Well, he didn't. He didn't remember anything about anything. That was the anxiety, or part of it. He did not remember anything at all. There was only that secret worry, that gnawing, fidgeting, terrifying anxiety, beyond any consideration of his personal safety; that awful half-recollected responsibility about fifteen. Fifteen. He had no idea what the figure signified. That part had gone completely. But it was both urgent and vital: he did know that. It towered over the rest of his difficulties, a great dim spirit of disaster.

Now, to add to everything else, he was going to be hanged for slugging a policeman. He might have slugged him too; that was the devil of it. Anyhow, there was that fool bobby talking to a nurse about it as if it were a foregone conclusion. They expected him to call in a solicitor, did they? A fine chance he had of helping any solicitor to make a case, he who didn't even know his own name!

Moved by indignation and the odd singleness of purpose symptomatic of his condition, he got out of bed.

He moved very quickly and naturally, still partly wrapped in the shrouding comfort of semi-consciousness, and therefore made no noise at all.

He chose the nearest door, since even he recognized the prudence of avoiding the mutterers, and his bare feet were silent on the tiles of the passage. It was a wide corridor, clean and yet ill lit because the bulbs were shaded heavily and cast separate circles of light on the gleaming floor.

It was in one of these circles that he saw the hairpin. He stooped to pick it up mechanically and the wave of dull pain which swept over him as he bent down frightened him. This was a fine kettle of fish. What was going to happen now? He was going to pass out, he supposed, and be dragged back

3

and hanged for slugging a policeman. God Almighty, what a position!

The tiles, striking cold on his bare soles, pulled him together a little and he became aware for the first time that he was undressed and the coarse hospital pyjamas were his only covering.

He glanced at the row of shining doors on his left. At any moment one of these might open and the Authority emerge. It would be a dreadful supercilious Authority, too, properly clothed and antipathetic.

It was a real nightmare. This idea seemed feasible and he seized on it gratefully. The conviction relieved him of a great deal of worry. For one thing, it did not matter so much that his brain was so unreliable.

All the same, even in dreams certain problems are urgent and it was obvious that some sort of clothes were imperative if he were to have a dog's chance with the lurking Authority behind those shining doors.

He glanced round him anxiously. The walls were as bare as an empty plate save for the fire-buckets, and the alcove beneath that crimson row escaped him until he was upon it, and then the glimpse of the red-rimmed glass case within jerked him to a standstill. He stood before the cupboard transfixed. There was the usual paraphernalia inside. A black oilskin coat hung at the back and the toes of a pair of thigh-boots showed just beneath it, while the hose was draped round the ensemble in neat heraldic festoons.

The man in pyjamas ignored the invitation printed on the enamelled plate requiring him to break the glass. Instead he concentrated on the keyhole in the smooth red wood. When he lifted his hand to touch it he rediscovered the hairpin and a warmth of satisfaction spread over him. So it was one of those merciful dreams in which things came out all right – that was it, if it worked.

He had no time to speculate on his own somewhat peculiar accomplishments. The bent wire flicked over the lock easily, as if it had done it a hundred times. The absence of oilskin trousers bothered him, but the boots were tremendous. They

4

came well up over his thighs and the coat had a belt which took off and could be slipped through the boot-loops. The sou'wester cap which fell out of the ensemble struck him as amusing, but he put it on and buttoned the coat up to his throat with deep relief.

Any incongruity in the costume did not occur to him. He was still moving with the simple directness of emergency. There was danger behind him and something tremendously important ahead. He was going away from the one and approaching the other. It appeared both sensible and elementary.

The row of doors still remained closed. There was no sound anywhere and no draught. The corridor was blank and quiet, but all the same it breathed. It was alive. He had no illusions about that. Wherever he was, whoever he was, drunk, mental, or dreaming, he was still wide enough to be able to tell a live building from an empty one. There were people about all right.

The door of the case imperfectly closed swung open again and startled him as it touched him. That was no good. That would give him away at once. If that crackling nurse put her head out of the ward that would be the first thing her pince-nez would light on. He thrust it back into its place, using far more force than he had intended. The thin glass splintered easily. The gentle clatter it made on the tiles was almost musical, but the automatic bell, which he had failed to notice above the case, was a different matter.

It screamed at him, sending every nerve in his body tingling to the roots of his hair. It bellowed. It raved. It shrieked, tremblingly hysterical in the night, and from every side, above him, and beneath him, other bells echoed it in a monstrous cacophony of alarum.

II

The building was alive all right. His sense had not deserted him. Doors swung open, rushing feet swept down on him, cries, sharp demands for information, raised anxious voices, they whirled round his head like bees from an overturned hive.

He ran for it, with his oilskin coat flapping and scraping round his hampered limbs. He passed the lift cages and sped on to the staircase. As he reached the second landing he collided with an elderly man in a white coat, who caught his sleeve.

'Can't wait, sir.' The words escaped him as he wrenched himself free. 'Look after your patients,' he shouted as an after-thought as he took to the next flight.

Meanwhile the blessed bells continued. Their shrill clamour was inspiring. If only they kept it up until he made the ground.

He arrived in the main entrance hall sooner than he expected. Here too there was wild excitement. Someone had lowered most of the lights so that the large double doors could be thrown open, and a porter was exhorting everyone in sergeant-major tones to go quietly.

The man in the oilskins plunged across the tiled floor, guided instinctively by the nearest blast of cold air. A nurse stepped aside for him and a doctor touched his shoulder.

'Where is it, fireman?'

'Round the back. No danger. Keep them quiet. No danger at all.' He succeeded in sounding wonderfully authoritative, he noticed. He had almost reached the threshold of the emergency doors when a girl slipped in front of him. As he dodged round her she spoke quietly.

'Is it by the gate?' she inquired idiotically.

He glanced at her over his shoulder and received a momentary impression of a heart-shaped face and disconcertingly intelligent brown eyes.

'The fire's at the back, Miss. Nothing serious,' he said briefly and passed on.

6

It was a completely meaningless encounter and the girl might well have been half-witted for all he knew, but she left an uncomfortable doubt in his mind and he dived out into the darkness eagerly.

It was not a pitch-black night. There was a moon behind the thin coverlet of clouds and, as soon as his eyes became accustomed to the change, the shadowy greyness of the darkened town became fairly negotiable.

The scene meant nothing to him. He was in a large semi-circular drive in which a dozen cars were parked, while beyond roofs and spires rose up in velvet silhouette against the lighter sky.

He took the nearest car. It seemed the wisest thing to do at the time, although he had some difficulty in managing the controls, hampered as he was by the mighty boots. Still, the little runabout started and he took her gently down the slope to the open gates. He turned east when he reached the high road, mainly because it seemed more likely to be lucky than the other direction, and, treading hard on the accelerator, he rattled down the dim ribbon of asphalt which was just visible in front of his single hooded headlight.

He had picked a terrible car. The discovery was particularly disconcerting because he fancied he was in the habit of driving something different altogether. Not only was this uncomfortable little machine cramped, but the steering was alarming, with a full turn play on the wheel at least, while somewhere behind him a suggestive clanking was growing noticeably louder.

The road, which was broad and lined with dim houses set back behind overgrown shrubberies, was quite new to him. It might have been any road in England for all he knew. There was no traffic and no street lamps. He drove anxiously, coaxing the unresponsive machine to further effort. Now it was a real nightmare, the familiar kind, in which one struggles down a dark tunnel with terror behind one and feet which become more and more leaden at every step.

He had travelled half a mile or so before he met another vehicle and it was with relief that he saw a pair of darkened sidelights swaying down the road towards him. They turned out to belong to a bus. The interior was darkened, but as it came up with him he caught a glimpse of the dim number over the cab. It was a 15. The sight jolted him and for an instant recollection rushed at him in a great warm sweep of bright colours, only to recede again, leaving him desperate. Something was frighteningly urgent and important. There was something he had to do instantly and the responsibility concerned was tremendous.

For a moment he had had it almost within his brain's grasp and yet now it was all gone again, all lost. What he did know was bad enough, he recollected with something of a shock. The police were after him, apparently for murder. The clanking at the back of the car ceased to be ominous and became downright sinister. At any moment now the big-end must go and he would find himself stranded in the suburbs of an unknown town where his present costume would damn him the instant he was seen.

It was at this point that he became aware of the car behind. There was no way of telling its size or make, for its single eye was as dim and downcast as his own. He pulled in a little to allow it to pass, but the driver behind made no attempt to overtake and appeared to be content to keep at a distance of twenty-five yards or so. This was definitely alarming.

He estimated that he was doing a little over forty miles an hour at the outside, although from the way his machine was heaving and rolling her speed might well have been nearer three figures. Cautiously he slackened speed a trifle. The car behind slowed also and at the same time the death-rattle in his own back axle increased noticeably.

A smile of pure amusement twisted the mouth of the thin man in the oilskins. This was so disastrous that it was ridiculous. This was attempted cat burglary on roller-skates. The odds against him were immeasurably too great. He had no chance even to run for it in these colossal boots.

A side turning yawning in the darkness on his left decided him and he swung round into it for a final spurt. The driver behind him overshot the corner and a flicker of hope flashed

8

through his mind, but before he had reached the next road junction the following car was back on his tail again.

The open country took him by surprise. The hospital must have been nearer the outskirts of the town than he had imagined. It was coming now, he supposed as he drove down a tunnel of bare trees into the lonely darkness beyond. They must make their arrest at any moment now, and he prepared himself for them to shoot past him and stop. But meanwhile there seemed no point in pulling up himself and he continued on through deeply wooded country with his silent attendant just behind him.

As the minutes passed his resignation gave place to nervous irritation and he drove squarely in the middle of the road. Whenever a convenient turning presented itself he took it, but always his companion followed him. If he eluded the car for a moment or so by some adroit piece of driving, invariably it put on speed and caught up with him again.

He seemed to travel for hours, even weeks. It was bitterly cold and his mind, which was in darkness save for the one single pinpoint of illumination which was the immediate present, appeared to him for the first time as a machine independent of himself and about as unsatisfactory as the car he drove.

The dreadful thudding between the back wheels was now deafening. His speed had slackened considerably also and the engine was missing on at least one cylinder. A sudden dip in the road was his undoing. He hit the watersplash at the bottom without seeing it and a wall of spray rose up over him, rushed in through the radiator and obscured the windscreen. The engine coughed apologetically and died.

He sat where he was. After the crashing of the big-end the silence was sweet but uncanny. He waited. Nothing happened.

The clouds had cleared a little and in the moonlight he could see on either side of him low hedges, and beyond, the dark spikes of an osier bed. There was not a breath of wind, not a rustle. It was as still and cold as the bottom of the sea.

He turned his head cautiously and peered through the rear window. The other car was in its familiar place, a few yards behind him. It too was stationary and there was no telling who sat behind that single downcast headlamp. Then, as he watched it, the car began to move. Very slowly it crawled down the road behind him, turned its long sleek body gently to one side, and, entering the water so quietly that there was hardly a ripple, it came up close to him so that the driving seat was on a level with his own.

III

The side windows of the two cars slid down simultaneously and the man in the fireman's coat braced himself to meet whatever was coming.

'Would you care for a lift by any chance?'

The question, put with a certain grave politeness, came quietly out of the darkness in a clear young voice which might have belonged to some nice child.

'Do you know where we are? We're relying on you. I hope you realize that.'

The second voice, which was elderly and querulous besides being practically in his ear, startled half the life out of him, it was so close.

'Driving at night is difficult at the best of times,' it rambled on hollowly, 'and night comes so early this time of year. I must have hunted over this country as a young man, but that's many years ago. Many. I don't know what road we're on at all.'

After a moment's incredulous silence the explanation of this apparent hallucination occurred to the fugitive with a second shock. Whoever these good people were they either knew him or his car very well indeed. He replied cautiously, relying on his voice to identify him or not as the case might be.

'I'm afraid this car has died,' he said clearly and waited for their reaction.

'With a beautiful smile on its bonnet, no doubt.' The young voice sounded gently reproachful. 'Do you mind getting in the back? Mr Anscombe is in the front with me. We shall all be rather late for dinner, I'm afraid, and I've phoned Lee once. Leave George's car where it is.'

The man who could not remember pricked up his ears. There had been definitely a warning emphasis on the Christian name.

'Our George has a depraved taste in machinery,' he remarked tentatively as he clambered out of the farther door and came

11

round to the back of the second car. When he entered the warm darkness of the limousine the girl gave him the hint for which he had asked.

'It's not George's taste, poor child. It's his pocket,' she said firmly. 'Er – all undergraduates are a little trusting when confronted by a second-hand car salesman, aren't they? Still, it is very nice of him to lend it to you. I'm so sorry I missed you. I was waiting in the vestibule and only caught a glimpse of you as you shot through and you'd started off in George's car before I could catch you. '

She let in the clutch as she spoke and they moved away into the darkness.

'I'm sorry, too. Very silly of me,' murmured the man in the oilskins. He was feeling his way very cautiously. Clearly they were on dangerous ground and now was not the time for explanations. Whoever this blessed girl was she was certainly helpful and appeared to rely on him to play up to her.

He leant back among the cushions and strained his eyes in the darkness. Gradually he made out the two silhouettes against the windscreen. The girl was small but erect and the line of her shoulders was square, like a boy's. Of course! She was the young woman with the heart-shaped face and the disconcertingly intelligent light brown eyes who had spoken to him in the hospital vestibule. She must have been trying to tell him that this car was by the gate. No wonder she was treating him now as if he were mentally deficient. So he was, God help him. So he was.

The man who sat beside her was less definite in outline. He appeared to be a spreading bundle with a large head adorned by a flat cap which sat upon it like a lid. He turned presently and leant over the back.

'Rather a disturbing adventure,' he remarked conversationally. His windy voice was old and foolish but it was also dangerously inquisitive.

The man in the back of the car hesitated.

'It was, in a way,' he said at last.

'I know. I know.' The old man was determined to talk,

whatever the effort. 'Still, you did your duty. There's a great comfort in that. Probably the only thanks you'll get out of it. A Good Samaritan. . . .'

'Is his own reward,' supplied the girl without moving her head. 'All the same,' she went on carefully, 'I don't see what else you could have done. After all, if a stranger is polite enough to talk to one in a railway carriage and nutty enough to fall over one's bag and stun himself in getting out the least one can do is to take him to hospital.'

'I can think of less,' said the old man, grunting into his muffler. 'Can't you, Campion?'

'Yes, yes, I can.' The man in the back of the car was not thinking what he was saying. Campion. He seized on the name eagerly and tried to think that it was familiar. At first he was convinced that it was, and relief rushed over him. But the next moment he was not sure again and despair returned. It was an unnerving experience and he felt for a cigarette.

Finding that he had no pockets, he leant forward automatically and discovered in the dark a packet and a lighter tucked into the case at the back of the front seat. He was actually smoking before he realized the significance of his behaviour. He must have known the cigarettes were there. He had taken one as naturally as if he had done it a hundred times before. The explanation was obvious. He had. He was in his own car.

He lay back to think it over. His head was abominably sore but his mind was clear. It was only his memory which had deserted him and, if he could not remember, at least he could put together what facts he had.

The one clear conclusion to be drawn from present developments, he decided, was that he and the girl were up to something – or at least she certainly was. She was protecting him the whole time, feeding him with story after story and doing it very well, almost as though she were used to it. Perhaps she was.

The conviction that she was his wife came slowly. The more

13

he thought of it the more likely it became. Here she was, driving his car, looking after him like a mother, lying for him like a heroine. George's car indeed! For the first time since he had recovered consciousness in the hospital ward he saw a ray of comfort in his prospect. The abysmal loneliness of his position was spanned. Apart from his tremendous relief he was also suddenly delighted and he peered at her again in the darkness.

She drove very well, with confidence and with an unusual sympathy for the machine. He appreciated that. So many people approached the petrol engine as if it were something vindictive, to be mastered with daring and a firm hand. He liked her voice too. It was clear and well bred, without being affected, and it was also engagingly immature. Her face he could only just remember from his brief glimpse of her in the entrance hall of the hospital, but he liked the carriage of her head and the courage and dignity in those small square shoulders.

His spirits rose. If she were his wife he was all right. It had gone through his mind once or twice that he might be a crook of some sort. The notion had so depressed him that he was inclined to discount it as unlikely on those very grounds. But he had opened the fire cupboard with the hairpin and there had been that mysterious remark about money made by the bobby to the nurse. Why should it have looked odd when he had been found with a lot of money on him? Why should the authorities have taken it for granted that he had slugged a policeman? Had anyone seen him do it? Had he done it? He did not feel a particularly violent man. What sort of person was he, anyway?

The final question pulled him up with a start. He had no idea. Physically he appeared to be fairly tall and he was thin. He had plenty of hair and his teeth were his own. Without a mirror he could tell no more.

His impression of the girl was that she was young, perhaps very young, and he considered the question of his own age thoughtfully. He was fit and, apart from a natural shakiness after his experience, which, whatever it had been, had left him

14

with aching limbs and a reeling head, he felt fairly athletic. He wondered. He was clearly not a boy but, on the other hand, surely he was not old? Finally he plumped for twenty-nine. It was a nice age anyhow and he felt no more.

He began to feel better, almost adventurous. The big car was brushing aside the miles and he had half persuaded himself that the police-slugging episode was part of some past delirium when the elderly man stirred himself.

'I see where we are now,' he said contentedly. 'We must have come fifteen miles out of our way.' He broke off abruptly and laughed, the silly little high-pitched giggle of a foolish old man. 'I mean five miles, of course,' he added clumsily. 'I don't know what made me say fifteen.'

The man who had been told that his name was Campion glanced up sharply in the darkness and the shadowy tide of anxiety rolled up into his mind once more.

'It's not far now, anyway.' The girl's cool voice was comfortingly matter-of-fact. 'If you don't mind, Mr Anscombe, we'll put you down at your house and rush on to change. Aubrey has put the meal back to eight-thirty and we can't in all decency be late. We'll see you there, shan't we?'

'Yes, yes, I shall be there.' The old man sounded enthusiastic. 'I never miss an opportunity to dine at the Institute now that Aubrey is the skipper. I remember his predecessor, the great Doctor Hale. He was an able fellow but nothing like Aubrey. Lee Aubrey is one of the big men of our time.'

'Yes,' said the girl thoughtfully. 'Yes, I think he may be. He's not afraid to surround himself with brains.'

Anscombe grunted. 'A particularly brilliant man on his own account,' he announced didactically. 'We were more than lucky to get him here at Bridge. I remember the famous session when his appointment was announced to the Secret Conclave. As Hereditary Secretary to the Society I was very much congratulated, but I said "Don't thank me, Masters of Bridge" – that's the customary address, you know – "Don't thank me. Thank the man himself for coming to us."'

He settled himself in his seat and sighed. It was clear to Campion that he was talking of matters very near his heart.

Pride and more than a touch of pomposity glowed from him.

Anscombe? The name meant nothing to Campion. But Bridge, and the Institute, struck a vaguely familiar note. He fancied that they were well-known terms, something he had heard about all his life.

Presently the old man spoke again.

'Aubrey is a wealthy man too, you know,' he said. 'It's not generally known, but he donates the whole of his two thousand pound salary to some scholarship fund in the north. His private income must be considerable. Still, it suits him, you know. He has a unique position which no money in the world could buy, and a house which is virtually a museum-piece, also not for purchase. You're comfortable there, aren't you?'

'Very. It's a glorious house, isn't it, Albert?'

It took Campion some seconds to realize that she was talking to him, but his response, when it did come, was manfully enthusiastic.

Mr Anscombe turned in his seat.

'You're tired,' he said. 'That experience of yours took it out of you. That sort of thing often does. London is exhausting, too. What are you wearing? A mackintosh? I can hear something rustling but I can't see you. It's very warm in here. Why don't you take it off?'

'No. I don't think I will, thanks.' To his horror he heard himself beginning to laugh, but again the girl came to his rescue.

'Leave him alone,' she said. 'He's in disgrace. He's taken the wrong car, led us miles out of our way, and now he dozes off smelling like a bicycle shop. You'll have to give up oilskins, Albert, at any rate for wear in a confined space. Still, we're practically there. This is your gate, isn't it, Mr Anscombe? You wouldn't think it awfully rude of us if we didn't take the car into the drive, would you?'

'Oh, of course not, of course not. I'm late myself. Thank you very much for all your kindness. I feel I forced myself on you this afternoon, but you've been so very good, so very good.'

He was hoisting himself out of the low seat with difficulty

as he spoke and his hollow foolish voice squeaked and trailed away as he landed himself safely on the pavement and closed the door. Through the window the remaining passenger caught a glimpse of him disappearing between high stucco pillars towards a steep dark house beyond.

'Silly little man,' said the girl suddenly. 'He's left his parcel. I shan't be a moment. I'll take it to him.'

'That's all right. I'll do that,' Campion said hastily, fumbling for the door handle.

'You can't in those clothes.'

'Yes, I can. He won't see me. Or if he does he'll have to realize I'm an eccentric. Where's his baggage?'

She turned towards him in the darkness.

'It's books, I think,' she said. 'Here you are.'

He took the square parcel and staggered out after the departing figure. It was brighter than he thought and he did not call to the man but came up the small drive quietly. The front door was already closed when he found it, and, rather than knock, he laid the package on the step and hurried down the drive to the waiting car again.

With the departure of Anscombe the very car seemed more comfortable. The girl let in the clutch softly and they slid away. The man, who was still trying to remember if his name really was Albert Campion, leant forward. Now that he was alone with this delightful if unrecognizable wife of his he felt unexpectedly embarrassed about coming to the vital point. She was having such an extraordinary effect on him. He was so very glad of her, so childishly content and happy to find her. He wished to God that she would take his head on her heart and let him go to sleep. It was ridiculous to have to ask her to tell him her name.

'It's all very difficult,' he began awkwardly.

'I know.' Her agreement was so heartfelt that it silenced him. 'It's frightful, and there's absolutely no time to talk and get it straight. We're here already and we daren't be late, it'll look so fishy.'

She swung the car up a steep incline and through a columned gateway as she spoke.

'I only found out where you were by a miracle. I'd been waiting down at the station as we arranged. I got rid of Anscombe until four o'clock, but after that I had to carry him round with me, telling him one dubious tale after another. I had to bring him because he insisted. He said he had to see his dentist and he asked Lee Aubrey if I'd give him a lift. Lee made a personal request of it and I couldn't refuse without sounding suspicious. So there he was.'

The car had not stopped. As far as Campion could see they were rolling through some sort of park. The girl was still talking. She was nervous and a little breathless.

'He's a terrifying old boy, isn't he?' she demanded. 'Flat mental deficiency for ninety-nine per cent of the time and single flashes of acuteness. You don't know whether it's silver showing through the disguising tarnish or the last few flecks of plate on the old tin spoon. Our only hope is to get down to the meal and behave normally. Have you got anything under that decontamination outfit? Can we leave it in the car?'

'It all depends where we're going,' he said. 'I'm in pyjamas . . . awful grey flannel things.'

'What?' She stopped the car in her astonishment and turned to him. 'What happened? You're not hurt?'

'Oh lord no,' he said, warmed by her anxiety. 'I'm all right really. I only got knocked out.'

'Oh that was it, was it?' she said, much more relieved than he had expected her to be and far less surprised. 'The man in the paper shop simply whispered "hospital". I didn't get an opportunity to talk to him at all. The place was full of people and there wasn't time. It was nearly five then and I had the wretched Anscombe inside. That old man knows something, I swear it.'

'More than I do,' said Campion grimly.

To his surprise she caught him up. 'Yes,' she said. 'That's what I thought. We'll bear him in mind. I say, I am glad you're all right. It never went through my mind that you might have gone to the hospital as a patient. When I saw you charging out in the deep-sea-diver costume I thought some kind friend had lent it to you to hide the tramp's garbage.

I've got your change in the luggage hatch. That's what was worrying me so when you didn't turn up before Anscombe returned. I didn't see how I was going to get it to you before he saw you. Well, it's silly to change now, isn't it? You'll have to smuggle yourself in.'

The man laughed. She was charming and he was very tired.

'Anything you say, lady,' he said. 'Where do we go?'

'I think that side door,' she said, 'don't you? The one that leads up out of the yard where we leave the car. I know it's bad form for house guests to use the back stairs, but we'll just have to look badly brought up if we're seen. You could always shout "Fire!" again of course, but that might not help in the long run.'

He sat watching her silhouette as she manœuvred the big car skilfully into a narrow entrance by the side of a large dim building. She was an astonishing young person, as practical and energetic as a child and utterly without affectation. He thought her voice was the coolest and most comforting sound he had ever heard.

She parked the car and he climbed out, still and unsteady, into a neat old-fashioned stableyard with cobbles under his feet and the low graceful lines of Georgian outbuildings just visible in the faint light. By the time he emerged she had already opened the luggage hatch and was tugging at a suitcase within.

He took it from her and would have put his free arm round her shoulders, but she did not notice his gesture and it occurred to him that he did not usually exhibit such open affection. He was wondering a little at himself when she called him from the house.

'Come on, Albert. It's awfully late.'

He found her waiting for him in a dark arched doorway. 'Two steps up,' she said. 'Come on. It's got a black-out gadget which turns out the light when you open the door.'

As the wood closed softly behind him the small passage in which they stood lit up and in a soft yellow glow the comfortable flagged and panelled interior of a perfect Georgian house emerged. A baize door opposite him clearly cut off the reception half of the establishment and a narrow flight of oak stairs on their left led to a similar door on the first floor. The girl made for this upper door and as she ran up the staircase he suddenly saw her and recognized her, the first real and familiar thing to emerge in the terrifying darkness of his mind. Her thin young back under the perfectly cut brown tweed of her suit, her red curls, and her small brown hand on the banister were all suddenly well known and inexpressibly dear to him.

'Amanda!' he said.

'Yes?' She swung round on the top of the stairs and stood looking down at him, a picture of arrested movement, her light brown eyes questioning and every line of her heart-shaped face alive and young.

He laughed and came hurrying up the stairs after her.

'I only wanted to hear you answer to your name.'

The smile faded from her face and he thought she looked a trifle embarrassed.

'I'm not really rattled,' she murmured unexpectedly and as if he had reproached her. 'It's only that it's all so horribly important and imminent. You've come back all carefree. Did something good happen?'

'No, I'm rather afraid it didn't. This is light-headedness,' he said, and followed her through the second baize door into a small world of past elegance.

Amanda crossed the upper hall, where stripped pine panelling, Chinese carpet, and sage-green drapery made a Georgian setting without either the stuffiness or the full-blooded ostentation of that great period of nouveaux-riches, and opened a door under an archway.

'Yes, they've put your things out, thank God,' she said, peering across another expanse of carpet. 'Lee has got the servant problem taped, hasn't he? It's the combination of love *and* money, you know. They not only adore him but he pays them the earth. You get dressed and so will I. I'll give you ten minutes. We can't wash much: that's all there is to it. Then I'll come back. I must see you before we go down. Bless you.'

She was gone before he could stop her, whisking into a

room on the other side of the hall while her vivid friendly personality still warmed and comforted him like the glow of a coal fire.

Albert Campion went into the room that presumably was his own and looked at the dinner-jacket laid out neatly on his bed. The tailor's tab inside the breast pocket assured him that it was his and that he had bought it in the preceding spring. Now that he had been on his feet for some little time his weakness had become more apparent and, with the departure of Amanda, his earlier lost feeling returned. He began to dress carefully, moving slowly and with a certain amount of difficulty. After a minute or so he gave up trying to fathom any further deeper mysteries than those concerning the whereabouts of his underclothes and washing tackle. He had to hurry. Amanda was coming back in ten minutes and that was time enough to get all the serious questions settled. He clung to the thought of Amanda. As his wife she was the one satisfactory, friendly truth in a world of villainous fantasy.

Meanwhile the obvious thing to do was to get himself safely changed.

He accepted his reflection in the shaving mirror discovered in the adjoining bathroom without seeing it, as do most men every morning of their lives. His self-searching mood had disappeared and his sole anxiety was to get his chin smooth. The cool comfort of well-fitting clothes soothed him and he had tied his tie and was getting into his jacket when a knock sounded on the door. He sprang to open it with an eagerness which wrenched his stiff body unmercifully, and stepped back in blank disappointment an instant later. It was not Amanda, but a dinner-jacketed stranger who smiled at him familiarly and wandered into the room.

'My dear chap, I'm so glad you've got back,' he said, revealing a voice several tones deeper than the average, and so flexible that its charm was instantaneous. 'Trouble all cleared up?'

Campion nodded without speaking. Even if some flicker of memory had not struggled to help him, he would have known the newcomer was his host as soon as he set eyes on him. The tall, big-boned figure, with its suggestion of elegant negligence, was impressive and went with the house. He recognized the type, or rather the species of original spirit, immediately.

Lee Aubrey was a personality; that is to say he exuded a force and a spiritual flavour as actual as if it had been warmth, or a small electric current. His big head was extravagantly moulded, the features fine but large and overdrawn, and his smiling eyes were kindly rather than friendly. The most striking thing about him was that he could not, apparently much to his regret, provide any stretch of common ground on which to walk with normal men. There was no suggestion of equality in his bearing but rather an exaggerated humility, as if he were in the habit of going down on mental all-fours to conduct any simple conversation. Now, as he stood lounging awkwardly against the mantelpiece, he was laughing a little, indulgently ashamed of himself for his clumsy efforts to relax.

'I was rather glad to put food off for half an hour,' he said. 'Fyshe from the War House has been down. Extraordinarily inferior mind. A decent chap. Quite sound, of course, but thunderingly dull. It took Butcher all day to tell him what he wanted to know, while any intelligent undergraduate could have mastered the thing in a couple of hours. It's absurd, isn't it?'

He laughed again, half apologetically, for making the criticism.

'Absurd,' said Campion.

It was coming back to him, or some of it was. This was the Principal's House in the Bridge Institute of General Research, that remarkable and ancient institution which, from being a provincial curiosity, part charity and part museum for a hundred and fifty years, had blossomed forth in the early part of the century into one of the most valuable centres in the country. The recollection came as Amanda's name had come; not as a raising of the curtain of darkness which hung between the front and the back of his mind, but as a sudden rent in it which flashed a whole scene from the brightness

22

within, only to close again a moment later as the folds resettled. It was all very confusing and alarming.

Lee Aubrey was looking at him intently.

'You're most frightfully tired,' he said gently. 'Or is something wrong?'

'No, no, I'm all right.' Campion was surprised at his own vehemence, but it seemed desperately important to keep his secret.

'Oh that – that's fine.' The other man was as hurt as a child. 'Won't you come down? By the way, did you get your letters? There were two or three for you this morning. John should have brought them up here. He's probably left them in my study. I'll get them for you myself. Shall we go?'

He was lounging towards the door, self-conscious and uncomfortably gauche like an adolescent.

'No, I can't for a moment. I'm waiting for Amanda. We've got to talk to each other.'

Even in his confused state the words appeared a little bald to Mr Campion. Aubrey swung round and his eyes were suddenly sharp and frighteningly intelligent.

'Oh, I see,' he said and immediately he became deeply if consciously kind again. 'I see. I'll go down and hold the fort until you come.'

He went out gently, and, it seemed to Mr Campion, with compassion.

Left alone, the man in the bedroom returned to his earlier problems. He thrust the firefighting kit into the bottom of a wardrobe and was about to close the door on it when a sound behind made him turn. It was Amanda. She was there just as he had expected her, in a long smooth white dress which seemed right and familiar and made her look about sixteen. She was wonderfully easy to look at. That discovery struck him as new and surprising and he felt irritated with himself that it should be so.

'Oh, that's grand,' she said, nodding at him approvingly. 'I was so afraid you might potter a bit, as you usually do. What are you up to? Admiring yourself?'

He glanced behind him and saw the point of her remark.

23

The door of the armoire had swung open, revealing a dressing mirror within.

'No,' he said and paused abruptly. He had just caught sight of himself with her standing beside him. He was older than he had thought. He saw a horrified man of thirty-five or so, tall and remarkably thin, with a lean wooden face on which there were far more lines than he had expected. She, on the other hand, might have been still at school.

'You look much more intelligent than usual,' she remarked. 'Don't you think so?'

'God help me, do I?' he said involuntarily. 'I am rather shocked, as a matter of fact.'

He saw the amusement die out of her face.

'That's not fair,' she said unhelpfully.

'What isn't?' he said, turning to her and catching her hands.

To his surprise her embarrassment increased and she released herself slowly and stood before him, a steady determined young person, serious and annihilatingly frank.

'Albert,' she said, 'I know this isn't the time, and that all this business going on is far more serious at the moment, but I've got this on my mind and I want to clear it up. You know you were going to marry me next month?'

The information, coupled with the ominous form in which it was offered, appalled him. His disappointment and loneliness was so acute that it produced a physical chill and he stood looking at her without realizing that his face was a complete blank.

'Was I?' he said flatly.

She did not speak and he had the dreadful impression that he had struck her, or had behaved in some other disgraceful way quite out of character with himself or her.

She drew back from him and for a moment he felt panic-stricken that she was going to walk out and leave him.

'Don't,' he said wildly. 'I didn't mean that, Amanda. I'm completely at sea. I don't know where I am or who I am or what I'm doing.'

'Oh I know.' She was herself again, impulsive and warm

24

and friendly. 'I know and I'll see you through this. You can rely on me absolutely all the time. That is true. You do know that?'

She thrust her arm through his and he felt the urgent, nervous strength of her young body against his side.

'I'll do anything, Albert. This is desperate, the most important, the most serious business you've ever come up against, and I'm with you. I wouldn't be here if I wasn't. It's disgusting of me to talk about the marriage when you're nearly off your head with worry about the other thing, but you know how hopeless I am about hiding anything and I couldn't bear to behave like a hussy even for ten minutes. You see, we've never had a love affair, have we? I've just been going to marry you ever since I was seventeen. We've known each other so long, and quite frankly it was me who ever suggested getting married at all. You'd almost forgotten about it in the strain of this other business, hadn't you? My good ape, don't be polite about it. It's silly when we're so used to one another. Well now, I want to call all that off. I don't have to explain any more than that, do I?'

Albert Campion let the honest young pronouncement sink into his shuttering mind.

'How old are you now?' he asked.

'Twenty-five.'

'As old as that? And you've been going to marry me for eight years.'

'Well, yes. Don't be silly, you know I have, more or less. We don't go talking like this as a rule but it's got to be mentioned some time. It wasn't really fixed by either of us and it was simply that I've never considered marrying anybody else. The question has never sort of come up, has it? But now, well, I thought I'd like to lay off, and like a complete mug I've come rushing in to tell you at this ungodly moment when you're exhausted and nearly off your head with worry about something which really is terrific. I'm sorry and ashamed, but anyway it's done. I've made it clear and that's all right.'

'You've been going to marry me for *eight years*.' He did

25

not repeat the words aloud but they glowed at him from among the shadows and he strove helplessly to reconcile the information with the man he had so recently discovered himself to be. If he was a half-wit now, he seemed to have been a lunatic for some considerable time.

'And now you're not.' Again he did not utter the phrase, but its finality petrified him. As he came to the surface he had a momentary flash of insight.

'Now you want a free hand?'

She glanced up at him and her brown eyes were level and truthful.

'Yes,' she agreed steadily. 'I want a free hand. Come on, we must go down. Lee's waiting.'

'Oh, just a moment.' The appeal escaped him in desperation. 'There are one or two things I've got to know. You see, when I got myself . . .' He paused with the words "knocked out" drying on his lips as he saw the pitfall and realized how she had forestalled him. He could hardly tell her now. To reveal his helplessness at this juncture would be both to plead weakness and to appeal to her pity, and to appeal to pity is very loathsome in love. He was appalled to discover how much love there was to be reckoned with. They seemed somehow to have achieved the mutual confidence of marriage without it, and now at a stroke it was destroyed; now, when probably for the first time he was realizing how much he had come to depend upon it.

'When you got yourself what?' she inquired.

'Nothing. It'll do later.'

She put her hand in his. 'You're a dear,' she said with that sudden candour which he had rejoiced at in her. 'I knew you'd be like this. You've always been rather magnificent, Albert, and you still are. Isn't it a mercy that you've never . . . I mean that you're a bit sensible, and . . . er . . . well, not exactly cold, but . . .'

'Fish-like,' he said bitterly and let her lead him, lonely and wretched, downstairs towards that sinister 'other thing' which was still lying like an ominous bundle behind the dark curtains of his mind.

has spent the world, while they glanced at them from among the glasses and as this was as bound to the brief-nearer tolerance its garter and given such a slight to be it the work of a favourite particular past and line, but he had possibilities that no more to him. One was

IV

The drawing-room of the Principal's House at the Institute of Bridge was typical both of its owner and of the foundation; that is to say, it was a genuine period piece which had been considerably improved by modern austerity and modern money. Its fluted columns and Wedgwood plaques had been stripped and cleaned and each piece of furniture that it contained had been chosen with care and a splendid disregard of cost either one way or the other, so that an old fruit-wood chair picked up for half a crown rubbed shoulders with Mozart's own spinet, acquired at considerable sacrifice.

When Campion followed Amanda in he walked into one of the few recognizable atmospheres of that nightmare evening. Intelligent academic formality, than which there is nothing more indestructible, closed over his head like a sea of glue.

Five people stood about sipping sherry from beautiful old apple-green glasses, and the soft light of candles in silver sticks flickered on determinedly unfashionable clothes and proud, clever, conservative faces.

Lee Aubrey came over to them at once, excusing himself briefly to the middle-aged woman with whom he had been talking. He smiled briefly at Amanda and turned to peer at her companion with one of his typical glances, as if he were humbly taking a little look at the soul and finding much to sympathize with there.

In the normal way Mr Campion, who was acute in these matters, would have recognized the phenomenon and enjoyed it all for what it was worth, but tonight he was not himself and he felt suddenly savage.

Lee was disarming.

'This is fine,' he said. 'Now it's just Anscombe to come. I don't think you've met everyone, have you?'

He performed the introductions with casual efficiency and four faces, one male and three female, peered up into Mr

27

Campion's own in dreamlike succession. A pair of round dark eyes under grey brows registered on him as he bowed to the third masculine member of the party, and he received a blurred impression of a wedge of a man with a great chest and dwindling legs. But the women meant nothing to him. One was elderly, with an untidy white haircut and black eyes, but she barely spoke to him, fixing her attention entirely on Amanda.

Lee carried him over to the other side of the room, ostensibly to find some sherry.

'Rather a depressing assembly, I'm afraid,' he murmured diffidently, 'but it simply couldn't be helped. This is municipal intelligentsia, my dear chap. The Bridge Institute may do work of national importance but it's still the so-called philanthropic little plaything of the Masters of Bridge. There's something frightful about hereditary possession.'

'I wonder the State doesn't take it over,' said Campion and realized that the observation was idiotic as soon as he had made it.

Aubrey looked at him with bewildered incredulity.

'Naturally they'd like to,' he said, 'but it belongs to the town and it's pretty much of a financial asset, isn't it?'

'Yes, of course. I'd forgotten.' In spite of his care the final word carried more emphasis than Campion had intended and again his host peered at him with concern.

'My dear good man, you're exhausted,' he said. 'For heaven's sake have a drink. Would you rather have something other than this? I don't want to be an infernal nuisance, but isn't there anything I can do?'

It went through Mr Campion's mind to say 'Yes, find out how I killed a policeman, old boy, and while you're about it have a squint to see if I've cracked my own skull,' and to observe what happened, but he checked this irresponsibility. He felt as if he were just half drunk, he decided; sober enough to realize that it was definitely not wise to talk.

'Very kind of you,' he said, 'but I'm all right. A little tired, nothing else.' He had spoken more loudly than he would normally have done and his host recoiled as the words sounded clearly in the hushed and frigid air.

'I see,' he said very gently. 'I see. Do forgive me. Oh yes, wait a minute, here are your letters. I brought them along.'

He took a handful of mail out of the coat pocket of his loose dinner-jacket as he spoke and withdrew at once, with his odd self-conscious diffidence.

Campion glanced at the letters with a slowly growing sense of satisfaction. All but one were re-addressed to him from 17a Bottle Street, Piccadilly, and the sight of his name on several envelopes appeared to lend him, however unreasonably, a certain faith in his own identity.

He opened the letter which had not been re-addressed but had come to him direct at the Bridge Institute and stood looking at a clumsily typed sheet which no one but an executive who normally employed a secretary would have dared to send out. It was headed baldly: 'My office. The Yard. Tuesday,' and ran on: 'Dear A.C.. Interesting conversation this afternoon with Pugh, whom T. brought in. Fancy a man called Anscombe is your best bet. He is Secretary to the Masters. Oldish, I think and with a sister. For God's sake get busy. Keep your eyes on the calendar. The figures 15 turn my belly whenever I see or hear them. Nothing else this end. Saw the Minister again. Hardly recognized him. Enjoyed seeing fellow of that type exhibiting the weaknesses and humanity of the common bloke, .but put the wind up me all the same. Forced to rely on you only now. Every other line has gone slack and the time is so short. If you fail, for my part I shall wait until the balloon actually does go up and then swim quietly out to sea. This is a tripey way of putting it but can't bring myself to put down what I really feel. If this thing happens it is the END and I mean that. I'm not a religious chap, as you know, but I'm praying now literally and if any blasted bobby on the beat wants to see me do it he's welcome to come in here and look at his Dep. Commish on his knees. Damn you, succeed. S.'

Mr Albert Campion read the letter through twice. The words themselves were convincing enough but there was something else. Something about the note was more than ordinarily startling. Suddenly he recognized what it was. Stanislaus did not write like that in the ordinary way. He accepted the name without realizing that it had not been written in full and concentrated on the really alarming peculiarity. Stanislaus Oates was an old man, a prim, elderly policeman of the oldest school, and he was hysterical. That was horrible, as dreadful as seeing a quarter of the Nelson Column sticking up raggedly against a lowering sky. He crumpled the paper into a ball and thrust it into his pocket until he should get near the fire to destroy it. There were cold waves playing up and down his spine. This was truly frightful. Some terrible responsibility rested upon him and not only had he no recollection of what it was but he was helpless, incapacitated by an obscene mental weakness from doing anything about it.

Amanda's laugh on the other side of the room cut into his thoughts. He looked across and saw her. She was talking to Lee Aubrey, who was leaning towards her, his big-featured face young and revealing, and a belated puppyishness apparent in his attitude. A servant was at his elbow trying to attract his attention and Campion saw him come out of his mood and turn with a startled expression to follow the man out of the room.

Amanda glanced after him. She was radiant and excited, the entire march of her magnificent common sense and reliability set aside for the sweet, foolish fandango which any lesser woman can dance when she is so minded. Campion stood looking at her and it seemed to him that in that moment he actually struggled up and out of a whole customary system of living and emerged a small naked essence of the basic man. She should not do it. She should not desert him. Pride, manners, custom, the habit of a lifetime, and the training of an ancient system be damned. Amanda was his. He needed her, and God help the man or the woman herself if there was any smashing up of that combine.

He was walking over to her when Lee Aubrey came hurrying in and accosted him. He listened to the murmured words with the sudden chill which a vision of delay presents when an extra snag arises at a time of crisis.

'The police?' he repeated. 'I can't see the police now.'

30

'But my dear chap . . .' Aubrey's deep voice was urgent, 'please, not here.'

Campion followed him out into the wide hall and saw through an open doorway across an expanse of black and white flags the familiar gleam of silver and blue.

'The whole thing was some idiotic mistake and I can't spare the time,' he said savagely.

Aubrey stared at him, his eyes surprised but shrewd.

'I don't know what you're talking about, Campion,' he said patiently. 'They've come about Anscombe. The poor old boy has just been found dead in his garden and you and Amanda appear to be the last people to have seen him alive.'

V

'Anscombe?'

As the echo escaped Campion, the personality of the old man as he remembered him slid into the front of his mind with startling vividness. He saw again the ragged silhouette with the flat cap atop as it had heaved towards him so ingratiatingly over the back of the car seat. The recollection of the crumpled letter in his pocket also became very clear before his eyes, like a close-up of a document on a movie screen. He could re-read the operative words: '. . . a man called Anscombe is your best bet'.

His new mood of reckless determination, which he suspected was completely foreign to his nature, was still in complete possession of him.

'Dead?' he said aloud. 'He would be.'

Aubrey made no direct reply but Campion thought he saw the whites of his eyes for a second.

'All the same, my dear chap,' he said at last his tone only faintly reproving, 'we must do what we can. There's a sister, and heaven only knows what other complications. Come on.'

The immense blue greatcoat containing the police sergeant moved out of the doorway as they approached and the bright room spread out before them. Lee Aubrey's private study was an impressive chamber at any time, with its arched bookcases, unexpected curios and deep green hangings. It was a room with an air, a room used to soothing and entertaining people of widely different types and standards, a diplomat among rooms, gracious and superior, capable of stimulating as well as subduing, but none of its charm cut much ice with the man who stood waiting for them as he warmed the back of his legs before the open fire.

Campion knew he was a County C.I.D. Superintendent the moment he set eyes on him. He knew that as surely and in the same inspirational way that he had known Amanda's name or where to find a cigarette in the car. There was no mistaking that tall, bright-eyed, smiling superiority combined with a meticulous physical neatness. This last was a muscular and sartorial spit-and-polish, almost naval in its perfection. The stranger was the country policeman at his highest, an impressive specimen anywhere.

Aubrey, whose gaucherie had given place to a remarkable energy apparently engendered by the emergency, thrust his visitor forward.

'Superintendent Hutch,' he said briefly. 'This is Mr Campion, Hutch. Here we are. What can we do?'

'That's a question, isn't it?' said the Superintendent, revealing an unexpectedly soft country accent, and Campion, glancing up sharply, became aware of the brightest eyes he had ever met smiling into his own with a startling intensity of horse-sense behind them.

The remark was clearly not intended to be taken at its face value. For an appalling instant it occurred to Campion that he had been betrayed and that Aubrey had got him to come quietly by a pretext. His face became wooden and he waited, his hands in his pockets, for the next move.

When it came it surprised him. Superintendent Hutch laughed a little. He might almost have been embarrassed. Glancing down at a disreputable piece of paper in his hand he said formally: 'You are Mr Campion, are you, sir?'

'It's a hundred to one on, I should think, God help me.' Campion did not say the words aloud, but they came into his mind involuntarily and he smiled, only to freeze a moment later. The Superintendent, catching his expression, had echoed the grin, secretly, alarmingly. His manner then became uncomfortably informal and he spoke as important policemen are apt to speak to cornered delinquents, affably and as if they were part of the family.

'I just want the usual, you know,' he said cheerfully. 'A brief account of your last meeting with the deceased. Where did you leave him and when?'

He had a jaunty manner which sat well on his slightly comical countryman's face, with the long duck's-bill nose. He

33

was evidently a local character and was very fond of himself.

Campion took the plunge without a pause. Hesitation, he felt, instinctively, was death.

'I last saw Anscombe at his own gate,' he began glibly. 'We'd come from – er – the town.'

'What town?'

He had not the least idea. The shaky lands spread out before him and he wavered.

'I think we ought to have Amanda here.'

'Amanda, sir?'

'Yes, my fiancée, Miss . . .' The hopeless pitfall loomed too late.

Lee Aubrey was staring at him, but his surprise was not at Campion's astounding ignorance.

'I had rather hoped to keep Lady Amanda out of this as long as possible,' he said briefly. He showed his annoyance and there was a suggestion of colour on his high cheek-bones.

Lady Amanda? Lady Amanda who? The utter hopelessness of the situation might have defeated Campion at that moment had it not been for Aubrey's irritation. Who was Lee Aubrey to spare Amanda? What was this blasted proprietory talk? Damn him and his chivalry!

'Ah yes, of course, my mistake. That will be Lady A. Fitton, won't it?' murmured the Superintendent, glancing down at the slip in his hand.

'No. It's Lady Amanda. As the sister of a peer she takes her Christian name.' Aubrey gave the snippet of information casually and the touch of schoolmaster came oddly from him. 'Lady Amanda was driving this afternoon. She gave Mr Anscombe a lift into Coachingford when she went to meet Mr Campion off the London express. They were delayed and didn't get back until after eight. These are the brief facts. Mr Campion can give you anything else you need, I think. You won't need to trouble her at all, will you?'

The last words were barely a question. He spoke with the complete assurance of authority.

The Superintendent shifted his weight. He was not a young man and there was a deal of experience in his long head. Cam-

34

pion, who had been sidetracked momentarily by the two valuable names 'Fitton' and 'Coachingford', was now impressed by his hesitation and it dawned on him that as Principal of the Bridge Institute Aubrey was no ordinary power in the land.

'I think I ought to see her, sir, if you don't mind.' Superintendent Hutch's soft voice was apologetic and he had a shy way of grinning, as if he had a secret joke on somewhere.

Campion, who was not at all sure that he had not, found the habit disconcerting.

Lee Aubrey clearly found his insistence astounding. He swung round on the policeman.

'Mr Anscombe died naturally, surely?'

Hutch looked uncomfortable. 'We're not absolutely certain, sir. He didn't do it himself, that's one sure thing. The Chief Constable is on his way over now. More I can't say, can I?'

'Good lord!' Aubrey thrust his hands into the pockets of his loose dinner-jacket. Then he whistled and stood for a moment irresolute, staring at the blank wall. At length he turned abruptly. 'I'll fetch her,' he said. 'Mr Campion will tell you all he can. Apart from everything else this is rather unpleasant. The man lives on the Institute estate.'

He went out, leaving Campion with the two policemen. Hutch said nothing. He stood studying his notes, his head bent earnestly over the small bundle of old envelopes and loose half-sheets of paper on which he appeared to have made them. His hesitation was unnerving. Campion was fully alive to the dangers of his position. Any question about the drive home from Coachingford must, if he stuck to the story Amanda had told Anscombe, introduce the suicidally dangerous subject of hospitals. It was the delay he dreaded most. He was getting a sufficiently clear angle on himself to realize that whatever he might or might not have done, it was no ordinary straightforward crime of violence, and meanwhile there was clearly something of importance for him to do, and to do immediately, if only he could get some sort of line on what it was. What troubled him particularly was that he had a growing conviction that he had been nearing success when disaster had overtaken him. There was a sensation of discovery in the back of his

35

consciousness, an impression that things were moving. More-over, the curtain between this misery of ignorance and a very clear vision indeed was tantalizingly thin.

Hutch was looking at him with his now familiar half-smile. He was waiting as though he expected Campion to speak first. The man who could not remember took a deep breath.

'How did Anscombe die?' he inquired.

The policeman grinned. There was no other word for the terrifying secret leer which spread over his face.

'We were going to ask you about that, Mr Campion,' he said.

In the moment of paralysed silence which followed, the step in the doorway behind them came as a merciful release to Campion, and the brisk new voice sounded comfortably common-place.

'Hallo, Super. Mr Aubrey here? Oh, it's you, is it, Campion? What a bad business, eh?'

It was the greeting of a familiar, anyway, and Campion turned towards the newcomer anxiously. He saw a heavy round man in early middle-age, with a distinctive ugly face and impudent eyes beneath brows as fierce and tufted as an Aberdeen's. He conveyed energy and efficiency and the sturdy decisiveness which goes with a simple point of view and no nerves. It occurred to Campion that he looked like a man who did not believe in ghosts, but for the rest he was as much a stranger as anyone else in this new and confusing world. At the moment he was very full of the story.

'I'm supposed to have dropped in for coffee,' he said, 'but the chap who let me in tells me you haven't started to eat yet. He told me this dreadful tale about Anscombe, too. Poor old boy! He couldn't face it, I suppose. Or am I letting cats out of bags?'

The Superintendent eyed him.

'It wasn't suicide, Mr Pyne.'

'*Wasn't* suicide?' The newcomer seemed first astounded and then embarrassed. 'Well, I'm glad to hear it,' he said. 'What a *gaffe*! Lucky there were only you two to hear me. I'm always putting my foot in it like that. There's been a lot of gossip about, you know. You've heard it, haven't you, Super? About the Secretaryship of the Masters.'

36

'Seems to me I did hear something.' Hutch was very cautious.

'You must have done.' Pyne's eyes were amused beneath his tremendous brows. 'It's been told me in strictest confidence by everyone I've met in the last three months. I heard that the job, like all these hereditary offices, took a fine old packet to keep up, and that the old man was on the verge of a smash and had made up his mind to resign. Naturally, as soon as I heard he was a deader I thought he'd done it himself. One would. It breaks an old man's heart to give up a position carrying a bit of kudos like that, especially when it's been in the family for generations. The Bi-Annual Meeting of the Masters is some time this week, too, isn't it?'

'Tomorrow.'

'Is it? Very likely. They're such a secret high-and-mighty body that they don't trouble to publish a little thing like that.' He laughed. 'I like it,' he said. 'It appeals to the kid in all of us, that kind of mumbo-jumbo, even if it is only a sort of glorified parish council.'

The Superintendent looked frankly scandalized and Pyne, catching Campion's eye, burst out laughing. It was a pleasant, open sound, a trifle high-pitched like his voice but full of limited humour.

'We're philistines, we Londoners,' he said. 'The Masters are sacrosanct down here in Bridge. I'm sorry, Super. I'm behaving disgustingly. Poor old Anscombe! I didn't know him well, of course. I'd only met him once or twice. You didn't know him at all, did you, Campion?'

'I appear to have been the last person to have seen him alive.' The remark seemed to be the most cautious he could make in the circumstances, but it was not altogether fortunate. Amanda, who followed Aubrey into the room at that particular moment, heard it and said the first and natural thing to come into her head.

'I was there too,' she said, 'unless you saw him in the garden when you followed him in.'

Everybody looked at Campion. Aubrey and Hutch looked because they knew where Anscombe had died and Amanda and Pyne looked because the others were looking.

'That s right,' said Campion. 'I followed him into the garden with a parcel he'd left in the car. I didn't catch him, though, so I put the package on the doorstep and went back.'

There was another pause after he had spoken and again it was broken by Pyne.

'What an extraordinary thing to do, old boy,' he said, and laughed awkwardly.

Campion hesitated, remembering his reason for not ringing the door-bell, and meanwhile Amanda leapt to the rescue.

'We were so late,' she explained. 'I was jittering in the car in case we didn't have time to dress. I begged Albert not to be a moment and he wasn't.'

'How long would you say you were, sir?' The Superintendent was making hieroglyphics on the back of one of his depressing envelopes.

'I don't know exactly. A minute and a half, perhaps. I went straight up the path and I came straight back again.'

'You didn't meet anyone or hear anything?'

'No. What was there for me to hear?'

Hutch was magnificently deaf to the question.

'I think I'll ask you to step across with me, if you don't mind, sir,' he said briskly. 'I'd just like to see exactly where you put that parcel. We haven't come across it yet.'

'I'll come too, shall I?' Amanda's young voice was eager, as usual, and Campion found it very comforting. She at least was definitely on his side.

The Superintendent was dampening, however.

'No, Miss – er – Lady Amanda. That'll be quite all right,' he said firmly. 'I won't disturb Mr Aubrey's dinner party more than I can help. If I want any more from you I'll know where to find you, shan't I?'

'You'll come back later on, then, Hutch.' Aubrey spoke for the first time since his return from the drawing-room and Campion, glancing at him, saw that he was annoyed by the whole situation. It was such an unexpected reaction that he noticed it and filed it for future reference. Such magnificent aloofness from the ordinary point of view was impressive. However, Aubrey caught his glance and evidently realized that he had betrayed a weakness, albeit a somewhat godlike one, for he smiled at Campion awkwardly and murmured apologetically: 'It's absurd, but I believe I'm worrying about my wretched duties as a host. One finds oneself doing incredible things like that.' His complete frankness was disarming, as also was his sudden return of gaucherie. All the same he did not change his mind and Campion saw himself delivered over to Hutch, alone and unprotected.

While he had someone with him to use as a stalking horse he felt he had at least an outside chance of getting by with his damning disability undiscovered, but alone he felt that the Superintendent must detect him in five minutes. Some of his old alarm must have shown itself in his face, for as he turned from Aubrey, Pyne suddenly laid a reassuring hand on his shoulder.

'I'll come along with you,' he said. 'Any reason why I shouldn't, Super?'

The touch of belligerence in the question was unmistakable and Campion was aware of Hutch's bright eyes regarding him curiously. He forced himself to meet them squarely and to his intense relief and surprise the policeman shrugged his shoulders.

'None at all,' he said grudgingly. 'We'll go at once if you don't mind. The Chief Constable will probably be there by now and we can't keep him waiting.'

He led the way and they followed him, Pyne still holding Campion's shoulder.

As Campion passed Amanda she looked up at him and winked. It was such a swift gesture and her face remained so composed both before and after it that he was hardly sure it had happened. At the same moment Aubrey touched her arm and drew her back into the hall towards the dining-room.

The three men made the short journey on foot. It was a ghostly night. The moon had come out of the clouds and was riding high and serene, her blunt horns cutting into the sky, but the ground mist had become thicker, so that the Super-intendent, marching along in front, looked like a ridiculous bust of himself, his head and shoulders alone clearly defined in the cold light.

They passed down the drive with the gravel crunching under their feet and out of the misty sea around them other buildings, some of them very square and modern, rose up on either side in the middle distance.

Pyne shook his head. 'You can't help handing it to Aubrey,' he remarked, panting a little, for they were walking fast. 'In seven years he's turned this place from a museum into a living brain factory. There's more valuable work done in these twelve acres than in any other place in the country. He's got breadth of vision, that chap. I've never met such a personality, have you? It gets me every time.'

Campion hardly heard him, but his voice, friendly and matter of fact at his elbow, was very reassuring. He wondered how long he had known the man and what degree of friendship was theirs. It seemed ridiculous to think of it but they might be partners, or school friends, or members of the same profession.

They passed through the wrought-iron gates and, turning on to an old and narrow pavement made of the thin rectangular flags of other days, they came up to the entrance through which Campion had last seen Anscombe disappear. There were several cars drawn up against the kerb and a shadowy figure in uniform came out to challenge them.

While Hutch was talking to him, Campion grew acutely aware of Pyne. The stocky man had become unnaturally still. He was standing on the pavement looking up at one of the high stone pillars of the gateway which rose up in the moonlight.

'Interesting?' he murmured to Campion, and there was just a shade more than the ordinary casual question in the remark.

Campion looked at the gate pillar and saw nothing more than the heraldic leaden eagle on the top. It was a nice piece of period decoration but too small and in no way remarkable.

'Charming,' he said politely, and turned back to the man. The light was deceptive, but he thought he saw a gleam die out of the bright round eyes.

The Superintendent's minion had stepped aside by this time, however, and the little procession moved on into the dark garden. Just before he passed behind it Campion glanced at the pillar again. He caught it at an angle and saw upon its smooth surface something he had not noticed before. His heart jolted violently and once again all the old dark anxiety, which was mingled with an exasperated yet fearful curiosity, swept down on him, strangling him like a garotter's scarf. In shallow relief, and now outlined by the shadow which the angle gave it, the house number showed up clearly. It was a 15.

Campion's first reaction after the shock was one of complete relief and his first impulse was to turn to Pyne as to a proven friend, a brother in some misty conspiracy and the first man in whom he could confide, but second thoughts brought misgivings. The dead man, Anscombe, had also indicated that he attached some special significance to the number, and he had not been a friend – or at least Amanda had not seemed to think so. It occurred to Campion that he was pinning a lot of faith to Amanda. Pyne was friendly and evidently knew him well, perhaps even better than the girl. He fancied he was accustomed to having many friends. He decided to await his opportunity and put out a feeler on the subject. God knew it was as well to go cautiously!

Just then there was not much time for investigation. As he entered the drive Hutch crossed over to him and walked by his side, while, to his intense discomfort, he found that the sergeant had come up at his other elbow, separating him from Pyne.

'Just show us exactly what you did, sir.' Hutch spoke formally and it occurred to Campion that the words were very familiar, as if he had heard them many times before, which was absurd. He did what was required of him and pointed out the exact spot in the corner of the doorstep where he had deposited the bundle.

'It was not a big parcel,' he said. 'It measured about six by five, I should think. I took it that it was a couple of books.'

Hutch seemed satisfied. 'You just went away without ringing,' he remarked.

It occurred to Campion that the literal truth, which was that he happened to be dressed up as a fireman and did not wish to be seen, might be misunderstood, so he repeated his original story about the hurry. The Superintendent made no comment.

'One does things like that every day,' said Pyne, obviously with only the best intentions. 'They only sound so jolly fishy when something happens. You're being damned mysterious, Superintendent. There's no question of foul play, is there?'

'There's always a question, sir.' Hutch sounded reproachful. 'I'd like you to see him, Mr Campion. He's been taken into the house. Lead the way, will you, Sergeant?'

Even in his uncertain state Campion realized that the request was extraordinary from a policeman to a layman. It seemed hardly likely that Hutch had reverted to the ancient custom of confronting the suspected murderer with the body of his supposed victim, and it went through Campion's mind for one wild moment that he might himself be some sort of eminent pathologist, but he dismissed the theory immediately since the idea conjured up no answering memory.

Yet, as they stood in the brightly-lit bedroom, overcrowded with furniture and still full of the medicine bottles, books, and intimate personal impediments of the dead man, again Campion was touched with that sense of the familiar. He knew the scene was pathetic and expected it to be so. Moreover, he felt no qualms as he looked down at the body on the solid old-fashioned mahogany bed.

Anscombe was lying on his face and the pillows had been removed, so that his head received no support. He was still clothed in the light raincoat which he had worn in the car, and it and the suit beneath it had been cut to facilitate an examination of the larger vertebrae.

The four men, Campion and the Superintendent, Pyne and the sergeant, stood round the bed in complete silence. If Campion and the police were stolid, Pyne was rattled. His heavy cheeks were several shades paler and his paunch drooped. He whistled through his teeth.

'Horrible,' he said. 'He's broken his neck, hasn't he? How on earth did he do it?'

42

The Superintendent turned away from the sprawling body with the dreadful unnatural angle of the head and looked at Campion earnestly.

'There's a little bit of a lawn at the left of the drive,' he said. 'I don't know if you noticed it? It's very dark there, hidden from the road by the wall. Well, in the middle of this lawn there's a sort of ornamental basin, a lily-pool I think they call it. It's in a saucer-shaped hollow and there's a ring of very shallow brick and stone steps leading down to the actual water. We found him on his back, lying across the flight, if you see what I mean.'

'As if he'd slipped on the lowest step and hit the back of his neck on the highest?' Campion put the question without noticing the clarity of the picture in his mind.

'Exactly,' said Hutch, and glanced meaningly at the body.

'What an astonishing thing to do!' The explosion came from Pyne. 'In the first place what was he there for?'

'That's what we're hoping to find out, sir,' said Hutch shortly and he looked again at Campion, who, catching the expression in his eyes, could not make up his mind if it was suspicion which he saw there or merely anxious inquiry.

At any rate, he did not let it bother him. At that particular moment he had something even more alarming to consider. Ever since he had first seen the body he had felt less lost and more sure of himself, as if the dark curtain across his brain were already practically transparent, and now it had come to him up out of the shadows, but with all the conviction of certain knowledge, that he knew perfectly well how the man had been killed and what the weapon was which had murdered him. He did not attempt to argue with himself. He simply knew two things for facts, just as he knew that milk was white and ink was black. He knew that Anscombe had been struck from behind on the base of the skull by a man of full height and considerable strength. The blow must have dislocated the vertebrae and the actual cause of death was probably asphyxiation. Moreover, the murderer must have been experienced: that was the certainty which stood out in his mind. The murderer was an old hand, a killer, a professional. As for the weapon, it must have been a length of lead pipe, possibly stocking-covered since there was no mark on the man's collar.

Campion could see the thing quite distinctly in his mind, a long thin murderous bludgeon bound with bicycle tape as like as not.

The Superintendent's questioning eyes still resting upon him brought him out of his reverie with a jerk and he felt his clothes clinging clammily to his body as a possible solution to this new mystery presented itself. Suppose he *had* slugged the policeman? Suppose not only that, but that he had also slugged Anscombe? That was what had happened to Anscombe all right; he had been slugged.

Campion collected himself. It was absurd. He could not have done it. Even if his mind was not playing him monstrous tricks he could not have done it in the time. Amanda knew. Amanda had said distinctly that he had come back at once.

The Superintendent was waiting, his comic country face as grave as a judge's.

'We found him on the steps,' he said. 'The doctor's still waiting to think over his opinion. What would you say, Mr Campion?'

The younger man stood still, moistening his dry lips with the tip of his tongue. At that moment, if it had not been for one thing, he would have made a complete statement of his condition and the terrors crowding through his head. The thing that prevented him was the letter in his pocket. A glimpse of Pyne's worried fat face had reminded him of it just in time. Pyne must know. After that deliberate question about the 15 on the gatepost, Pyne must know. He must get Pyne alone. He forced himself to eye Hutch calmly. It was a touchy business, God knew, like handling high-explosives in a fire.

'If Anscombe fell rigidly,' he said, 'arching his back to regain his balance, you know, then he just might have done it like that. Still, we're in the hands of the doctor, aren't we?'

He could have bitten out his tongue for using that 'we'. He had no idea why he'd done it. The moment it left his lips it stuck out like a signpost. However, if Hutch saw it he ignored it. He seemed relieved but unhappy.

44

'Yes,' he said, sighing. 'That about sizes it up. Would you care to see the steps?'

Since he had clearly made up his mind to show them, there was no way of avoiding the inspection, but as they crowded into the little pit of darkness at the side of the house and stared by the light of muffled torches at the meaningless jumble of stones and bricks, as unreal and confusing as pantomime scenery in the unnatural glow, Campion edged closer to Pyne. It was difficult to choose a sufficiently non-committal opening, but at last he ventured a sighting shot.

'Not much like the old days,' he said heartily.

Pyne seemed engrossed with the exhibit, or at any rate he took some seconds to reply. Then his cheerful murmur came briskly out of the darkness.

'When we were in the States together, you mean?'

'Yes.' Campion did not wish to be drawn into any further reminiscences until they had had time to talk, but it was not going to be so difficult after all. They were old friends; that was the main thing.

His immediate hopes were defeated a minute or two later, however, when they were all three walking back to the Principal's house together. At the Institute gates Pyne took his leave somewhat abruptly.

'I must get back at once,' he said. 'You know what work is, Superintendent, and you know where to find me if you want me, don't you? I'll see you in the morning, Campion. This is a bad business, Super. I believe it's turned me up a bit. I'm a novice, you know. I feel like a kid at the hunt who's been blooded.'

He stumbled off down the road. The policeman looked after him and laughed soundlessly.

'I'm afraid we've upset that stomach of his,' he said. 'Serve him right for nosing in. Look here, Mr Campion, I shan't come back with you now because I've got to wait for the Chief. I don't know what's delaying him. He ought to have been here hours ago. I only came along here because I wanted a word with you in private if I could get it. I wasn't quite accurate up at the house when I said we hadn't found the parcel. I wanted

45

an excuse for getting hold of you. We had found it, of course, just exactly where you'd put it. I didn't want to go into it up there because in some ways it's rather peculiar, and I thought you might be particularly interested. Do you know what it contained?'

He bent closer and a trick of the light gave his face a menace which it did not normally possess.

'Close on four thousand pounds in cash,' he said softly. 'I found it interesting because we had another case earlier today in Coachingford when a lot of money cropped up. It's been a very funny business altogether over there, with one of our fellows laid out and an unknown in hospital. When I come along I'll tell you about it.'

To Campion it seemed that the great starry arc of the sky above him reeled over and back like the lid of a bacon dish, but if the Superintendent knew what he said his game of cat and mouse was inhumanly effective. He gave no sign of meaning more than his actual words, but just before he turned on his heel and left his victim to go up the drive alone he made one further remark which was, if anything, even more annihilating than the first.

'I wonder at that fellow Pyne sticking to us like that,' he said earnestly. 'Curiosity seems to drive some people off their onion. He only met you three days ago. He told me that himself last night. And he doesn't know me at all. You wouldn't think any man would thrust himself forward like that, would you? I'll be seeing you later, then.'

VI

'I'm afraid Hutch has let us down. It's abominably late.'

Lee Aubrey broke a long silence with the remark, which he delivered with an effort, as if he had been thinking of it for a long time. He, Campion, and Amanda were sitting round the fire in the drawing-room with the candles burning low and the uncomfortable silence of the night bearing down upon them. They had been there for perhaps an hour. Campion had returned from Anscombe's house just as the dinner guests were leaving and had found himself let in for a more or less formal *tête-à-tête*, his host the one person in the way.

He was more than anxious to talk to Amanda alone. Every time he set eyes on her she became clearer and dearer to him. Whatever other values were upset, whatever other mistakes he made in this new nightmare world of his, she was real and solid, a living part of that self which he was rediscovering so painfully.

She was sitting curled up in her chair between the two of them, very much alive but gloriously composed. She looked very young and very intelligent, but not, he thought with sudden satisfaction, clever. A dear girl. *The* girl, in fact. His sense of possession was tremendous. It was the possessiveness of the child, of the savage, of the dog, unreasonable and unanswerable. He glanced irritably at Aubrey.

The great man had risen and was leaning against the mantelpiece. He was frowning at first but then once more that little smile of tolerant self-contempt curled his narrow lips. Suddenly he laughed.

'Well,' he said, 'we've thrashed it all out, haven't we? Anscombe appears to have fallen down and broken his neck: that's all it amounts to. I'll go up and see poor old Miss Anscombe in the morning. Until Hutch condescends to report we can't do anything else. You look fantastically tired, my dear fellow. Why don't you go to bed? Amanda and I will give the wretched Hutch another half-hour. Don't you think so?'

The final question was put directly to Amanda and as he looked at her his expression softened so much that the change was positively theatrical. However, he seemed quite unconscious of betraying himself and it was as if he were not in the habit of considering himself objectively ever.

Amanda avoided his eyes and might almost, for the light was deceptive, have blushed. Her involuntary behaviour seemed to annoy her, however, for she looked at him squarely.

'Very well,' she said.

Campion sat up. In the ordinary way he might well have been startled, for there are few hosts who send their guests to bed so blandly, but now, in his confused state, he was bewildered. Aubrey had spoken with authority, like – yes, that was it – like royalty, or a headmaster; not with rudeness, but as if he had special privileges.

At first Campion had every intention of refusing baldly and of forcing himself upon them, but Amanda swept the remaining ground from under his feet.

'Good night, Albert,' she said.

He went up to his room and sat on his bed with the door open, as if he were a schoolboy in the throes of a first love affair. Until that moment he had not properly assimilated her announcement of earlier in the evening. So many things had happened since then and the dreamlike quality of his new existence had seemed to allow of lightning changes of front and back. Now, again, it returned to him that Amanda was real, and, being real, she was consistent, the one concrete thing in a world of fantasy. She meant what she said. She was not going to marry him. Beside this actual disaster all the other inconsistencies – the mad cat-and-mouse behaviour of the police, the too friendly Pyne who had tricked him into a betrayal and then disappeared on heaven knew what tortuous and subversive mission – faded into fantasy. On the top of his blinding desolation crept a new fear. It was a fear for Amanda. It occurred to him that it was the first completely unselfish thought he had had since the disaster, or, of course, ever in his life for all he knew. It was linked with something he knew about her, some vulnerability he had forgotten, and with some-

48

thing he knew about Aubrey. There was something from which he must protect her. She was a responsibility of his, quite as much a responsibility as that other which was rapidly assuming such enormous proportions. Apparently he was a responsible person. It seemed a pity he had lost half his mind.

He got off the bed and walked out into the upper hall. He strode up and down there for what seemed an eternity, his footsteps deadened by the heavy carpet. The lights were very bright, with the cold brilliance which seems to be a part of the middle of the night, and when the drawing-room door opened he walked over to the banister without hesitation and looked down.

'Good night, Amanda.'

Aubrey's deep delightful voice was soft and packed with meaning. He was leaning against the doorpost with his head bent and a lock of his thick hair drooping boyishly forward. He had taken Amanda's hand and was swinging it backwards and forwards in the careless inarticulate fashion which Gerald du Maurier used to use so effectively in so many of his scenes. He was not a man who would ever appear handsome, but his whole pose was negligently graceful, which was odd in such a large-boned loosely constructed figure.

Campion got the impression that Amanda was a trifle flustered and also that the condition was hitherto unknown to her.

'Good night, Lee,' she said, sounding positively schoolgirlish in an effort to be matter-of-fact. Then, turning away, she hurried upstairs, to arrive pink and a little breathless before Campion in the upper hall.

She was astounded to see him and obviously accepted the first explanation which came into her head.

'What's the matter?' she demanded. 'What's happened?'

'I want to talk to you.'

'All right. What is it? I say, nothing else awful, surely?' She appeared to expect disaster and hurried into his room as if she thought to find concrete evidence of it there.

He followed her and closed the door. Had there been bolts upon it he would have shot them.

'There's one thing you've got to tell me,' he said. 'I've been trying to find out all the evening.'

'What?'

'What day is it?'

She stared at him. Her light brown eyes were wide with astonishment at first, but as he looked at her the fine brows came down in a straight line above them and the fiery colour spread over her face.

'Did you hang about on the staircase simply to ask me that? You're behaving rather extraordinarily, aren't you?'

He was, of course. He saw that the moment she pointed it out. To the uninstructed his behaviour and the all-important question could have only one explanation; that he was acting like a jealous child. He felt unreasonably angry with her for his own helplessness.

'I want to know the day and the date of today,' he said doggedly. 'You're the only person I dare ask. What is it?'

'It's the thirteenth, I think.' She was furious, and the dignity which her control lent her was the coldest thing on earth.

'Friday, I suppose?'

'No. Tuesday. Now I think I'll go to bed.'

Tuesday the thirteenth. That meant Thursday the fifteenth. A day. A day to do what?

Amanda moved over towards the door. He thought she was going out without a word and was helpless to stop her. He was completely unprepared, therefore, for what was evidence of one of the most lovable traits in her make-up. On the threshold she turned and quite suddenly grinned at him.

'I've gone all theatrical, Albert,' she said. 'What is up?'

He groaned. 'God knows,' he said truthfully.

Amanda came back into the room and sat down on the edge of the bed.

'Are you all right?' she demanded. 'Don't forget you have had a dust-up. I don't want to fuss you – I know how you hate it – but you do look a bit green, you know. I've noticed it all the evening and haven't liked to mention it.'

He cocked an eye at her. That was a piece of his own character slipping into place. He was one of those men with a horror of being fussed, was he? Yes, that was right; he felt he might be like that. She hadn't liked to fuss him. She was pretty marvellous. A great surge of desire for comfort from her broke over him. She was alive. She was his only link with reality. It was on his tongue to risk everything and come out with the awful truth when her next remark silenced him.

'I'm sorry I behaved so badly. I've got a bit self-centred. I thought you were playing the fool because I was falling in love with Lee.' She spoke without any affectation and was free from any suggestion of the coyly blunt. Her eyes were as candid as her words.

'Are you?'

'I think so.' There was a quiet softness in her voice, a gentle satisfaction which he knew he had never heard in it before.

'Why?'

She hesitated and finally laughed. 'It's a thing I couldn't possibly tell you if you weren't yourself,' she said. 'I mean if I didn't know you as well as I know myself almost. He's like you, isn't he?'

'Is he?'

'I think so, very. Except for the one important thing.'

'What's that?'

She looked up at him and there was a sort of rueful shyness in her young face.

'He loves me so. He's doing his best about it but it's bubbling out all over him and making him shy and silly, like an undergraduate or a peasant or something. And since he's a great man – because he is brilliant, you know – well, that makes it pretty irresistible.' She paused and shook herself. 'Let's not discuss it. It's not a bit in your line and things are getting up speed, aren't they? I feel disgusted with myself for getting – er – overtaken by this thing, but it's like that. It does – er – overtake. Tell me about Anscombe.'

'He was murdered.'

'What?' She sat staring at him. 'But that's impossible! Who?'

'I don't know.'

Amanda clasped her knees and her heart-shaped face looked small and worried as she rested her chin on them.

'Of course I'm not competent to judge anything in this business,' she said unexpectedly, 'since I don't know the full strength.'

'My dear,' he said with elaborate deference, because he was still tingling from the blow which seemed to have hurt the secret forgotten part of himself even more than his conscious needy present, 'I only wish I could tell you.'

'Yes, well, you can't,' she said briefly. 'You're under oath and that's final. I don't mind. I know you well enough to work under sealed orders. Otherwise I'd hardly have done the unforgivable thing and got Lee to invite us down here without telling him you were working on something in town. I've got your assurance that it's desperately important; that's good enough.'

Campion was standing with his back to her and did not dare look round.

'Let's see,' he said mendaciously, 'how long have we known Lee?'

'You mean how long have I known him,' objected Amanda. 'You've known him three days, as you very well know. I came down here from Dell on some work on the new armour for the Seraphim planes. There was a man working at the Institute we had to get hold of. I made friends with Lee then.'

She was talking gibberish apart from the all-important dates, as far as Campion was concerned, and he wondered how far he dared press her for information. Fortunately she helped him unconsciously.

'Have you told anyone about the hospital episode this afternoon?'

'No.'

'Nor have I. And I was thinking, Albert, I don't suppose Anscombe did. So suppose we stick to our original plan, which is, if you remember, that I took you into Coachingford on Sunday night to catch the London express. That was immediately after you had the wire which was waiting for you when we arrived. Then yesterday I was supposed to fetch you from the same station after your return. At dinner tonight I was very vague about our delay, but it was a sticky gathering anyway and didn't matter. Still, if it does come up we'll have to call it tyre trouble. How's that?'

'Excellent,' he said dubiously and waited for her to continue. 'How did you get on at Coachingford?' she inquired at last.

He shrugged his shoulders and she nodded gloomily.

'Like that?' she said. 'Never mind. It'll come suddenly. I don't like this Anscombe business, though. That's horrible. Just when we thought he knew something.'

He turned on her. 'What made you think he knew something?'

'I don't know. I just got that impression.'

'Not – "fifteen"?'

'Fifteen?' She seemed surprised. 'Fifteen what?'

'Fifteen men on a dead man's chest,' he said and half wondered if he had invented the ringing phrase.

'Yo-ho-ho and some nice sound sleep,' said Amanda. 'You can't do any more tonight, anyway, if the whole world's at stake. You go to bed.'

Campion leant heavily on the back of the chair which he had been fingering. His wooden face was haggard and he looked tired and frustrated.

'My God, I wonder if it is,' he said.

She gave the question serious consideration.

'It seems a bit presumptuous, but it might be,' she said.

Campion felt the beads of sweat break out on the line where his forehead met his hair.

'That's the kind of damned silly premonition I've got,' he said.

Amanda smiled at him. 'If it is, I'd rather it was in your hands than anybody's,' she said honestly. 'You've got all the cards, Albert, and fundamentally you're so . . .'

'So what?'

'So sort of sufficient at heart. So cold. You'll get by.'

After she had gone he sat very still in the silent room and the strong light beat down upon him with chilly clarity. The warmth had gone out of the dream again and he was back in the familiar nightmare. He knew what it was like now. It was like one of those trick films wherein familiar objects are photographed from an unfamiliar angle. The strange shadows thus cast made vast secret shapes, forming a horror where there is none and, worse still, concealing a horror where horror lies.

Now that Amanda had gone he wondered why he had not confided in her. It was not only because of Lee and because he dreaded her pity as he dreaded insufferable pain. There was another reason. He reached down into the darkness in his mind and drew it out from its skulking place in all its hideousness. It was a fear. If she knew of his mental state, if she knew of that overheard conversation in the hospital, and had it presented to her with the facts as they both knew them about Anscombe's death, then would she still regard him with that candid trust which was the most precious thing about her? Or would the gleam of a doubt come creeping into her brown eyes before her loyalty doused it? That was the risk he had not dared to take. He was the man involved and he would not entirely trust himself.

The whistle cut into his thoughts. The low note, which was just sufficiently unlike a bird's to be uncanny, sounded twice before it brought him to his feet. He switched out the light and stood listening. It sounded again just beneath the window.

He pulled the heavy curtains aside, unlatched the old-fashioned shutters, and threw up the sash as quickly as he could.

The whistle began and ended suddenly and there was a long silence. The house cast a deep shadow and the space below the window was black as the pit.

'Is that you, sir?' The voice was very quiet and almost directly beneath him. 'Are you ready? I've been waiting round the other side. I must have mistook your meaning. We'll have to get a move-on if we're to get the job done tonight. Can you come at once?'

'What? Yes, yes, all right, I'll be with you in a moment.' Campion drew in his head, closed the window and replaced its various shroudings. Then he went downstairs with the soft-footed tread of a professional burglar. In his mind was a single unqualified question-mark, for the voice had been the utterly unmistakable one of Superintendent Hutch.

VII

Campion came out of the front doorway noiselessly. He picked his way over the gravel to the silent turf of the lawn and stood waiting. If this was arrest the whole world was as light-headed as he was.

The Superintendent's jaunty figure emerged from the black shadows round the house and dropped into step beside him. He did not speak, but, taking Campion's arm, led him into the narrow line of darkness below the row of close-growing poplars which lined one side of the path. He walked very fast and did not open his mouth until they were a good two hundred yards from the window. Finally he sighed.

'Very nicely done, sir,' he said with approval. 'I didn't know you had come out until I set eyes on you. It's as well to be careful. We don't want to give a lot of fancy explanations. Once you start that game, it's my experience that you have to go on remembering what you've said for years afterwards.'

Campion made no specific comment. He grunted non-committally and pressed on towards the gateway.

As he had hoped, Hutch continued to talk. He revealed a friendly soul and a justifiable pride in his rise to eminence in the force.

'That's why I'm doing this little job myself,' he remarked. 'It's not that I haven't got half a dozen men I could trust to be both efficient and discreet, but I don't want them to take the risk, don't you see? When it's something unorthodox and a little bit delicate it's the Chief's job every time. Don't you agree?'

'Oh, every time,' said Campion heartily. He wondered where in God's name they were going with such determined speed.

They turned away from Anscombe's house at the end of the drive and plunged off downhill in the opposite direction. Hutch kept to the shadowed side of the street and his long strides were silent as a ghost's. Most English country towns

55

are picturesque in the moon's eye, but this winding hill was like a part of an old fairy story in the cold yellowish light. Tudor shops with overhanging upper storeys and windows like those on a galleon squeezed prim Queen Anne houses which wore shutters and graceful fanlights. There were mounting blocks and lantern posts at every dozen yards, and through carved archways occasional glimpses of cobbled courts and stone gardens. It was probably the most hackneyed picture-postcard subject in the world, but Campion saw it with the eyes of a child and its charm startled him. The crazy roofs were like witches' hoods huddling together for whispered consultations and the dark windows winked their panes at him from a bygone world.

Meanwhile the Superintendent's silence became oppressive and Campion ventured a leading question.

'Why exactly is this trip so delicate?'

'Perhaps that isn't the word I ought to have used.' Hutch seemed a little put out and for a moment Campion was afraid that he had silenced him.

As they turned across a wide market square which might well have decorated any calendar the policeman opened out a little.

'I don't like to talk under windows,' he said. 'In a place like this everyone knows your voice, let alone your life story. You don't quite understand the position of the Masters in this town, do you?'

'No,' said Campion truthfully, 'I'm afraid I don't. Most of the offices are hereditary, aren't they?'

'All of them.' Hutch appeared to respect the fact. 'It's a very interesting survival,' he announced, a touch of the professional guide creeping into his voice and mixing oddly with the confidential police low-down which was his natural manner. 'Their records go back nearly five hundred years. This is the only example of what you might virtually call a free city in the British Isles – other than London, of course. We're in a funny position, you see, stuck here on a navigable river which yet isn't quite big enough to make us a port.'

'Yes, of course,' Campion held his breath. They were half-way across the Square now and in a moment or two windows would be over their heads again.

'That fellow Pyne,' said Hutch, 'he called the Masters a glorified municipal council, you may remember. So he can, but if he realized how glorified they are he'd keep his mouth shut like the rest of us. Do you know, Mr Campion, there's not a man in this town selling so much as a packet of cigarettes who doesn't do his business solely at the direct discretion of the Masters? They're kings, that's what they are, little kings. Between 'em they own the whole place and the Institute makes 'em rich. Why do you think there's no cinema in the whole of Bridge? Because the Masters don't want to alter the character of the town. They own the land, they appoint the magistrates, they control the licences, and it's their say-so. Same with the trippers. You'll never see a charabanc in Bridge although it's the most famous beauty spot in the whole of the south-west. The Masters don't want charabancs. They know their towns-folk. In fact they are their townsfolk. They're all related – the whole town is related – and charabancs aren't allowed.'

He paused in his stride and lowered his voice.

'Of course, being so old and so rich and having all the ancient ceremonial and secrecy and so on, it makes them very powerful. They've got such a pull. They always put up a Member of Parliament and they subsidize a Chair at one of the Universities – oh, they've got a finger in all sorts of pies! They're thick as thieves with the Government and in fact I shouldn't be a bit surprised if they weren't one of the most powerful bodies in the whole country in their own quiet way.'

'Quiet.' Campion repeated the word aloud unconsciously. It was coming back to him, or rather it was all there now. He knew it all, just behind the shadow in his mind. The Super-intendent's urgent words were like a new facet on some old stone which he knew well.

Hutch snorted. 'They're quiet all right,' he said. 'There's never been a meeting of theirs discussed at a tea-table, let alone reported in the press. It's amazing what you can keep quiet if it's in your interest to do so. That's why I called our little job tonight delicate. We haven't got too much time either. This way, sir. It's quicker.'

He took Campion's arm again as he spoke and drew him down a narrow alleyway between two dark houses whose sugar-loaf roofs bowed to each other overhead.

'This brings us out directly into the Nag's Pykle,' he said. 'Round here.'

Another sharp turn brought them out into the open moon-light again and Campion, still with his new child's eyes, was brought up short before what is perhaps one of the most dramatic natural pictures in England.

A broad road, still paved and flanked with squat houses, rises slowly to the Corn Exchange and the Nag's Head Inn. The Hostelry, fourth oldest in the country, is three storeys high and its centre gable, gallant but drunken, leans appreciably west-ward, lending the whole structure a note of ancient and irresponsible festivity both laughable and endearing. Behind this, and behind the Corn Exchange and the low tower of St Nicholas's Church, stands the Nag itself. The bare hill rises up stark and unexpected, like the head of the giant horse it is said to resemble. It is threadbare limestone and is entirely naked save for the double line of ragged pine trees on the crest which in Bridge are called The Mane. In broad sunlight it is impressive and even menacing, but that night, by the moon, it was breathtaking.

Even the Superintendent was tempted to comment.

'Extraordinary formation,' he observed. 'When you come on it like this you can almost believe the old tale about the bridge. You know that one, don't you? Oh well, if you don't it's interest-ing,' he added with some satisfaction. 'It shows you how far back the name of the town goes. There's the river mouth be-hind there, as you know, and that other hill on the opposite bank is called The Manger. It's got a big hollow in the top. You can see it on a clear day. The story goes that there was a great flood here once that cut the town right off from the mainland. There was a terrible famine and no one could put out in a boat because of the storms. Right at the last moment, when every-one was practically dead, the Mayor – or local saint or somebody – said his prayers extra strong and lo! and behold, "with a roar like a million drums", the Nag raised his head and shot out his great neck and put his nose in The Manger over on the other side of the river. Those who were still strong enough ran along his mane and brought back food for the rest. The Nag kept his head in The Manger until the floods went down and then one night, when everything was quiet and everyone was asleep, like it might be tonight, he drew it very quietly back again. That's the legend of how the town got its name, and there's certainly no bridge in the place except the little hump-backed one down by the mill on the Coachingford road.'

He laughed a trifle self-consciously.

'I always think of it when I come along here at night,' he said. 'I like that bit about the "roar like a million drums". You can just imagine it, can't you? I don't know that there's much moral to the tale, unless it's that the Nag looks after Bridge. So he does, of course, to this day. Very much so. But it's remarkable how an old tale like that gets handed down. I wonder you hadn't heard it. It's very well known. One of the big composers wrote a bit of music about it. Holst, was it?'

Campion said nothing. The story, coupled with the unexpected sight, was strangely moving. He knew he must be hearing it much as a savage might, or as the early unsophisticated inhabitants of the town must have done. It was damnably convincing. He felt quite a thrill of superstitious fear.

Meanwhile, the Superintendent's attitude towards himself was growing more incomprehensible at every step. He was friendly, not to say obliging, and, moreover, the farther they came the less certain of himself he appeared to be. But where they were going so fast and so secretly remained a complete and utter mystery.

Campion was naturally tempted to begin careful pumping operations, but he was alive to all the dangers. He knew so little about anything at all that the most innocent remark could easily prove a disaster. He ventured one little feeler.

'Mr Aubrey rather expected you to come along earlier this evening,' he said.

'I daresay he did, sir.' Hutch became an official again. 'I had one or two things to see to. I'd hardly left Mr Anscombe's house when something else cropped up.'

'Oh?' Campion tried to show interest without anxiety and the Superintendent rose to the fly.

'I had a call from Coachingford,' he said briefly. 'They're having a bit of a manhunt all round here tonight. As far as I could get it on the telephone the case seems to have all the usual features, but it's a worry in wartime. There was the stolen car abandoned on the high road and all the rest of it. They'll pick him up in the morning when they can see what they're doing. They're circulating a full description . . . here we are, sir, this way.'

The final announcement was providential, since it covered Campion for the necessary moment. He had started like a cat, he noticed with concern, and he had a conviction that his nerves were not usually so unreliable.

They had passed the Inn now and had taken a side turning which ran round the eastern base of the Nag. This street was particularly ancient and here the buildings hung together, shrinking into the very sides of the hill. The shop before which Hutch had paused was a grocery and in its bow windows the familiar cartons of breakfast foods, condensed milk, and sugar substitutes looked ridiculous. Such a place should have sold love philtres at least.

The Superintendent took Campion's elbow and led him into a minute alley which ran down between the shop and its neighbour. This passage was so narrow that they could not walk abreast and at one point, where the wall bulged, there was scarcely space for Campion's shoulders. Hutch was treading like a hunter. His tall figure passed like a shadow and his feet made no noise. Campion followed him with equal technique.

At the end of the alley they came into a yard. It was little more than a well, with the Nag rising sheer on one side and the building crowding down upon them on the other.

Hutch produced a torch no larger than a rifle cartridge. It's pin-point beam lit up a keyhole in a surprisingly modern door set in an ancient frame. A short key slid into position and the lock turned over. They passed inside into the spicy, slightly rancid atmosphere of a store-room. Campion followed the Superintendent blindly. His passage now had all the actual qualities of dreaming. He had no idea where he was and the velvet dark was warm and faintly anaesthetic.

They seemed to go on walking for some time and his impression was that they were following a narrow path amid all kinds of obstacles. Another door brought them to a flight of wooden stairs and a surprising change of atmosphere. It was still warm, but the air now smelt of paper and floor-polish and the gentle, exciting odour of old wood. It was a long climb and Hutch began to relax some of his elaborate caution.

'We're right in the hill now,' he said unexpectedly. 'You wouldn't think it, would you? We'll go right on up to the Council Chamber, shall we? There's nothing much down here.'

'By all means.' Campion spoke absently. He was struggling with incredulity. 'Where are we?' he demanded, throwing caution to the winds. 'In the Town Hall?'

Hutch laughed. He seemed to take the question as a witticism.

'That's about the size of it, really, isn't it?' he said. 'The Masters run the show in Bridge, not the officials in Basket Street. At one time, you know this used to be the only administrative headquarters in the town. I believe they used to hold the courts in the Council Chamber. It's very interesting if you're keen on ancient history. The whole place is formed from the natural caves in the hill. The air shafts are artificial but they're prehistoric. You'll be impressed by the room. I've only been in it once, and that was last year when I had to come up before the society and make a report. The carving is remarkable, I believe, to those who know.'

'Is this the only entrance?' inquired Campion faintly.

'Not likely.' Hutch paused in his stride. 'You know about that, surely? Excuse me, sir, but don't you know your guidebook? I thought everyone knew about the Doors of Bridge, as they call them. It's one of the features of the place. It's my opinion that it's those four doors which give the Masters their peculiar fanciful quality. After all, there's nothing extraordinary in an ancient body meeting in a room built in a hill.

61

In the old days it served as a fortress, and stood a long siege in the Jacobite rebellion. But those four doors, each one marked by an innocent-looking house, give it a sort of romantic touch, if you see what I mean.'

'What houses?' inquired Campion, who appeared to have given up subterfuge.

'Well, there's the pub for one.' Hutch was torn between astonishment and delight at the discovery of such ignorance. 'The old Nag's Head is built across the main door. You can see it in the back room, a lovely bit of carved wood. Takes up all one side. That's the ceremonial entrance where the Masters go in on a meeting night. Then there's the Gate House, where Mr Peter Lett lives. He's the hereditary gatekeeper. That door leads out of his drawing-room and isn't often used. His house is round the other side, in the Haymarket Road. The third door is off the Rectory. It's a sort of gallery there, next the Church. And the fourth lies behind the Wain House, farther off down the street. Mr Phillips, who is the hereditary groom, lives there. It's all very old-world and out of the ordinary, if you come to it new, but of course when you're as used to it as we are you don't see anything in it. It's just a custom, that's all.'

Campion felt an absurd desire to sit down on the stairs. He wondered vaguely if all ancient history sounded as picturesque as this when it was heard for the first time, and, if so, if most children lived in this perpetual state of astonishment.

'We came in by a fifth door, then,' he murmured.

'We came in by the back door,' said Hutch firmly. 'Not many people know about it and I daresay it's comparatively recent – not above seventy years old perhaps. Like everybody else the Masters have to have cleaners and they have to have goods delivered. I imagine they must have bought the shop at some period and installed a caretaker there. It's an old-fashioned business. It's been in the same family for years. I came in that way tonight because it seemed safest. I don't want to have to give a lot of explanations and I'm sure you don't. This is the last step, sir. Now to your right.'

He produced a larger torch as he spoke and Campion was startled by the height of the gallery in which they stood. It seemed to have no ceiling but to go on up and up into infinity. There was a pleasant dull sound of wood on wood, a faint squeak from a protesting hinge, and then a great rush of cool air as they passed into the room within.

Hutch swept a broad beam of light round them and Campion stepped back. The place was enormous. It was church-like and colossal. He received a confused impression of black panelling, the lower halves of mighty pictures, full-length portraits of heroic size, and, overhead, canopies of ragged banners, still bright and gallant after their passage down the centuries. The centre-piece turned out somewhat tamely to be a table. It was a mighty affair of glistening black oak and it fitted snugly on a carpet which must have been very nearly the size of a tennis-court, but apart from this it was normal enough and almost ordinary. Twenty-five chairs encircled it and at the head, before a seat larger than the others, was a pile of papers and a very prosaic speaker's water-bottle and glass.

The silence was remarkable. It hung over them like a smothering pall. There was not a breath anywhere, not a crackle of shrinking wood, not a scurry of dust upon the stone floor, nothing. Hutch sighed deeply. It was evident that he was about to make some pronouncement and Campion nerved himself to meet whatever might be coming.

The man's words when they arrived, however, took him completely by surprise.

'Well, sir.' He sounded a trifle breathless. 'Here you are. I've risked my warrant to get us in and I hope you'll forgive me if I say for God's sake get whatever you have to do done as soon as possible, so we can get out before the light. I don't like to think what would happen if we got caught. No one would lift a finger for us. But you know that even better than I do, I expect.'

63

VIII

Campion did not move. The actor who drives up centre-stage in the middle of the big scene, and who stands there blankly with the urgent silence growing more acute at every second, feels much as he did then.

His first coherent thought was even more terrifying, however. Since he had evidently engineered this illegal entry himself, and had apparently persuaded a Superintendent of Police to break the dearest law in the British Constitution in order to achieve it, it must obviously have some vital importance and he himself must possess much more than ordinary influence. There was something he had to do here, more probably something he had to find out, and there was no knowing what stupendous matters hung upon his success. Already it was long past midnight. The morning of the fourteenth had begun. The fifteenth, as far as he knew, was zero-hour.

It came to him that he must lay his cards on the table and take the consequences. He turned to Hutch, prepared to speak, but as the first difficult words formed in his mind the Superintendent began again.

'I don't like to criticize,' he said, his apology making the reproach a hundred times more poignant in the circumstances, 'and I know men in your position have to keep their mouths shut, but, just as a question of policy, don't you think it would have made things a lot easier if your department had seen fit to trust the Chief Constable and myself with just a little more information? You can see how it is. We're quite blindfold, aren't we? We're instructed to give you every assistance, every assistance no matter what you ask, and so we will, but it would make things simpler if we had a glimmer of what you were up to.'

He paused hopefully but, when the man before him did not reply, went on earnestly.

'Look at that business this evening, for instance. I haven't been in the Force for close on thirty years without being able to recognize a corpse which has been slugged when I see one. But what am I to do? There's a ready-made loophole there and we've got a young doctor. If I shut down on the inquiry I can let the whole investigation collapse without any trouble. But am I right in doing that? Is it in the country's interest or is it nothing to do with the case? I don't know. I'm asking you. I'm in the dark. I gave you every opportunity but you didn't give me any lead.'

Campion pulled himself up as the solid ground gave way at his very feet.

'I can't tell you,' he said helplessly. 'Don't you understand? I am simply unable to tell you.'

Hutch stiffened. He was like a soldier at attention.

'Very good, sir,' he said. 'I'm in your hands. Carry on.'

Campion took the torch from him and advanced towards the table. It seemed the obvious thing to do. As he came up with it its enormous size became more apparent and panic seized him as he looked across that vast expanse of shining wood. It was so empty, so utterly uninformative.

He glanced towards the papers neatly arranged before the main chair and experienced his first ray of hope. They were not all the usual blanks. On the top of the pile was a fold of foolscap neatly headed 'Agenda'. Anscombe had done his last duty for the Masters.

By the light of the torch he read the list of items down for discussion at the morrow's meeting. It began archaically enough with 'Prayers to Almighty God' and went on to the orthodox 'Senior Master's Opening Remarks', 'Minutes of the Last Meeting' and 'Correspondence'. But the third entry was more unusual. 'Ceremony of the Bale of Straw', it stated simply, and continued, as though the one were the counterpart of the other, 'Report on the New Sewage System for the Lower Town, temporarily suspended by War'. The 'Institute Report' followed, and the fifth item recorded 'Extraordinary Council: Resignation of John Robert Anscombe, Secretary.'

The sixth heading brought Campion up short, his brows rising as he read the round characterless copperplate.

'*Suggested Purchase from the Government of the French,*' it ran briefly. '*Spice Island of Malaguama. 950,000,000 francs.*'

This somewhat staggering project brought him to the foot of the page and he turned it casually, unprepared for any further statement, but there, staring at him and in the same childish hand, was yet another consideration for the Masters of Bridge.

'*Main Business of the Evening,*' he read and saw underneath it, in a large carelessly drawn circle in red ink, the haunting figures 15.

Below were two further lines, clearly referring to some traditional closing ceremony: '(1) *The Oath*' and '(2) *The Toast Sec. 5. Perish All Those Who Doe Wrong Unto Us.*'

He refolded the sheet, put it back into position and stepped back. His knees were trembling. It was all here, he felt certain, all under his hand, and yet he could not recognize it. The other half of the talisman was lying just out of his reach in the monstrous darkness of his own brain.

Hutch remained stiffly at his side. Campion could feel that the man was uneasy, alarmed at the enormity of his own share in storming this sacred fastness.

Campion peered round him in the gloom.

'There are other rooms, of course?'

'This is the only actual habitable room, sir. The others are only caverns. They go right on down to the Trough.'

'The Trough?'

'Yes, sir. That's the local name of the big cave on the estuary bay. It runs a long way under the hill and the old river road leads past it. At one time it used to be a great place for picnics and so on, but the water comes right up to the entrance at high tide and there were so many cases of people getting caught down there that the Masters declared it shut and ran a railing across the entrance, which isn't very wide. A place like that gets very dirty and untidy if you leave it open to the public.'

'I suppose so. Can you get down to it from here?'

'I don't know, sir. No one's allowed in here, you see. I don't think you can. As far as I know you can get on to a sort of gallery which looks down into the Trough, but I don't think there's any way down from that. When I was a boy we used to dare each other to get up into the Masters' store-rooms, but it was a terrific climb and you needed a rope. We never got very far.'

'I see. I'd like to go on a bit, though. Is that possible?'

'It's possible, sir.' Hutch did not add that it was also insane in his opinion, with the seconds racing by so dangerously.

A new doggedness had come over Campion and he hunched his shoulders.

'We'll have to risk it,' he said.

Hutch was an experienced man and he worked quickly, but it was not an easy adventure since he was as ignorant of the geography of the place as was Campion, and their first need was to get out of the Council Chamber without stumbling inadvertently through any one of the Four Doors of Bridge.

They found the way by considering the formation of the cavern in which the chamber was set and came at first to an astonishingly efficient furnace-room with a chimney built up through a prehistoric airshaft in the hill. From there they passed on into a passage which had been roughly lined at some much earlier period, and thence an iron ladder took them down into the Masters' store-rooms.

These long caverns were unexpectedly well ventilated and confirmed Campion's suspicions that the whole Nag was nothing less than a fortress, probably dating back to Neolithic times.

A brief inspection disclosed that the main use to which the Masters put their space was the storage of wine. The first gallery contained rack after rack of dusty black bottles and a smile appeared on the Superintendent's strained face as he looked at them.

'They must have done themselves proud for generations,' he said. 'I bet there's a fortune here. As a matter of fact they do own vineyards all over the world, I've heard.'

Campion did not comment.

At the end of the gallery the entrance to the next cavern was small and had been boarded up at some time. Hutch ran his

67

torch beam over the edges of the torn wood lying in a neat pile on the uneven floor.

'This hasn't been down long,' he remarked. 'They've been making room for more liquor, I suppose.'

It certainly looked like it. It seemed hardly credible, but the thin shafts from the Superintendent's two torches disclosed pile upon pile of small packing-cases, each sealed and labelled with a grower's name and burnt with the same hieroglyphics. Most of it appeared to be hock and it was clear that the Masters had had the forethought to see that no European upheaval could interfere with their serious drinking.

Hutch gaped. 'There's a cargo of it,' he said, sounding thoroughly shocked. 'A perishing cargo. Hallo, sir, what's the matter?'

Campion had paused in the middle of a step. His body had become rigid and he stood immovable, his head raised.

'Listen,' he whispered.

Hutch became a rock. He had extinguished his torch and now both men waited in the suffocating darkness which filled the world about them like black wool.

'What was it, sir?' The Superintendent's agonized demand was only just audible.

'A petrol engine. Listen.'

Very faint, so muffled that it was more of a sensation than a sound, the throbbing reached them.

'It's beneath us,' said Campion briefly. 'Come on.'

'Sir . . .' Hutch was a good man and he knew his duty, but there is one State Department which does not recognize its servants if they make mistakes. He did not belong to it and thirty years' blameless record was at stake.

'Give me the torches. You stay where you are.' It occurred to Campion briefly that it was odd that he should issue orders so naturally and should be so certain that they would be unquestionably obeyed. He went on alone, moving like a wraith but very quickly, with a sure-footed stealth which betrayed long practice. He did not see the second iron ladder until he was almost upon it, and he paused with his heart in his mouth, peering down into the abyss.

The throbbing had ceased, but in the cold underground air there was a slight but unmistakable breath of exhaust. He went down the ladder for what seemed a very long way and found himself in a passage no wider than his outstretched arms.

Here the taint was stronger and he moved very cautiously, keeping the pin-point of light from the small torch on the ground at his feet. An abrupt right-angle turn brought him up with a start. The fumes were much stronger now and, mingling with them, was the fresh sharp tang of the sea.

He pressed on and came out suddenly into what felt like a vast open space. The air smelt like a garage and his tiny ray of light suddenly lengthened as the path ended in a yawning hole before his feet. He paused, breathless, and switched off the light.

There was no sound, no sign of life, nothing except the strong reek of petrol. He hesitated. If the place was occupied his presence must already be discovered. He took the Superintendent's larger torch in his left hand and, holding it at arm's length so that the beam should arise a good three feet away from him on the wrong side, switched it on.

What he saw was so unexpected that he almost dropped the torch. He was on a narrow ledge, high up on the rock wall of a cave which could only be the Trough of the Superintendent's description, for it stretched away to a narrow railed opening far away in the distance. This in itself was not altogether unexpected, but what was extraordinary was that directly below him, hidden from the entrance by a natural partition which jutted out into the main body of the cave, was a large pocket or alcove, snug and secret, which housed at the moment something under three hundred three-ton lorries of varying types and ages, but clearly in good running order and ready for the road.

Campion swung the torch over them and the finger of light rested on bonnets and cabs, on yawning bodies and solid wheels. The narrow shaft of light ran up one row and down the next, wavered dangerously and swept on again.

Campion forced himself to finish his inspection, but that single glimpse at the end of the row had been enough. He had seen the face of the man, crouching back into the shelter of an overhanging cab. It had been a white face in the bright light and it had been familiar. It had flashed into his vision bringing a name with it; a name and a deep feeling of no enthusiasm, as someone once said so expressively.

'Weaver Bea.'

As he repeated it under his breath it sounded absurd and unlikely and yet in all the turmoil in his mind it remained familiar and unpleasant.

It was at this point that the full realization of his own utter inefficiency came home to him. The curious singleness of purpose which had hitherto characterized his condition was wearing thin and he began to take a more normal view of the situation in which he found himself, inasmuch as he began to suspect himself at every step. He saw himself making mountains out of molehills, and, what was even worse, pitfalls into mere depressions. Moreover, the physical effect of the experience had begun to tell on him again. His head ached maddeningly and he was not too certain of his legs.

He crept back the way he had come but, although he paused to listen when he reached the right-angle bend, there was still no sound from the great hidden garage he had left.

As he felt his way up the narrow iron ladder he tried to assimilate what he had seen since entering the Nag. It was both tantalizing and alarming. He had the uncomfortable feeling that it might all be very ordinary if seen with the clear eyes of a normally informed person. Any municipal stronghold of great antiquity could probably appear fantastic to the completely ignorant. Yet, on the other hand, every half-observed aspect of the place might well possess some all-important significance which he ought to recognize at once. There was the number 15 on the agenda: that must be of interest. And the man he had just seen: if his presence was normal, why had he hidden?

He struggled on and by the time he heard the Superintendent's heavy breathing just ahead of him he had made up his mind. There was only one course open to him which was not criminally negligent. He must get into touch with Oates at once. He ought to have done that immediately on receipt of the letter, of course. He wondered why he had ignored this obvious solution and suddenly remembered Anscombe and his own invidious position in that matter, which had focused his entire attention on the personal aspect. Hutch had only just explained that, of course. Good God, he was mad! Here he was, stumbling about in the dark seeing monsters where there were bushes and innocent shadows where there might be death-traps, and all the time the precious hours were racing past. He was a lunatic, very possibly a dangerous lunatic. Mercifully he was gradually getting the intelligence to recognize the fact.

The Superintendent was eager for news but even more eager to get out of his highly compromising position. He led the way back with alacrity and they passed across the Council Chamber like a couple of homing foxes.

'Lorries?' he said in astonishment when Campion had replied to his question. 'How many?'

'Several.' Campion could not explain his own urge towards caution.

Hutch shook his head. 'I don't know anything about them,' he said. 'It's the Government work, I expect. They're doing a lot of experiments with synthetic juice up at the Institute – at least that's the gossip. The Masters own the Institute, and, come to think of it, the Trough wouldn't be a bad place to hide a lorry or two. You're suddenly in a great hurry, sir. You weren't seen, were you?'

'No,' said Campion truthfully, 'but I've got to get a move on now.'

The Superintendent opened his mouth to make an inquiry, but the experience of long service saved him the indiscretion. Moreover, they were approaching the store-room behind the shop again.

They got out without incident but Hutch was not pleased to find it almost dawn. Fortunately it was misty and the two men plunged into the chilling vapour as thankfully as if it had been a smoke-screen especially provided for their benefit.

As they passed down the broad highway of the Nag's Pykle

the squat houses blinked at them through the haze and the town of Bridge looked a little less like a fairy-tale than it had done by moonlight. It was old and very picturesque, but the unreality, the frankly fantastic atmosphere of the night before, had vanished with the moon.

Campion was relieved to see it and to credit his returning intelligence with the change. He felt definitely ill. His head was throbbing and his body ached. However, he knew what he had to do. Amanda was his card. Amanda must take him to Oates. It was odd that the very recollection of Amanda should wrap such comfort round him. He must get out of that, he supposed, if she had made up her mind, and yet . . . it was absurd. All that was ridiculous. Amanda was not only his: she *was* himself. Amanda . . . oh, he couldn't be bothered to work it out. He must get to her . . . get to her . . . get . . . to . . . her.

Hutch caught him as he stumbled, and as they stood swaying together on the cobbles Campion was aware of some inner reserve of strength like a separate person within his body reaching down, down, and dragging his submerging faculties to the surface again. It was a staggering experience, like being rescued from drowning in a dream.

The Superintendent's face, which had loomed very large, gradually resumed its normal proportions and his voice, which had receded to a distant hail, slipped back into tune.

'You've overdone it, sir, that's what you've done. We're just by the station. You'll have to sit down. You can't go on for ever without sleeping or eating; no one can.'

The tone was plaintive and gently nagging.

'You'll go sick on your feet, and then where shall we be?'

He was leading his charge all the time with the firm efficiency of long practice and they advanced upon the unexpectedly modern Police Station, set among the Tudor scenery, in spite of his companion's incoherent protests.

A Police Sergeant met them on the doorstep and there was a muttered conference between him and his chief.

'Is there?' Hutch said at last. 'I see. Yes. Yes, of course. Put it through at once. We'll take it in the Charge Room.' He turned to Campion anxiously. 'There's a personal call waiting for you, sir,' he said. 'It's from Headquarters. Can you manage it? Are you all right?'

Campion had no clear impression of his passage through the station. He came back to himself as he sat staring into the black mouthpiece of the shabby telephone.

'Yeo here, Mr Campion,' said a voice in his ear. It was so small and quiet that it might have been the whisper of conscience. 'Yeo. Have you got the Chief with you?'

'Oates?' Campion's own voice was strong and apprehensive. It seemed to him that he was shouting.

'Yes, sir. He's gone. We can't find him. He left his room here in the small hours of yesterday morning and hasn't been heard of since. Is he with you?'

'No, he's not here.'

There was a long pause. It seemed to stretch into centuries and shrink again into a minute's space. He had time to become aware of the light streaming in through the tall windows and of the green distemper on the wall at the end of the room.

The faraway voice spoke again.

'Then it's you alone now, sir. You're the only one now who can do anything. None of the rest of us here even know the full strength. I don't know if you think that's wise, sir. The Chief was in sole control of his agents.'

Campion could not reply and after a pause the little voice came again.

'Any . . . luck, sir?'

Campion closed his eyes and opened them again as once more the secret reserve which lies in every human body was pumped up into his veins.

'Not yet,' he said distinctly, 'but there's still an hour or two.'

Then he slipped forward across the table, his head in his arms.

IX

He woke holding Amanda's hand. He was so relieved to find it there, so comforted to see her, alive, friendly, and gloriously intelligent, that for a blessed moment he remained mindless and content. He lay looking at her with placid, stupid eyes.

'You're ill,' she said, her clear, immature voice frankly anxious. 'I've been trying to wake you for hours. What shall I do? Phone Oates?'

That did it. That brought him back to the situation with a rush. Everything he knew, everything he had discovered or experienced since he had awakened in the hospital bed, sped past his conscious mind like a film raced through a projector at treble speed. The effect was catastrophic. It took his breath away and left him sweating.

'No,' he said, struggling into a sitting position, while the whole top of his head seemed to slide backwards sickeningly. 'No, that's no good. I mean don't do that. I'll get up at once.'

'All right,' she agreed, and he looked at her with deep affection. She was quite obviously worried about him and in her opinion he should have stayed where he was, but he was the boss and she was not arguing. She was so pretty, too, so young and vividly sensible. He liked her brown eyes and wished she would kiss him. The reflection that he had probably lost her for ever was such an incredible disaster that he put it away from him, unconsidered, and tightened his grip on her hand childishly.

'How late am I?'

'About an hour.' She released herself gently. 'You start the tour of inspection at ten. I'll run you a bath and then go down and scrounge you some breakfast. You've got twenty minutes before you leave the house.'

'Tour of inspection?' he said dubiously. 'What – er – what do I wear?'

He had hoped for a clue, but for once she was unobliging.

'Oh, just the simple uniform of an Admiral of the Fleet, I should think, don't you?'

Her voice floating back from the other room was followed by the roar of his bath water.

'Or you might stick to the old fireman's outfit, of course. That's bright and cheerful without being vulgar. I say,' she added as she came in again, 'what about those things? The servants here look as though they take a valet's interest in one's wardrobe. It'll look so bad if you come in and find them neatly laid out on the bed. Shall I take them down and stuff them in the toolbox of the car?'

'I wish you would. They're in the cupboard,' he said. 'You're very helpful, Amanda.'

She did not answer for a moment, but when she emerged from the armoire with her arms full of oilskins her cheeks were bright.

'I'm still the Lieut,' she said, facing him squarely. 'You get up and see to that bath or we'll have a flood. Time's very short.'

Short! As the door closed behind him he realized how short time was and cursed himself for sleeping. He could only just remember the later events of the morning. Hutch had brought him home in a car and had put him to bed like a mother. Mercifully they had not given him alcohol at the Police Station. That might well have killed him with his head in its present condition. The Sergeant in charge had apologized, he remembered, and had substituted a stimulant fashionable in official circles at the moment, sweet weak tea. There had been gallons of it. The glucose had probably saved his life.

He said 'probably' because getting out of bed proved to be a major operation. However, the sleep had done him good. Miraculously he had lost his terror of his disability. Now he was merely exasperated by it. He did not realize that this phenomenon was nothing less than a return of his original singleness of purpose and that it was a far more dangerous condition. He only saw that there was work to be done, that he was alone to do it, and that time was desperately short.

By the time he staggered downstairs he was fairly clear about his immediate plan of campaign. The Masters were his best bet.

They knew the secret of 15 if anyone did, since they were making it their main business of the evening. Lee Aubrey must be persuaded to tell him all there was to be known about the Masters. For the rest, since they had obviously arranged a programme for himself when he had been in full possession of his senses, that programme must be part of his original plan and the only thing to do was to go through with it.

He found Aubrey waiting for him in a brown and yellow morning-room. He was standing by the window looking with tragedian's eyes at Amanda, who sat behind the silver. His greeting was gravely commiserating, as though he knew that lesser men had weaknesses and he could be tolerant and even a little envious of them.

Campion, watching him with his new child's eyes, saw what Amanda liked in him and sized it up like a General inspecting enemy fortifications before the commencement of hostilities.

He made a hurried breakfast and, only half-way through the meal, realized that it was Lee who was waiting for him.

'It's too bad we can't take you with us.' Aubrey spoke to the girl with a frankness of regret which was almost indecent. 'But I'm afraid it's impossible. We're not exactly wedded to the Government, but we're rather definitely under its protection, in the eighteenth-century sense, and my instructions only apply to Campion. It's all quite, quite mad, of course. I sometimes wonder if the fellows who set out these restrictions aren't using a little too broad a rule. There's not enough brains to go round, you know. That's the fundamental weakness in the Government and everywhere else.'

'Oh, that's all right,' said Amanda cheerfully. 'I don't want to see your old Institute. The whole show sounds like a municipal school of conjuring to me.'

Lee hesitated and it was only after a moment that his charming smile spread over his large curling features.

'You shocked me,' he said with disarming naïveté. 'I get very parochial down here. One does. To hear the Masters called "municipal" gives me a sacrilegious thrill.'

'They achieve almost international status, financially at any rate, don't they?' Campion's thought was running on spice islands and he spoke unguardedly.

Lee raised his head and gave him one of his surprisingly intelligent stares.

'They're very wealthy, of course,' he said primly.

'Yes, well, there you are. A penny here and a penny there, it all mounts up over a period of years.' Campion had intended to sound ignorant, but even he was unprepared for the degree of fatuous idiocy he managed to present.

Lee looked genuinely embarrassed and glanced at Amanda apologetically.

'When you're ready we'll go,' he said, and later, as he and Campion walked across the turf together, he took it upon himself to explain gently, choosing his words carefully as though talking to a child. 'Historically the Masters are amazingly interesting,' he began, reproval in his pleasant voice. 'The family which was the leading spirit at their foundation never completely rotted away. The Letts have never produced any great men, but nor have they had any downright wrong 'uns, and there's always been one moderately intelligent business man in every generation. The present fellow, Peter Lett, is just a good sound average brain like his uncle before him, and his grandfather and great-grandfathers before that. They've all been religious, respectable, and very parochial, while of course the curious hereditary and semi-secret structure of the society has been a tremendous safeguard. Financially the Masters have had their bad periods but they've never gone quite under. Their basic line is so good.'

'What's that?'

Aubrey seemed astounded. 'Patents, of course,' he said.

'Patents?'

'Well,' he was laughing a little, 'it was monopolies to begin with, naturally. Queen Elizabeth gave them their first big break. One of the kids in the little charity school they started up turned out to be the great Ralph Godlee, who invented the Godlee loom. The Masters got a monopoly on the manufacture of things for the Queen and it revolutionized the wool-weaving industry over here, speeding up the production by about five

77

hundred per cent and making the town's fortune. The word "abridged" comes from it. It shortened the process. But you know all this as well as I do.'

Campion coughed. 'At the moment there are gaps in my education,' he admitted modestly. 'Do go on. I find this fascinating. They've continued like this, have they? – first educating and then fleecing the inventor?'

Lee made a deprecatory grimace and quite openly thought for a moment or so. He was extraordinarily unself-conscious in that one way. His thinking was obvious, almost pantomimic.

'That's not quite true,' he said at last. 'One must be fair. Let's say that instead of patronizing the arts they've always gone in for science and have been lucky in having been able to produce a few valuable inventors who have always made their own fortunes as well as adding to the general fund. The Masters had their great successes in the Victorian industrial age, naturally. It's only comparatively recently that they've become so very wealthy. They bought very sensibly at that time, always going for overseas property, tea plantations and so on. At the moment I think the Institute gives more than value for money every time. Look at the facilities the chosen inventor gets here. Once his idea is approved, every mortal thing he needs is given to him gratis. His patents are acquired for him and he hands out a percentage. Just now things are more than booming, naturally. The Carter cheap process for extracting petrol from coal is going to be an enormous thing, and we've one or two pleasant little explosives on the carpet. The whisky bottle you can't refill is another one of ours too; that's a great money-maker.'

Campion listened to him fascinated. He knew it, he had heard it all before, he was sure of that, and vaguely it was all coming back to him. It reminded him almost of a rubbing of an old brass. Shadowy outlines of facts were coming up on the blank surfaces of his mind. If only he felt a little more sure of his legs, a little less as though he were ploughing through clouds of cotton-wool which gave beneath him!

'I don't approve of the Masters in principle,' Lee was saying pedantically. 'I don't like pockets of wealth like that in the

78

country. But, to do these fellows justice, their little constitution does good work. The Ceremony of the Bale of Straw is a nice archaic idea, for instance. All the mummery of the fraternity is connected with the Nag, you know, and they have a ruling that at every half-yearly meeting the Masters shall "put down a bale of straw in the Nag's stable"; that is to say they shall do something to improve the amenities of the town of Bridge. That's why the place is so luxuriously drained, watered, and lit. There's not a scrap of slum property in the area. Fortunes are being spent on the place and the rates are negligible. Here we are. See the sentry? That's what working for the War House does for you.'

They had come up over the ridge of high ground which stretched up behind the poplar trees and had reached the private roading leading to the Institute, a cluster of roofs surrounded by a high moss-grown wall. The original building was now no more than a museum, but all around it clustered other houses, workshops, and laboratories, representing every phase of British architecture. There was the usual preponderance of Victorian-Gothic and a generous sprinkling of modern pill-box.

A soldier with fixed bayonet stood on guard before the ornamental iron gates. Lee Aubrey smiled at the man as they passed.

'Gloriously mad, isn't it?' he murmured. 'There's something rather sweet and childlike about the modern world, don't you think? "Halt. Give the countersign. Pass friend. Eena-deena-dina-do, you're a spy." It's so monstrously young.'

'Childish perhaps, but hardly sweet,' said Campion absently. 'Where do we go first?'

'My dear fellow, that's entirely up to you. My instructions are that I'm to show you anything that you care to see. Take your choice. On your left you have the bad-tempered but otherwise wholly delightful Carter working with his team of galley-slaves. They'll be polite because I'm by way of being Headmaster, but they won't be hospitable.'

Aubrey was enjoying himself. He was exaggeratedly proud of the place and its magnificent organization.

'On your extreme right, in that depressing building which looks like a Methodist chapel, is poor old Burgess. He'll talk all night. He's having trouble with his reaper. The late trials were nothing less than a fiasco and he may have struck a serious snag. Before you is the library, the office, the filing department, and the drafting-rooms. And right over there, as comfortably distant as space will permit, is the star turn of the moment, the War House's little white-headed boy, our young Master Butcher, mucking about with Anderton's latest variety of potted hell fire. I have to keep an eye on him and see he controls his quantities. It's incredible stuff. Half a teaspoonful can make as much mess as a bucketful of T.N.T. Hence the sentry on the door.'

He paused expectantly and Campion stood irresolute. This was a continuation of the frustration dream of the night before. As far as he could see, the whole thing was being handed to him on a plate and yet he could not put his finger on it.

'It's almost an embarrassment of riches,' he said aloud, and added hastily: 'What's in the dovecote?'

The building so unkindly described had caught his attention because of a certain amount of life going on before it. A lorry loading sacks was drawn up in front of the door.

Lee frowned and the man at his side was aware of the wave of irritation which passed over him. It was a physical thing, as if his personal magnetism had been switched off and on again.

'You've got a nose, haven't you?' he said, half laughing. 'You're one of those people who always move the chair which covers the hole in the carpet and go straight to the cupboard where the dirty washing-up has been hidden. I offer you the exciting drawing-room exhibits and you go direct to the one dull ugly scullery in the place. That's our cross, the blot on our dignity. We've been compelled to shelter fifty beastly little amateur workers simply because we happen to have a lot of room. Think of it! In that sacred building Richardson perfected his adding machine, and now half a hundred little girls who can hardly write are addressing envelopes there for the Ministry of Health. As if there weren't five million other places in England which would do quite as well. I tell you, I have them shepherded in and out by a police matron and a stalwart Corps of Commissionaires. Like to come and look at them?'

'Not very much,' said Campion. They had reached the building by this time and through the long windows he could see rows of bent heads and piles of Government envelopes. It looked dull work, but in his present mood highly preferable to his own, and he envied them.

As they skirted the lorry a woman with untidy white hair came out of the arched doorway. She was faintly familiar and he recognized her at last as one of Aubrey's dinner guests of the night before. She was startled to see them and came up with that half hesitant, half eager humility which is more common in far younger women.

'We're getting on very nicely, Mr Aubrey,' she said appealingly and blushed.

Campion was surprised. Missing on four out of five cylinders though he was, he could still recognize those symptoms when he saw them, and she was not that kind of woman. A great many ladies who are old enough to know better frequently become hopelessly infatuated with brilliant middle-aged bachelors, but they are seldom of the experienced, intelligent type of gentlewoman which he saw before him. He recollected that she had been very interested in Amanda the last time he had seen her. He glanced at Aubrey, to find him frigid.

'Splendid, Mrs Ericson,' he said briefly and passed on, leaving a flavour of distaste in the air. 'Patriotic voluntary work,' he murmured under his breath to Campion as they turned the corner. 'Intense stuff.'

'She looked intelligent,' said Campion and Lee considered the matter.

'Oh, she is,' he agreed brightly. 'She's a widow of the late holder of one of the Masters' minor offices and quite a power in the town. Very well read, you know, nice, educated, but emotionally unstable, I fancy. Now this is Butcher's domain, which I take it is your main interest. I say, I admire your magnificent reticence, Campion. It's impressive.'

The final observation was made impulsively and as if he meant it.

Campion said nothing and hoped that his silence might pass for modest appreciation. There was a dull throbbing in the back of his head and he had begun to wonder if his vision was not a little deceptive. All the colours in the bright sunlight tended to blur together dangerously. He took hold of himself again. This was hopeless! There was something to be done and, as far as he could gather, only himself to do it. It was a fine thing if he was going to fall down on it through a goddamn silly bang on the head.

It was a longish walk to the square concrete tower at the far end of the Institute grounds and when they reached it their inspection was not illuminating. Butcher himself turned out to be a cheerful youngster with the face of a ploughboy and thick pebbled glasses. He had a youthful respect for Aubrey, whom he clearly admired, and was pleased to show his laboratories and workshops.

'These are the best of the bunch,' he said, diving into a rough cupboard in a corner of the main room on the ground floor, which had been deserted and open to the path as they came up. 'I keep them in their racks because they really are pretty sensational. We call 'em Phoenix Eggs. Don't drop it, old man, will you? It's quite safe unless you dig that pin out, of course, but it's as well not to bounce it about because it's only a specimen and you never know.'

Campion looked down at the metal egg so suddenly thrust in his hand. It was a little larger than a hen's and unexpectedly light. Butcher was fondling another, fitting it lovingly into the hollow under his thumb.

'It's important to be able to chuck it a decent distance,' he explained. 'It's pretty powerful. The blast is colossal and they even make quite a crater. It's wonderful really. You can make almost any building look silly with only one of these. It's the Anderton variety of liquid air, but we've improved on it – or at least we've utilized every aspect of it. I could hit that old museum over there with this and after the balloon had gone up, oh boy, you wouldn't know it! This is refined warfare, that's what this is.'

He retrieved Campion's specimen, juggled with the

two of them absently, and replaced them in their nests.

'They're putting up the machines for these now,' he said. 'I've got some nice little aero models coming along in the basement, but we're still working on the detonators. Anything else in particular that you'd like to see?'

'No, I won't keep you from your work. You've given me more than fifteen minutes already.'

The young man's expression did not change and Campion shook hands and turned away. A sixth sense, or rather that mysterious body-mind which so often seems to take charge when one's normal brain goes back on one, was looking after him. His reserve and non-committal tone were far more impressive than any show of appreciation could ever have been and young Butcher retired to his underground laboratory wondering if the Authorities really put quite the trust in him which their behaviour so far had caused him to suspect.

It was Campion who led Aubrey out into the sun again. He had listened to a quantity of technical detail from Butcher, all of which might be important to an enemy but was not so to him. Whatever Butcher knew was also known already, presumably, by the War Office and was therefore none of Campion's business. What he must be looking for was something which was hitherto unknown to them. Fifteen? He must keep his mind clear and hang on to that. Fifteen: that was still his only definite clue. Fifteen, and the people who knew what it meant. Butcher was evidently not one of them, but there was someone else who was.

As he raised his eyes and looked down the narrow concrete path which ran like a chalk-line across the green turf, he saw the man he was thinking about. He appeared so quickly that it was difficult to say whether thought or vision came first. His jaunty roundness was recognizable at a tremendous distance and he came bouncing along towards them without haste.

X

'That fellow Pyne,' said Campion.

'Really?' Aubrey's distinctive face clouded. 'What on earth is the man doing wandering round here alone like this? They've let him in to look for me, I suppose. They mustn't do that, as they very well know. He's talked his way in, you see. How extraordinary these fellows are! I'm quite prepared to like him, but he mustn't make himself a nuisance. I loathe having to tell a man to clear out.'

'Who is he?'

'Pyne? Oh, rather an interesting bird. Remarkably intelligent in his own way. Probably dishonest. Works like a fiend.' Lee had dropped into his objective mood again. His remarks were quite free from affectation and he spoke with the judicial simplicity of an admittedly superior being. 'He's evacuated his office down here. It's an amusing little organization and he makes a very good thing out of it. He calls it Surveys Limited. I suppose you've heard of it?'

'It's faintly familiar,' said Campion not untruthfully. 'What do they do? Arrange one's life for one?'

Lee laughed. 'Only in part,' he murmured. 'They're an advice and information bureau. If you want to build a factory or start up a business in an unknown locality they'll get out all the dope on the place for you. They're remarkably thorough. Apart from the usual stuff, they tabulate the most intimate details, including some very shrewd work on public opinion and estimates of local wealth. In fact they'll sound every possible depth for you in strictest confidence. Pyne told me once that he had ten thousand agents all over England. That probably means that he's employed about half that number at some time or other during his career. I imagine any man to whom he's ever given five bob for personal views on local conditions is included in the aggregate, but still, to do him justice, he does seem to get the commissions. Mildly entertaining?'

Campion nodded briefly. He was not in the condition to be mildly entertained and Pyne was almost upon them.

By morning light he did not look quite so amiable and easygoing. At first Campion was inclined to blame his own unreliable observation on the night before for the change, but as soon as the newcomer began to speak he was not so sure. Pyne was still hearty, but now there was suppressed anxiety and a touch of antagonism there as well. He greeted them without preliminaries.

'Any developments?' he demanded as soon as he was within speaking distance.

'In which direction?' Campion was relieved to find that his own powers of controlling both his face and voice were considerable.

'Well, what about last night? What about Anscombe?' Pyne was keyed up and his round eyes were as shifty and inquisitive as a sparrow's.

A thin trickle of fear dribbled down Campion's spine. Until that moment he had entirely forgotten the incident. The enormity of the omission appalled him. Anscombe and his disturbing manner of dying had gone clean out of his mind. Good God! If he had forgotten that, what else had he overlooked? To his relief Lee looked faintly shamefaced also.

'Oh Lord! Miss Anscombe!' he said. 'I *must* go down to see her. It's early yet, but what a merciful chance you reminded me. Once one gets behind this wall one passes into another world, you know. Don't you feel it, Campion? The mind simply settles down to consider ideas and their technical development. Poor old Anscombe. I knew him reasonably well, but in here and at the moment he's absolutely remote.'

Pyne wiped his forehead. 'You're lucky,' he said dryly. 'I've been thinking of him all night. I don't like the look of that death. If the police are satisfied, of course, it's nothing to do with me, but I rather wondered if they were?'

There was a question in his last remark and Campion, who recollected just in time that no one present knew of his late night meeting with Hutch, ignored it. Lee Aubrey was less cautious.

'Anscombe was of the type who never commit suicide,' he said didactically.

Pyne glanced at Campion.

'Murder was the thought in my mind,' he said.

Lee coughed and moved on up the path. He was offended. His mouth was pursed and he looked shocked.

'My dear chap,' he protested, giving the protest just sufficient reproach to make it also a rebuke, 'hysteria at this time in the morning is inexcusable. And there's one other thing while I think of it, Pyne. You really must not come in here unless I bring you personally. It's simply not allowed. The British Government has put its foot down on the subject. I don't want to know how you got yourself admitted, because I don't want to have to report the poor beast on the gate, but for heaven's sake don't do it again.'

It was as near a schoolmaster's scolding as Campion had ever heard administered to a grown man. Pyne gave no sign that he had heard. He remained round, pink, and dangerously suspicious.

'There's been a manhunt all over this district for the last twelve hours at least,' he remarked presently as they walked on. 'A fellow wanted by the police escaped from St Jude's Hospital in Coachingford last night. He pinched an old car, abandoned it at the water-splash on the lower Bridge road, and disappeared. They're still searching for him. Doesn't that strike you as suspicious?'

Lee burst out laughing, an almost feminine spitefulness in his amusement.

'Oh, come,' he said, 'that's abominable thinking. Some wretched man is escaping from the police and therefore it's only natural to suppose that the first thing he does is to sneak into a garden and murder old Anscombe, who happened to be there. It's childish, Pyne. It won't wash. You're upset, my dear chap. That obtrusive stomach of yours is out of order.'

The little fat man jerked in his belly, but his eyes did not lose their alarming shrewdness.

'I was thinking, Campion,' he began, 'you must have come

86

over from Coachingford about the right time. You didn't see anything of this man, did you?'

'No,' said Campion. His tone was mild, he noticed.

Lee sighed with exasperation. 'My good Pyne,' he said, taking the other man's arm with weary familiarity which had in it the very essence of condescension, 'you're making an unholy ass of yourself, you know.'

'I don't believe I am, Aubrey.'

'Then you must take my word for it.' Lee was smiling dangerously. 'Campion is personally known to me and I give you my word that (a) he gave no lift to any escaping suspect, and (b) that suspect did not reward him by bumping off poor old Anscombe in his own front yard. Moreover, that suggestion is ridiculous, it's absurd, it's mad, it's nuts. Forget it, and let the police do their own chores.'

Pyne allowed himself to be led out of the Institute gates and across the turf towards the house. If Aubrey was offending him he did not show it.

'I don't know Mr Campion well. If you do, I've nothing more to say,' he remarked at last in a perfectly unruffled tone. 'But have you read the description of the man the police are looking for?'

'No, I haven't. I don't think I want to particularly.'

'I found it interesting.' Pyne's placid obstinacy was insuppressible. 'The man they want is thirty-five years old and six-foot-two high. He has a pale face and sleek blond hair, and his chief characteristics are that he is very thin and yet powerful.' He paused and when no one spoke added ingenuously: 'When last seen he was wearing fireman's oilskins.'

Lee crowed with delight. 'And a brass helmet as well?' he demanded. 'This is lovely. Pyne, my poor friend, you're giving me an enormous amount of innocent pleasure. Do go on; I wouldn't stop you for the world.'

The plump man turned to Campion.

'What do you think?' he inquired.

Campion appeared to give the matter serious consideration. They had reached the ridge of high ground and were now sauntering down towards the poplar trees. He had his hands in his pockets and they were clenched so that the nails dug into his palms. His heart was thudding in his side and before the dark curtain hung across his mind his conscious thoughts were as chaotic and useless as those behind it were lost. He was dithering, and that fact frightened him far more than this dangerous little man's questions.

'What name would you put to that description?' Pyne persisted.

He was waiting for an answer. He was waiting for an answer. He was waiting for an answer. A minute had gone by, a whole minute. A minute; perhaps another minute. Campion could not think. Good God, he could not *think*. This was horrible, terrifying. He could not think. The machinery for thinking had broken down. He was helpless, lost, at the mercy of this dreadful little creature with the cruel, predatory eyes of a bird.

What name? What name? What *name*?

'Almost any, I should say,' he murmured, unaware that he sounded more bored than anything else. 'John Smith, Albert Campion, Weaver Bea.'

There was complete silence. It lasted so long that he was able to drag himself out of his floundering panic and glance round before anyone spoke.

Lee Aubrey was mooching along with his shoulders hunched under his sleek, almost foppishly cut jacket. He was clearly embarrassed by the personal turn which the conversation had taken. The ridiculous name which had slipped out so dangerously had not registered upon him.

But with Pyne it was very different. For the first time his shining composure was destroyed. He had changed colour and his eyes were no longer merely suspicious. He turned his head and looked the other man full in the face.

'I've obviously made an idiotic mistake, Mr Campion,' he said. 'That scene last night unnerved me a bit, I expect. You and I ought to have a talk some time. Why don't you come down to my office? I think you'd be interested in it. We might have a spot of lunch together in the town.'

'That's an idea,' Lee cut in before Campion could reply. He spoke with the hearty relief of the host who thinks he sees a way of amusing the temporarily unwanted guest. 'That business of his will entertain you, Campion. I found it fascinating. Pyne's a most amusing beggar when he's not being melodramatic or playing detectives.'

Campion was silent. He had no illusions whatever about Pyne. The man was on the right track and knew it. It was a tight corner. Delay at this point was the one thing he knew would be fatal, and delay there certainly would be once the county police discovered in him the particular man for whom they were scouring the country. Headquarters might back him up to the hilt, but there would have to be explanations first and explanations would lead to the discovery of his condition, whatever else they disclosed. Whatever else? That question was too alarming even to consider and he shrank from it.

With what was obviously a habit with him in difficult moments he looked around for Amanda. To his relief he actually saw her, turning the corner of the house. He was not surprised. That was the miraculous part of Amanda; she always seemed to materialize at the right moment. It was as though they were partners in some long practised game, with years of experience and co-operation behind them. She hailed him and with a muttered word of excuse he hurried over to meet her. She spoke quietly as he came up.

'I say, the Superintendent's here. He wants to see you alone – apart from Lee, I mean. He won't come in and he's waiting round by the side door. Would you go to him?'

Would he! The idea of the lanky Hutch as a rescuing angel, robe, feathers, and all, did not seem in the least incongruous at that moment.

'Oh, bless you,' he said so fervently that her brown eyes widened.

'Sticky?' she inquired under her breath.

'Not so hot, anyway,' he admitted. 'Stay with them, will you, my darling? Don't let Pyne open his heart to Aubrey.'

He saw the faint flicker of astonishment in her expression and was puzzled by it until he realized that it was the heartfelt, grateful endearment which had surprised her. That was a revelation which brought him up with a jerk and his sudden sense of desolation was not lightened by the conviction that he deserved it.

He saw Hutch as soon as he turned into the yard. The plain-clothes man was sitting on the running-board of a huge old Buick and the sun shone down on the unexpectedly resplendent colours of his tweed suit. He rose as soon as Campion appeared and sauntered forward.

'Hallo!' Campion's greeting was unusually hearty. Here at least was an ally, however blindfold.

'Good morning.' A guarded quality in the policeman's tone struck a warning note which set every nerve in his body on edge. 'Can I have a few words with you, sir?'

'Of course. Why not? Carry on.' Campion felt he was talking too much and could not stop himself. 'What's the excitement?'

'No excitement, sir.' Hutch eyed him curiously. 'I'd just like you to take a look at this, if you will. We don't take any notice of these things as a rule, naturally, but in this case there are certain circumstances which made me think I'd bring it round to you.'

Campion glanced at the sheet of paper which was thrust into his hand. It bore a short typewritten message.

'DEAR SUPERINTENDENT,—
'When the Home Office issued you with instructions concerning Albert Campion, did they by any chance also send you a photograph? That's all. Think it over.'

There was no signature and it was undated. Campion read it through twice. It was Pyne, of course; probably written the night before after his own idiotic slip when he had fallen into the little trap concerning their previous association in the U.S.

The inference was obvious. Pyne saw there was something fishy about him and suspected him of impersonation, impersonation of Albert Campion. That was pretty good, pretty funny. He could soon put a stop to that, anyway.

Could he, though? The new danger opened out like a morass in front of him.

He gave back the sheet of paper with a steady hand, but his

head was hurting intolerably and he could feel the sweat on his forehead.

'Well?' he inquired.

Hutch produced another paper. This proved to be a police chit which detailed in the usual unenlightened phrases the chief physical characteristics of the man who had escaped in fireman's oilskins from St Jude's Hospital, Coachingford.

Campion read them aloud.

'Well,' he said again. The throbbing in the crown of his skull had turned to shooting pains of excruciating violence and the outlines of the Superintendent's jaunty figure were shimmering as though in a heat haze.

Hutch looked up. His eyes were searching and he took a long time to make up his mind to speak.

'I haven't got a warrant, of course,' he said at last, 'so I'd like to ask a favour of you. May I go over your room, sir, just to satisfy my own curiosity? I – well, to put it frankly, sir, when I was getting you to bed last night I noticed the whole room reeked of oilskins. I can't get that out of my head.'

Campion laughed aloud. It was not a very convincing sound, but at least it was spontaneous.

'Search with pleasure,' he said. 'Search the whole house. I'll square you with Aubrey. How long have you been in the police, Hutch?'

'Twenty-eight years and two months, sir.'

'Have you?' The implied criticism, as from a superior officer, had its effect. Campion felt rather than saw the man waver. He laughed again and with better humour. 'You trot along and set your mind at rest,' he said. 'If you find the uniform bring it to me. I'd like to see myself in fireman's rig. If it shouldn't be in the bedroom, well, try the rest of the house and then the grounds.'

Hutch shrugged. He was verging on the sheepish. He took a step towards the side door, changed his mind and came back.

'Just answer me two questions, sir. Then I'll apologize.'

This was more dangerous. Campion kept his tone light.

'Anything you like, Superintendent.'

'What is the name of the C.D.I. in Room 49 at Head-quarters?'

'Yeo.' It was a shot in the dark but he had not hesitated. The name had been dragged up out of his mind as he forced himself to hear again the small voice on the telephone the night before.

Hutch stood looking at him oddly. There was no way of telling whether he had succeeded or failed.

'And the second?' Campion took the bold line. To pause, he felt, might be fatal, and whatever happened he could not be held up now.

Hutch moistened his lips and lowered his voice.

'What's your own S.S. number, sir?'

Campion smiled. He had no idea, no idea in the world.

'At the moment I rather fancy it's fifteen,' he said, and laughed.

He saw he had blundered badly. He saw the consternation slowly dawning on Hutch's pleasant face as the enormity of the situation dawned on him, since it included his own inexcusable deception and the incredible indiscretion he had committed in taking an unauthorized person on the visit of the evening before. Campion saw the next move, imminent and inescapable. He saw himself detained, held up helpless while the vital hours raced by. His tormented mind shuttered. It was as though the dark curtain became for a moment an open venetian-blind. It rattled, flickered, and was shut again.

He hit out.

His fist possessed a cunning he did not anticipate. It was a beautiful, expert's blow which rippled from his left shoulder with the entire weight of his body behind it.

Hutch, who was still reeling under the nervous shock, was taken completely unawares. He went down like a tree, the silly expression of astonishment still on his face.

Campion did not look at him. He was not aware of him. From that instant he moved automatically. He stepped into the Buick, trod on the accelerator which was also the starter, and leant back.

The car bounced in the air and he took the drive at sixty. At the gates he turned to the left as if he knew exactly what he was doing and drove with uncanny precision and great speed through the town, under the lowering Nag, over the small mill-bridge and on through twisting country roads, all without hesitation or any conscious thought. His mind was a peaceful blank. Never afterwards had he any recollection of the journey. He travelled as migrating birds seem to travel, with blind knowledge. The brain behind the curtain was in charge and the conscious man might well have been in a hypnotic trance. From first to last he was peculiarly dexterous.

He entered the big industrial town of Coachingford by the Roman road and negotiated the by-pass circus without difficulty. One or two policemen saluted the car, with its small priority notice in the corner of the windscreen. He drove without hesitation through a knot of tiny streets, paused correctly for the lights, and took the complicated turnings with precision.

At an open garage in a dizzy square he slowed, drove the car into a shelter and climbed out. He did not feel his feet on the pavement and did not wait for his check. Moving with the un-hesitating singleness of purpose which renders a man so natural that he is next best to invisible, he crossed the road, turned down an alley, came out of it into a busy but impoverished street, and pressed on until he paused before a small and dirty shop which possessed a row of empty display boards outside and a dreary collection of cigarettes and dusty sweets in the window. He glanced up and down the road and then went inside.

The cold darkness of the shop, with its characteristic smell of printer's ink and tobacco, brought him suddenly out of his state of somnambulism. He stopped dead and stood staring about him with startled eyes. He had no idea where he was, nor how or why he had come. A grey face peered at him from behind the back of the counter and the two men remained looking at one another in mutual doubt.

The shopkeeper, who was old and thin and ineffectual, seemed quite as bewildered to see his visitor as Campion was to see him.

After the first shock of returning intelligence Campion grew

93

afraid. He was a man not used to fear in any form and its deep cold fingers gripped his stomach paralysingly.

The shopkeeper cleared his throat nervously and came edging round the counter.

'You'll want the boss,' he said. 'Come inside.'

Campion moved forward unsteadily and the other man raised a greasy flap in the counter. The back of the shop was very small and dark and the two panels of frosted glass in the door which the old man indicated looked like some bright avenue of escape. Campion all but charged them, hurling himself into the room within, while the shopkeeper drew the door silently behind him. It was in many ways a dreadful little room, papered with sections of grey fruit and still furnished with all the misguided decorations of the 'eighties. Practically the entire floor space was taken up by a large table, covered first with a red cloth and then with several sheets of newspaper.

Sitting at this table, collarless and in shirt-sleeves, was a very remarkable person. He had a white melancholy face hung beneath a glistening bald skull, and his eyes, which were narrow and expressionless, were dull as coal-dust. At the moment he was engaged in cleaning and oiling a heavy service revolver which looked as if it had been well loved for many years. He raised his eyes as the door burst open, but did not move his head or speak. Campion said nothing. He leant back against the panels of the door. His ears were drumming and the beating of his heart seemed to keep time to the intolerable throbbing in his head.

The man at the table breathed heavily through his short nose.

'So you've come back, 'ave yer?' he said.

XI

Campion did not speak. The walls of the tiny room were converging on him. The air was too warm and too heavy to force open his lungs. The face of the man at the table swelled terrifyingly, widening and widening like the white of an egg in a pan. Soon it must fill the whole universe and suffocate him beneath its flabby weight.

Campion's lips moved in a final despairing cry of protest, but no sound came.

Across the red table-cloth the fat man gazed at him with new interest. Suddenly he laid aside his gun and slipped quietly to his feet with that surprisingly smooth agility only found in old fighting men.

He came round the room and peered into the newcomer's face.

'Eh,' he said at last and the word was a grunt uttered deep in his throat. 'Come here.'

He lowered the young man on to a chair and propped his elbows on the table for him, while his own thick hands explored the scalp.

'You've 'ad a cosh, 'aven't you? 'Ow bad are yer?'

His concern was genuine and intensely practical. He was also very gentle without being in the least soft. It was like being delivered into the hands of some gargantuan Roman matron, or perhaps a friendly female bear.

'Answer up,' he commanded, prodding the nape of Campion's neck with a padded forefinger.

The injured man drew away from him wearily.

'Who the hell are you?' he murmured with just sufficient interest to drive home the genuineness of the inquiry.

'God Almighty!' The exclamation was no expletive but a direct and pious appeal to the Deity. The fat man plumped himself down on a chair and seized Campion's shoulders. His little black eyes were circular and a fine sprinkling of sweat appeared on his heavy face.

'Are you kiddin'? This isn't the ruddy time to play the goat, you know.'

Campion let his head roll forward. The pain of movement was almost welcome, since it cut through the dreadful breathless sense of weight which was stifling him.

'Do you know 'oo you are yerself?' There was a tremor in the thick voice so near his ear.

'Campion . . . It's written in my suit.'

'*Lumme!*' There was a brief pause while the older man assimilated the salient facts. Then he took command. 'Come on,' he said. 'Get yer collar orf and lie down. Don't try to use yer 'ead. It's no good to yer for a bit. You're all right. You're at 'ome. Don't start thinking. You're with yer own. Got that? With yer own. I'm goin' to put you on that sofa and cover you up while I get a crocus.'

'No.' Campion recognized the word without realizing that it was more than nine-tenths of his compatriots would have done. 'Can't have a doctor. Can't have any officials. They're all after me by now.'

' 'Oo?'

'The police.'

'Rozzers? You've made a mistake. You're punch-drunk. What 'ave you done?'

'Slugged a copper. Two coppers. The last one was the local Super, a dear good chap. I can't have killed him.'

'Killed 'im! 'Oo's talking of killing?' Generations of inbred fear of the one crime which is never forgiven to any man, however privileged, lay in the truculent demand.

'I am.' It was a relief to Campion to talk freely at last. 'Apparently I did kill the first one. Can't remember it. Woke up in hospital.'

'Horspital?' The fat man's heavy eyelids lowered a fraction. 'There was a man scarpered from the horspital in a fireman's outfit,' he suggested.

'Yes. That was me. Now I've slugged a Superintendent of Police. I can't remember anything after that until I walked in here. Who are you?'

The other did not reply directly. He got up heavily and as if he had grown older.

'You come and lie down,' he said. 'I want to 'ave a look at you. I'll get you as right as I can and then we'll talk. We'd better,' he added grimly.

Campion allowed himself to be led over to the dreadful imitation leather couch which took up practically all one side of the room, but the moment his head touched the clammy seat he struggled into a sitting position again.

'No time,' he said, unaware that the words were slurred. 'To-morrow's the fifteenth. Must get on. No time for this.'

'You'll 'ave all the time you want and more if you don't shut up. Lie still while I do a bit of doctoring.'

The bald man moved towards the door as he spoke.

'I'll just drop a word to old Happy Fanny outside to keep 'is eyes skinned in case they take sights of us. You don't know if you was followed 'ere, do you? No, that's right, you don't 'ave to tell me. You don't know anything. You lie still. I'll see to yer.'

It was warm and dark in the little room in spite of the time of day and the mean rickety french windows gave on to a weedy yard with a blank wall behind. Campion closed his eyes and was lost.

He came to himself to find artificial light burning painfully into his eyes. The fat man was on a chair, fitting a new bulb into a chandelier which hung over the table. It was a compli-cated arrangement of weights and pulleys decorated with dis-tressing pink frosted glass shades.

He clambered down cautiously and, groping under the table, produced a cone-shaped contraption of black paper which he fixed round and over the lighting arrangements, so that a brilliant pool lay in the centre of the table alone while the rest of the room was in comparative darkness. Having complied with these black-out restrictions, he returned to his patient.

'That's right,' he said with relief as he raised one of the pallid eyelids with a great thumb. 'You're not so dead as you was. I got you warm, see? Now I'm not giving you spirits because they might finish you, but I've got some muck 'ere you'd better drink. I've cooked it meself so I know what's in it.'

97

He went round the table and bent over a small grate where he had got a fire going. It was all very homely and grubbily comfortable.

Campion was puzzled by it, but not alarmed. The fat man, whoever he was, was a friend. He returned presently with a steaming jug which looked ominous but which turned out to contain nothing more extraordinary than strong old-fashioned beef tea, made according to Mrs Beeton. Campion was surprised to find that instead of being repelled by it he could drink it with enjoyment, and its effect upon him was extraordinary. As its warmth spread over him he felt strength generating in him as clearly as if new blood was being pumped into his veins. It occurred to him that he had not eaten properly for a very long time. His head felt clearer too; that was a mercy. Everything which had happened recently stood out in his mind with stereoscopic vividness. The curtain was still there, though, heavy and dark as ever, with the great nagging worry lurking just behind it.

The other man took away the jug and hitched himself on the edge of the table.

'Now,' he said, 'you and me 'as got to 'ave a talk. You think you've slugged a big cop, don't you? A Super? How sure are you?'

'I'm certain of it. He was just getting on to me and I saw delay ahead and no way out of it, so I let him have it and bunked. I can't remember anything after that. But there's no time for talk now. How long have I been asleep?'

'What was the cop's name?'

'Hutch. Superintendent Hutch. A delightful bloke. He wanted my number.'

'And you didn't know it?'

'Er – no.'

'I see.' He seemed more resigned than shocked. 'Well, they ain't 'ere yet, that's one thing. Old Fanny in the shop is a good look-out. Lucky we kept this place so dark. This'll take a bit of getting away with. Do you remember anything at all before you got your cosh?'

'No. Nothing. That is, I remember odd things like people's

names, and I remember the one thing, of course. I remember fifteen.'

'Fifteen?' The little black eyes were suspicious. 'That's more'n I do. That's something you never told me.'

'Oh, my God!' Campion turned his face to the wall. It was back again, the damnable frustration-dream motif. He felt like a man in a stone maze.

'Don't you excite yourself or you'll go under again.' His ally became the nurse once more. 'Keep what little bit of common you 'ave got, for pity's sake. I've seen some of this sort of thing in my time and I know what it's like. You've got no bones broke and your eyes are reacting all right. You've just forgot, that's all. There's nothing to get the serious wind-up about in that. Now, am I right? You feel as you do sometimes when you first wake up in the morning in a strange bed. Just for a minute you've got a hold of yerself all right but you don't know where you are nor what's gone before. You're like a man living in that minute, aren't yer?'

This somewhat homely description was so apt that Campion turned to stare at his questioner. The stranger's white face was very grave and his eyes were intelligent.

He nodded. 'Yes,' he said, 'that's just what I am like.'

His questioner's reaction was not entirely comforting.

'I've known it go on for months and wear off gradual,' he said unhappily, 'and I've known it come back as quick as it went. We'd better get hold of Oates at once. You're fit for nothing now.'

Campion explained the difficulty in that quarter and the other man's anxiety became acute.

'We're in the cart,' he said. 'In the cart good and proper.'

Campion groaned. 'Who are we, anyway?' he demanded. 'Who are you?'

The fat man did not reply for a minute. There was a curious half-smile which had nothing to do with amusement on his face. It was some little time before Campion recognized it for what it was. This odd stranger was deeply and sentimentally hurt.

'My name is Lugg,' he said at last. 'I've been a perishing

servant of yours for seventeen years.' There was an awkward pause and then he rose and stretched himself. 'That's all right,' he said magnificently, 'you're not to blame. I'd 'ave told you at once only I was hoping it'd come back to you. 'Ullo, 'ullo, what's that?'

The lights flickered and a deep full-throated rumbling echoed through the house. Both men started.

'Thunder,' Lugg pronounced as a whirlwind of heavy drops pattered against the glass behind the thick curtains. 'It got me wondering. It always does nowadays. Oh well, let it snow if it feels like it. We've got more than we can carry anyway, so what does it matter what else piles up?'

'How late is it? I can't waste time.' Campion was struggling to his feet as he spoke. 'Tomorrow's the fifteenth. Must get on. God knows how.'

'You stay where you are.' Lugg had picked up his revolver and was playing with it carelessly. 'Your head seems to 'ave gone so we'll 'ave to use mine for a ruddy change. Now look 'ere, we're in a very nasty position. I'm an accessory after the fact, don't forget that, so I'm going to tell you all you saw fit to let me know about the lark you're on before you lost your senses. You're going to listen, and we're both going to hope it's going to bring something back to you because if it don't we're both up the creek.'

He was right, of course. Campion had the wits left to realize it even while every instinct warned him frantically against delay. The thing he had to avert was enormous and catastrophic.

'Avert.' Once again it was a single word which arrested him. That was right. There was something he had to avert. Something tremendous.

Meanwhile Lugg was talking and his thick voice sounded comforting and sensible against the rumbling of the storm outside.

'I've only been by your side day and night for seventeen years and you couldn't trust me with the whole packet. Said you was under oath,' he was observing. 'If you hadda done, we shouldn't be in this mess, but I'm not reproaching you. That's not my way. Never 'as been. I've been here for five days and this is it, I should suppose. My instructions from you in London was that I should keep myself under cover 'ere and take all messages. Old Happy in the shop was to do all the front of the 'ouse stuff and I wasn't to show my face until I was told. Happy is quite okay, by the way. I picked this place of 'is myself. I used to know 'im years ago when 'e was one of the old Forty Angels gang up at Hoxton. 'E's straight as a die to 'is own sort. 'E's keeping the look-out now. There's been no one particular about since you came. You must have given them the slip completely, punch-drunk or not. Now listen. Since I've been 'ere you've only showed up twice. The first time was the day before yesterday. You came in with a portmanteau and that time you were wearing your ordinary clothes. You changed here into some duds that even my old dad wouldn't 'ave worn and went off with a little fish-basket under yer arm, looking as if you'd been on the tramp from one sick ward to the next for the last five years. Don't you remember?'

'No, I don't. I'm sorry, it's gone completely.'

'Never mind. Never mind. Don't strain it or you'll never get it. Just listen. I may say something that'll bring the 'ole thing back.' Lugg was very earnest and the suppressed anxiety in his matt black eyes belied his words. 'The second time I saw you you came sneaking in by these french doors 'ere, about three yesterday morning. I was sleeping where you're sitting now and I got up and fetched you a bit of food. I asked 'ow things were going, but you didn't open out at all. You seemed worried and distant-like, as though you was puzzled by the way things was running.'

'Was I – was I all right then?' Campion stirred as he spoke. This was one of the most unnerving experiences of all.

'Oh yes. You'd got yer 'ead screwed on then. You was as bright as I am. You just seemed sort of mystified, as though things weren't running the way you'd thought. About eleven in the morning you slipped out again, still in yer old clothes, and that was the last time I saw you right in the head.'

It was an unfortunate way of putting it, but evidently Lugg was one of those Britons without the celebrated national gift for euphemy.

'You left your little old basket,' he said. 'You locked it in the table drawer, but you took one or two things out of it and put them in your pockets. About tea-time yesterday Happy came in with a tale that 'e'd picked up in the shop about you being mixed up in a row down at the waterside. A rozzer had been killed and two or three men took to horspital.'

He paused hopefully, but Campion shook his head. In spite of the sudden chill which this confirmation of his worst fears produced in him, he still could not remember. Lugg breathed gustily.

'Never mind,' he said again but without any sort of conviction. 'Never mind. It'll come back sudden. Then young Amanda called for your suitcase with your good clothes in it,' he went on, 'and Happy told her some of what he'd heard—'

'Yes, I know. She came to the hospital.' Campion spoke absently and did not see the small black eyes flicker.

'Oh, you've seen 'er, 'ave you? Did you recognize 'er?' The jealousy was very faint, but it was there and Campion noticed it.

'Not for a long time,' he said. 'I – er – like a fool I thought she must be my wife.'

'So she will be in a week or two, if you're not strung up.' Lugg's dreadful directness was irrepressible. The words came into his head and he said them.

A shadow passed over Campion's lean wooden face.

'I rather think that's off,' he said shortly. 'She – she didn't realize what had happened, you see. She doesn't know now and I don't particularly want her to, so, should you see her, for God's sake don't refer to it. She broke the engagement.'

'*She* did?' Lugg was clearly incredulous. 'Why? 'As she seen someone else?'

Campion writhed. The discussion was distasteful and also, he discovered, quite unbearable. (Ah, Amanda! Oh, my blessed smiling sweet! Oh, sensible, clear-eyed, unembarrassed beloved! Oh, dear God Almighty, what is to happen to me without you?)

Lugg took his silence for consent, apparently, for he pursed his mouth and jerked his head with resigned regret.

'I see that coming,' he remarked brutally. 'It was your fault for mucking about. Courting a woman's like cooking something. There comes a time when it's done. After that you had ought to eat it. If you don't and keep it simmering on the side so to speak, you're apt to forget it and when you do come to look for it all the goodness is gorn away and you're left with nothing but a bit o' skin. And it annoys the young woman too. It doesn't do her any good.'

He paused and glanced at the other man's face.

'Sorry, cock,' he said abruptly.

Campion said nothing. Outside the storm was working itself up to fury and the rain hissed and spat against the windows like a host of serpents.

'Avert something tremendous.' The command blazed at him suddenly, wrenching him out of his small private hell. 'Hurry, hurry. Think, think. Pull yourself together. Get on with it.'

'Where's the basket—' he said. 'The whole story sounds nuts, but let's see it anyway. There may be something in it.'

Lugg looked at him curiously. 'Don't you know what's in it?'

'No, of course I don't. Do you?'

'I 'ad a look, naturally. I'm 'uman. The lock on the drawer could be turned with a bent pin.'

'Oh, all right, what's in it?'

'I didn't touch anything, of course,' he said, taking up a piece of wire which he kept conveniently on the mantelshelf. 'It got me wondering, though.'

He squatted down and poked at the lock. It was child's-play to open, as he had said, and he pulled out a wide drawer, revealing a fair-sized rush bag lying inside. Campion thrust his hand in the basket. An expression of blank amazement spread over his face and he shook the whole contents out on the table. A slippery, feathery heap of old one-pound and ten-shilling notes appeared before him.

'Six 'undred and eighty-four pounds exactly,' said Lugg. 'I counted it after you left.'

Campion took up a banknote and rubbed it between his fingers. Then he held it up to the light. Britannia's head and trident shone out of the watermark at him. None of the notes appeared to be new. Their uniform shabbiness suggested months of circulation.

'Extraordinary,' he said, looking blankly at the fish-basket. 'I took some more out with me, you say?'

'Yes. About seventy quid. You didn't trouble to count it – what was that?'

Both men stood listening. At first they thought there was no sound but the storm, but an instant later there was a gentle thud outside the inner door and the shopkeeper put his head in.

'Take sights,' he whispered. 'They're all round the house. Plain-clothes. I'll watch the front.'

Lugg swept the notes into the basket, thrust it into the drawer and pulled back the tablecloth. The whole movement was as smooth as if it had been done by a conjuror. He thrust a gun into Campion's hand and produced another from his hip. He touched the sick man's arm and nodded towards the french doors, laying his finger on his lips. Campion nodded obediently and moved silently into the darkness at the back of the room.

The gentle knocking on the glass sounded like the Last Trump when it did come.

XII

It was a quiet, insistent tapping on the french windows. The
gentle summons was very near and very intimate. It sped
through the weeping of the storm and stood close to them.

They waited in silence and let it come again, still discreet
but a fraction sharper, determined, inexorable.

Lugg glanced over his shoulder. Campion was well in the
shadow, so he picked up his gun and advanced towards the
window with all the easy confidence of an innocent householder
expecting a visit from the police.

He drew back the curtains cautiously, as a good citizen
should, allowing only the minimum of light to escape. For
some seconds he stood peering into the darkness, alert as a
dog at a rat-hole. Finally he unlatched the doors and pushed
one of them open a few inches.

' 'Ullo?' he demanded suspiciously.

There was no direct reply but there was a new movement out
in the storm and Lugg became tense, his bald head with its
fringe of greyish hair held oddly on one side.

Standing just below him in the driving rain was the figure he
expected. The drab mackintosh and slouch hat of the plain-
clothes man were there, but the stranger was not looking at
him squarely. He peered up slyly out of the dark and from his
white hand hung a large white handkerchief which fluttered
significantly in the downpour. It was impossible to mistake its
meaning.

Lugg backed slowly into the room and the newcomer came
in after, holding the white rag ostentatiously before him.

He took up a position some little distance from the table and
the heavy shade over the lights cut him off from the breast
upwards as far as Campion was concerned. As soon as the
window was closed behind him he held up his hands.

'You can take my gun,' he said distinctly.

Lugg searched him promptly and efficiently, setting down

the man's heavy Webley on the table well within the circle of light. Then with a glance at his visitor he produced his own gun and put it down beside the first. There was a long pause and then Campion also stretched out a hand in the darkness and added his weapon to the other two. He kept his face out of the light, however, as did the newcomer.

They made a curious headless group standing round the three guns, since all the light in the room was focused on the weapons and on their three pairs of hands. Lugg and Campion maintained their advantage and waited for the visitor to make the first move.

'I've got a message for the man calling himself Campion,' he announced at last. 'That's you, isn't it?'

'Never mind which of us it is,' corrected Lugg sharply. 'What's the dope?'

'*He* knows.' The stranger spoke meaningly, jerking a hand towards Campion. 'It's up to him, that's all.'

This was an unforeseen impasse. Campion's thin hands remained expressionless and Lugg's great ham-fists did not stir. The silence persisted. The room was hot and its very quiet was ominous and uncomfortable amid the bellowing of the storm which raged round the house. Lugg found it unbearable.

'The boys outside'll get wet,' he observed pleasantly.

'I'm waiting.'

'What do you think we're doing?'

'He's only got to make up his mind. He knows.' The visitor had begun to reveal a personality. He was not a big man and his raincoat hung on him in concealing folds, yet he managed to convey an impression of wiry strength curiously and rather horribly allied to ill-health. His voice was not without culture of a sort, either, but it had a thin tinny ring to it and when he coughed, as he did frequently, his lungs wheezed and groaned dangerously. Yet he was a force in the room. There was no question but that he knew what he was doing and was determined to waste no time.

Since his head and shoulders were hidden, his hands were his only distinguishing feature and these were frankly repulsive, being womanish, degenerate and quite abominably dirty.

A sixth sense warned Campion to hold his tongue. It was not that the half seen, headless figure was actually familiar, but the atmosphere of rank evil he brought with him was. Campion left the talking to Lugg, who seemed quite prepared to deal with it.

'Knowing's not always saying,' the fat man remarked, managing to infuse a wealth of craft into the observation. 'Your call, mate.'

'*He* knows,' the newcomer repeated and one of his repellent hands slid inside his raincoat.

The two others had their guns up off the table like one man. They waited, the two weapons levelled and the two barrels gleaming dully in the circle of light.

The visitor did not waver or hesitate. He went on with what he was doing smoothly. He seemed to have considerable experience of guns. His hand came out of his coat with something in it. He laid his offering on the red tablecloth and they all looked at it. It was a thick packet of old banknotes secured with a rubber band.

'Two-fifty,' he said, 'and we ask no questions.'

Lugg laughed. It was a genuine expression of surprised amusement and was entirely convincing. The newcomer was standing very still. Campion could feel him trying to pierce the shadow which shrouded both their heads. He made no movement himself and kept his gun steady.

Once again the dirty hand crept inside the sodden coat and presently another packet lay on top of the first. Once more the silence became suffocating.

The performance was very slow, definitely sinister, and, of course, in the circumstances entirely fantastic.

'Chicken feed,' said Lugg thickly and a third packet of notes appeared on the table and finally a fourth.

'That's the limit,' said the stranger at last. 'Take it or leave it. Suit yourself.'

'And supposing it's a deal?' Lugg was showing more finesse in an impossible situation than Campion would have expected from him.

'He quits his racket and gets out.'

'Where to?'

'London. Hell. Anywhere. We're not fussy.'

Campion's condition was making him slow-witted. It had taken him some minutes to realize that he was not dealing with the police, as he had expected. This man on the other side of the table, whose face he could not see, represented a new element in a complicated and terrifying predicament. He represented the element which until now had been maddeningly elusive. Here at last must be a definite materialization of the enemy. Campion's limping brain seized on the discovery and he struggled to make as many bricks as he might out of this meagre straw.

The stranger belonged to a very definite class. He was a thug, one of that mercifully small army of professional bullies who in previous ages were euphoniously called 'soldiers of fortune'; men, that is, who would undertake violence for a fee. It did not occur to Campion that it was strange that he should recognize so much. He accepted the fact without thinking, as a natural deduction based on some past experience which he had forgotten. He went on with his reasoning. Since the man was what he was it argued that he possessed employers, some intelligent organization which had the sense to use professional servants. The question now was what sort of organization? It was obviously anti-social, but how large? How dangerous? How big? International importance?

The old phrase came into his head and he rejected it. It was not quite right. National importance? That was it. He had heard something like that described lately and in some connexion which, taken together, had had an extraordinary effect upon him. It was an amazing experience. He was remembering something not mentally but emotionally. The ghost of an emotional upheaval was returning to him. It was both terrifying and exhilarating. The whole thing was recent, too, very recent. Anger was coming back to him and with it something else, something new and overwhelming, a passion. That was it. Something deeper than affection, something more primitive and disturbing than love of women.

For a moment he felt it again, experienced it as he had done some time so very lately, a burning, raging, invigorating thing, the stuff of poetry and high imagining, the fountain-spring of superhuman endurance and endeavour.

Once again a fact came to him without recollection. He knew something suddenly as surely and clearly as if he had arrived at it by a long process of thought.

He belonged to a post-war generation, that particular generation which was too young for one war and most prematurely too old for the next. It was the generation which had picked up the pieces after the holocaust indulged in by its elders, only to see its brave new world wearily smashed again by younger brothers. His was the age which had never known illusion, the grimly humorous generation which from childhood had both expected and experienced the seamier side. Yet now, recently, some time very lately, so near in time that the tingle of surprise still lingered, something new had appeared on his emotional horizon. It had been something which so far he had entirely lacked and which had been born to him miraculously late in his life. He saw it for what it was. It was a faith, a spiritual and romantic faith. It had been there always, of course, disguised as a rejected illusion, and must have lain there for years like a girl growing to maturity in her sleep. Now it was awake all right and recognizable; a deep and lovely passion for his home, his soil, his blessed England, his principles, his breed, his Amanda and Amanda's future children. That was the force which was driving him. That was the fire which was crowding him on through and over the obscene obstacle of his own un-natural weakness.

He glanced towards the man with the filthy hands. This, then, this professional crook, this must be a hair on the hide of the Enemy, and, like the zoologists, from this one hair he must somehow reconstruct a whole beast. For God's sake what organization was he up against, and what particular machination was it engaged upon now?

He pulled himself up, despair facing him. He was annihilatingly helpless. He knew so horribly little, even about himself. For instance, what sort of man was he, if this enemy, which was shrewd enough in all conscience, should so confidently expect to be able to bribe him?

A possible explanation of that final question occurred to him. It was so absurd and yet so likely that he laughed outright. Bending forward suddenly, he allowed the full light from the chandelier to fall upon his face.

It succeeded. Miraculously the outside chance came home, proving him right beyond all question. The effect on the man was immediate and sensational. He drew in a gulping breath and there was a faint rattle from the dreadful lungs.

'Campion!' he ejaculated in a thin voice. 'Campion. You *are* Campion.'

He dived forward to snatch up his gun but Lugg was before him, bringing down his own revolver across the grimy wrist as it shot out over the cloth. It was a tremendous blow which might well have cracked the bone, and the sound it made was one of those ruthless noises which are inexplicably shocking in themselves.

The man sobbed once, deep in his throat, with pain, and then, before either of the others realized what he was doing, he turned and rushed from them, leaving gun and money still on the table. He threw himself at the window and burst out into the storm, leaving the curtains bellying behind him as a gust of rain surged into the room. Lugg stood gaping after him. Presently he went over and closed the window. He swore steadily for some little time.

'What d'you know about that?' he said at last. 'Dirty little tyke! He made me sit up the moment I saw 'im. 'Oo's 'e working for?'

Campion felt himself giggling. The money and the gun and the ridiculous mistake were all absurdities out of a nightmare.

'I think I know that,' he said, recovering himself. 'I'm sure only one person could come to the conclusion that I was impersonating myself. Who was that man? I never saw his face clearly.'

'That was no loss.' Lugg was grimly amused. 'I know 'im, and I'd like to know 'oo 'e's sold 'is mortgaged little soul to this time. You know 'im all right. That was Weaver, B.'

He mistook Campion's blank expression for lack of recollection and hurried on to explain, all his old anxiety about the younger man's condition returning.

'You'll remember his brother better,' he said coaxingly. 'Weaver, T. A. They were both in the army together one time and they distinguished them like that, using the initials last. You remember them. I'll tell you 'oo they was both working for when we struck them last. Simister. The man we kept calling Ali Baba. Doesn't that ring a bell? Weaver, T. A., wasn't the class this chap is. He 'adn't the brains. He was killed with a tommy-gun when the Denver boys came over. This little sweep Weaver, B., went in for jam-jars afterwards. 'E's a wizard with a petrol engine. If 'e's in this there's something big going on in the car line. Does that bring anything 'ome?'

Campion thought of the fleet of trucks in the hidden garage under the crouching body of the Nag and he nodded. His brain was working feverishly. It was Pyne again, of course. Pyne was the man who had assumed that he was another crook trying to muscle in on a racket by impersonating Albert Campion. What about Pyne, then? What about his questions and his 'amusing organization'? And his snooping about at the Institute?

He glanced at the pile of money on the table.

'They're not broke, anyway,' he said.

'They are not.' Lugg's heartfelt agreement was unexpected. He was very serious and his small black eyes were open to their widest extent. 'They're a powerful crowd,' he said. 'Money to burn. There was a sort of share-out down here before we came, you know. The drunks filled every can in the place. Happy said 'e never saw anything like it. 'E reckons they're on to something colossal, something that'll need a lot of men from the way money has been splashing around.'

He gathered up the cash on the table and rolled back the cloth.

'Wicked to waste it,' he remarked virtuously.

The drawer was only just closed when the shopkeeper appeared behind them. His startled face came edging round the inner door.

'They've scarpered,' he said, using the rhyming slang which

still serves a fraternity needing a patois. 'Only one of 'em left. He's leaning against the wall a door or two down the road. What happened?'

'Nothing to interest you, my lad.' Lugg was heavily jocular. 'Someone came along to make what you might call an extravagant gesture, that's all.'

'I don't like it.' Their host was inclined to whine. 'It's dangerous. There's some pretty funny chaps in this town just now. I saw "Lily" Pettican walking down the street this morning.'

'Lily?' Lugg was clearly astounded. 'You've got the 'orrors,' he said.

'If it wasn't Lily, it was 'is brother 'oo 'appened to 'ave lost the same eye,' the old man persisted. 'Chew on that.'

'Go away.' Lugg was not amused. His small eyes were frightened.

'All right, but I've got something for yer. What d'yer say to this lot?' He wriggled into the room through the smallest possible aperture and presented one of those long narrow ledger-books in which small shopkeepers often keep their orders. It was open at the last page and he pointed to the final entry made in his own wildest handwriting.

'A.C.' it ran. 'The White Hart, private sitting-room. Immediately. Come clean.'

Both Lugg and Campion read the line and exchanged glances.

'Where the hell did you get that from?'

'From a woman.' The shopkeeper did not seem particularly surprised. 'She came in just before I shut the shop. I was just going to lock the doors after giving you the word the busies were about. She was about fifty, I suppose. Very respectable, you know. I hadn't never seen 'er before. She came up to the counter and said could I get 'er *Heartsease Novels* every week. I said I could and I got out my book to take 'er name. When I was ready she simply dictated that lot. After I'd written it down she said thank you very much and went out. A.C., that stands for you, doesn't it, Guv'nor? Albert Campion, that's your name.'

Lugg turned to his employer. He was completely startled.

'But they were 'ere,' he said stupidly. 'They didn't know you were A.C. then. Lumme, see what it means? See what it means? It's someone else. It's not them at all. "Come clean"? 'Oo the 'ell is it?'

The little shopkeeper looked at his excited face and shook his head.

'That's all I know, what I've told you,' he began. 'The White Hart's that big hotel in the middle of the town. Nothing could happen to you there, that's one thing mortal certain. It can't even be a try-on. More people know you than you know people.'

'You're telling me,' said Campion fervently.

XIII

'What are you going to do?'

The inquiry crept into the almighty muddle of confused thoughts and emotions in Campion's tortured mind and opened out like a great question-mark-shaped hole of nothingness.

He did not answer because both men were looking at him confidently and he saw that he should have no help from them in his decision. He was the Boss still; they relied on him.

He was trying to marshal some sort of order among his scattered forces when another secret question shot out at him. Just how ill am I? Just how serious is this damned injury? Am I going to curl up and die from it, and if so, how long have I got? He put that query from him impatiently. He guessed he'd find that out when the time came. Meanwhile, what *was* he going to do?

There was something just under his nose which he had missed. He felt it was there and he groped for it. When at last he found it it grinned at him with the dreadful cross-eyed leer of complete insanity. This was the fourteenth. Moreover this was the evening of the fourteenth. Therefore, all the arrangements for the catastrophe, or whatever it was which he was struggling so blindly to avert, must have been made already, and the thing itself be on the very point of happening. And yet Pyne, or the Enemy, whoever he was, had been prepared to try to buy him off even at this eleventh hour. That argued that he was still dangerous to this unknown. How? What could he do now, this minute? What was there to do?

He glanced at the remarkable message in the notebook and then at the man who had written it. The shopkeeper had come forward and the light was on his face. It was not so much that sterling honesty shone from his eyes. It didn't. He looked shifty and disreputable. But he was also puzzled. The message clearly fascinated him. He had no idea what it meant or from whom it came. He would like to have known. He, too, waited expectantly.

'I'll go down there,' said Campion.

'I'll come with yer.' Lugg was shaking off his carpet-slippers as he spoke. 'You'll be less noticeable if we go together.'

'I don't think so.' Campion spoke frankly. If there is one human peculiarity which cannot be disguised it is fat. A fat man is distinctive at any distance. Lugg could scarcely hope to pass anywhere unobserved.

'There's a busy up the street, don't forget,' said the shop-keeper.

'How do you know it's a busy?' Lugg was tolerantly con-temptuous.

'Because I see 'is face and I know 'im. 'E's been round 'ere once or twice. The other lot went away. 'E didn't.'

This was important information. The police were the one body who, so far as Campion knew for a fact, had definite cause to want to lay hands on him, but if they had actually located him it seemed highly peculiar that they should not come in and get him. The probable explanation was, of course, that they had not located him but were keeping an eye on one of the others in case they should try to contact him.

'I'll take you past the busy,' said the shopkeeper unexpectedly. 'I've got my own way out. I'll go first, you come behind. I'll lead you right to the White Hart. It's not easy to find if you don't know the town.'

'I'm to stay 'ere?' Lugg inquired dubiously.

'Yes,' said the shopkeeper.

Lugg looked at Campion silently. He was pathetic and Cam-pion could have murdered him. What right had he to lean like this, to sit childlike and helpless, relying on a superior intelligence? – which, God help them all, was no longer there. It was the original Campion's own fault. The new Campion felt he had the grace to recognize that. He had a vision of a damned superior young man who must always have been laughingly tolerant, gloriously sure of himself. The new Cam-pion turned from him with loathing. A fine chuckleheaded ass he must have been to surround himself with dear, faithful, pathetic followers incapable of independent thought; fawners, seekers after orders.

'I'll give you a couple of hours,' said Lugg, shattering the illusion. 'If you're not back then I'll come and save your ruddy life again. It won't be the first time. Don't forget you're not right in the 'ead now, either.'

Campion set out with the shopkeeper. Both he and Lugg appeared to have brought the art of avoiding police supervision to a high state of perfection. Campion was provided with a shabby raincoat and a peaked cap. It was no disguise but rather a badge of some unspecified but respectable office. As he put them on he became just another taxi-driver, bus conductor, chauffeur, St John's ambulance man or gas inspector hurrying home to get out of his working clothes.

The shopkeeper led him out of the back door into a minute yard and out of that into another and another, all symmetrical and uniform as a section of a dusty egg-box.

They came out finally into an entirely different quarter of the town, a solid residential district of ornate Victorian houses with transoms over the doors and high surprised windows with little apartment cards in them.

The shopkeeper scurried along in front. In his dirty overcoat and dented bowler hat he looked as frail and negligible as a piece of sodden brown paper blown along by the bullying wind.

The storm itself had passed but there was still a lot of rain about. There was just enough light to see one's way, but the going was not too easy and the pavements looked washed and sticky, like pieces of half-sucked toffee.

Campion did not notice the town. It took every ounce of concentration which he still possessed to follow the little wisp of a figure in front. His legs were heavy and his head swam.

He was so intent on the mere physical task that he did not notice the carved portico of the White Hart until he was almost directly under the famous sign and was so close to the doorway that he was forced to turn straight in through the light-trap arranged over the double doors. He was walking quickly and stepped slap into a bright lounge full of people, most of whom turned and looked at him inquiringly.

Every town in England has one hostelry like the White Hart. It is always a grand old inn where either Charles Dickens or Queen Elizabeth spent a night and which modern motor traffic has made once more fashionable. In these ancient houses rooms are knocked together, beams are uncovered, mighty fireplaces are filled with false logs with red electric bulbs tucked under them, and in the roughcast walls mock casements show painted musical comedy settings through their diamond panes. The food is usually good, the service appalling, and the atmosphere about as cosy and cliquey as the school hall on prize-giving day. Practically every man in the room was in khaki on this occasion. Campion, who had no recollection of ever having seen anything like it before, was completely bewildered. Fortunately his astonishment fitted his somewhat unsuitable costume and no one among the little parties clustered round the small tables gave him a second look. A growing youth in a tail suit far too small for him hurried forward inquiringly, anxious to direct him to the saloon bar round the corner. Campion looked at him helplessly and said the first thing to come into his head.

'I want someone in a private room. I've been told to come here.'

The boy regarded him dubiously and scuttled into a small office half hidden in a mass of oaken tracery far more suitable to the rood-screen for which it had originally been carved. He came out again with the landlord, a dapper elderly man with a military cut to his clothes and bored eyes.

'Yes?' he said.

'My name is Albert Campion.'

'Really?' His surprise was genuine and terror seized the man who had just come in. What a fool thing to do! What a lunatic he was! What a benighted idiot! Both sections of society thirsting for his blood, no time to lose, disaster imminent, and he had to go and give his name to the first stranger who raised an eyebrow at him. He was so appalled that he hardly noticed the landlord until he realized that the man had gone over to the foot of the main staircase and now stood waiting for him to follow.

They went upstairs in silence and paused before a crooked

door with the fine thin panels of the Tudors. The landlord knocked and bent his head to listen. Campion heard nothing, but presently the other man seemed satisfied, for he threw open the door and announced 'Mr Albert Campion' as if he had been a flunkey.

Campion went in. It was a wide, low-ceilinged room, badly lit, possessing an uneven floor, antique furniture, and a genuine coal fire. At first he thought he was alone and his misgivings rose up reproachfully. He turned to try the door but it was not even properly closed, much less locked. As he moved somebody coughed on the other side of the room.

It was a ladylike sound and he swung back just in time to see a small figure rising up out of the shadows of a winged chair which he had presumed to be empty. A little old woman stood before him.

He was astounded. She came nervously towards him, simpering a little, and with two bright spots of embarrassment in her faded cheeks. She held out her hand, but shyly, and as if she felt that she was being forward.

'This is so awkward,' she murmured. 'I don't think we've met?' Her voice trailed away and he became uncomfortably aware that she was put out by his mackintosh and the peaked cap in his hand. Socially the situation was absurd. Even factually it was peculiar.

They shook hands and stood looking at one another. The woman was over seventy and frail. Her thin grey hair was parted demurely and she wore a dark silk dress with bits of lace on it.

'You're not quite as I expected you,' she said nervously. 'Forgive me, I don't quite mean that. I'm sure I'm very glad to meet you like this. Sit down, will you? It's very cold, is it not?'

She was completely out of her element and very annoyed with herself for showing it. Suddenly she dabbed her eyes.

'It's all been such a shock,' she said unsteadily, 'but this is quite unpardonable. So silly of me. I really ought never to have come.'

'Oh Lord!' said Campion. He was under the impression that he had spoken under his breath, but to his horror his voice, clear, brusque, and unnaturally loud, echoed back at him from the shadowy walls. An inner door which he had not noticed before opened at once and, as though in direct answer to prayer, Amanda stood on the threshold.

Hallucination! The dreadful possibility shot into his mind and frightened every other consideration out of it. She looked so fine and fit and young and alive. Her brown suit matched her eyes and her head sat sanely on her shoulders. She was lovely, she was kind, she was friendly, a right thing in a ghastly unrealistic world. That was it; she was an oasis. No, of course, a mirage! One of those things you see before you die of thirst in a desert and the vultures come and pick your bones into decency before you decay.

'Oh beautiful,' he said and had not spoken the words so guilelessly since he had first said them, leaning out of his go-cart to look at the sea.

Her fine eyebrows rose into arcs on her forehead.

'I heard your voice,' she said. 'I'm sorry I wasn't here when you came. Have you and Miss Anscombe met?'

A great portion of the world slid into the horizontal again at the command of that cool voice and all the lovely machinery for living, like manners and introductions and calling-cards and giving up one's seat in the bus, began to whirr comfortingly in the background of the scene.

The old lady appeared to appreciate it as much as he did. She raised her head and smiled.

'I'm being very stupid, my dear,' she said. 'I hadn't realized how shaken I am. You must ask Mr Campion to forgive me.'

'I think he's been a bit shaken himself.' There was warning as well as apology in Amanda's tone and she considered the forlorn figure in the tight mackintosh with interest. 'I've got Miss Anscombe to come along herself to tell you one or two things, Albert,' she went on. 'Very kindly she came along to see me and . . .'

'I went to her because she looked so sensible and so sympathetic,' interrupted the old lady. 'I felt I ought to approach someone and naturally one has a horror of the police at such a time. I prefer to talk to a woman of course.'

'Of course,' said Campion so earnestly that again Amanda stared at him as if he were demented. He fought to get hold of the situation, but it was all hopeless. His memory had deserted him. He sighed. 'Why?' he added disastrously.

'Well naturally, Albert.' Amanda caught the dropping brick with both hands and struggled with it manfully. 'I mean, since her brother's death she's been frightfully hurt and shaken, and she hasn't felt like talking to just anyone.'

Her brother. Miss Anscombe. Of course! The name had not registered on him before. He understood at last. This must be the sister of the murdered man whom Lee Aubrey had kept talking about. It came into his head that Aubrey might have sent Amanda here now and the possibility irked him unreasonably.

The old lady tucked her handkerchief into her belt and leant forward purposefully.

'Mr Campion,' she said, 'I'm a very strong-minded woman and all my life I've gone out of my way to do what I thought was right.'

It was a formidable opening at the best of times and to Campion, who was not experiencing one of them, it sounded like a confession of early suicide. He nodded.

'Yes?' he said.

'Well, that's why I've come here now, to talk about poor Robert. We shall never know how he died. He was a very weak person in some ways and if he had taken his own life I should have been very sorry and very hurt, but I should not have been surprised.'

Campion remained unimpressed. He knew how Anscombe had died and that information was enough to startle this old duck into screaming hysterics. It was only when he caught sight of Amanda watching him earnestly that he realized what the old woman was trying to tell him. Of course Anscombe had known! Anscombe had been the best bet. Oates had said so. He turned to the old lady so eagerly that he bewildered her.

'Was your brother frightened of something?' he demanded.

She bridled and he was aware of her rather hard blue eyes with their bald rims and wrinkled sockets.

'He had something on his conscience,' she said. 'I always felt he was just going to confide in me but he never did. I have a very rigid code,' she added naïvely.

'Tell Albert about the money,' put in Amanda.

Money? More money? This cash motif cropped up all the time. It frightened Campion. The Tory Englishman never under-estimates the power of money as a weapon. It is his own, and when he sees it against him he feels betrayed as well as anxious.

Miss Anscombe cleared her throat. Having embarked on a distasteful duty she was determined to get every ounce of virtue out of it.

'He never told me that he was in financial difficulties, but it was very obvious some little time ago,' she began. 'I realized that he was hard put to it and I helped him to a certain extent. He was quite sick with worry, naturally, for we had a certain position in the town to keep up and he was a man who understood the importance of doing his duty to the community in that respect. Also he had the Secretaryship to think of. That is a very sacred responsibility, Mr Campion.'

'I suppose it is.'

'Our family have thought so for seven generations,' she said stiffly. 'If you don't realize what it must have meant to him to resign that office, you can hardly appreciate anything I'm trying to tell you.'

'He does understand,' cut in Amanda hastily. 'He's terribly tired and worried himself. Albert, for the love of Mike take off that awful mackintosh.'

He obeyed her and realized as Miss Anscombe looked at him that his suit was crumpled and his linen grubby. What in God's name did it matter? The old lady exasperated him with her ridiculous niceties in the midst of this maelstrom. Why didn't she cut the cackle and come to the horses? What had Anscombe known? Didn't she realize that there was no time to waste? He could have shaken the facts out of her and was within an ace of telling her so when she spoke again.

'When my brother suddenly became comparatively wealthy again I was astounded,' she said. 'I knew then that things were not at all as they should be. We come of a class, Mr Campion, which never acquires money suddenly, except by legacy. For a little while my brother was almost happy, but gradually a great change came over him. His conscience was haunting him.'

Campion stared at her. In spite of his preoccupation some of the urgent tragedy in her story forced itself through to him. He saw her world vividly, with painful clarity. He saw the narrow, self-important old man clinging to his inherited privileges amid a snowstorm of falling shares, rising prices, fleecing taxes, whispers in the town, nudges, older clothes, tradesmen waiting, and silly little economies which did no good.

'What did he do?' he said, his eyes reflecting some of the awe in her own.

'I'm not perfectly sure.' Now that she was holding him she was less antagonistic. They had become fellow investigators, gossips with a licence. 'For a long time I couldn't bring myself to consider it, but now that he's dead I feel I must tell all that I do know. I'm afraid poor Robert sold his honour and his integrity, Mr Campion. I think he must have used his position as Secretary of the Masters to permit some sort of smuggling to go on in those caves under the Nag. And then later I think he changed his mind and was trying to expiate the sin he had committed. I don't know how he died. If it was an accident it was the hand of God, but if he took his own life, or if someone else killed him, I shouldn't be in the least surprised. I've lived through several wars and one can't do that without realizing that the world contains violent men.'

Campion felt the muscles at the corners of his jaw contracting. This was truth. This was a break. At last a real break, if only he had the wits to assimilate it.

'Smuggling what?' he inquired.

'I don't know. I'm only guessing that,' she reminded him quickly. 'But there was a Mr Feiberg who came to the house once or twice to see my brother. That was in the spring of 'thirty-nine, when my brother was most hard pressed for money. After he left Robert began to talk about the Nag and about the smuggling that was done there in the seventeenth century. He covered it up at once, of course, but I never forgot it. Mr Feiberg came twice after that, but never after the war broke out. I mentioned him at once, of course, because he was an alien and my brother said definitely then "We shan't see him again".'

'Had your brother acquired his new money then?'

'Yes,' she said, 'yes, he had, but it was after that that his conscience began to prick him.'

'Long after?'

'No.' She paused. There was uncertainty in her whole poise. She waited until he was exasperated with her and then, with an apologetic smile, came out with the one remark in the world which could have brought him up on his toes and re-kindle a flicker of hope in his heart.

'I mustn't mislead you,' she said. 'I think his conscience slept until he heard of fifteen.'

'Fifteen?' His voice failed and he whispered the word.

She ignored the interruption.

'It must have been then that he saw his terrible mistake. I think he did everything he could after that. He decided to resign his Secretaryship. He drew out every penny he had in the bank, and he was bringing it back with him yesterday when you drove him home. Also this morning his bank manager called on me and told me in confidence that Robert gave instructions for all his securities to be turned into cash and the money delivered to him.'

'But that's extraordinary!' Amanda spoke before she saw the pitfall, and, having seen it, went on sturdily. 'I mean, that doesn't look like suicide. That suggests to me that he was going to clear out.'

'Yes.' Miss Anscombe was not offended. It was evident she had no very high opinion of her brother. 'It does, doesn't it? Unless, you see, he meant to give it all back to someone. We shall never know and I prefer to be charitable.'

Campion was not listening to them. His ears were still tingling from the shock of hearing that one most elusive, most tantalizing word of all, the keynote and symbol of the whole maddening enigma.

'Tomorrow is the fifteenth,' he said stupidly.

'I didn't refer to the date.' The old lady made the remark with complete conviction. 'I don't know exactly what fifteen refers to, but it isn't a day of the month.'

'How do you know?' Even then he did not believe her. The tension was still there, straining every nerve in his body, urging him to hurry.

'Because of the diary.' She had been holding the little pocket-book all the time and he had not noticed. Now he would have snatched it from her, but she was not to be hurried. 'Robert was a very unmethodical man,' she remarked with exasperating deliberation. 'I thought the book was empty at first but then I found just these two entries. Here's the first, just over a month ago. Look for yourself. It's almost as though the poor man bought the book just to write something melodramatic in it. That would have been very like him.'

Campion took the book and Amanda looked over his shoulder.

'Friday the 7th,' they read. 'Just heard of Minute Fifteen. See it all. What have I done?'

The following pages were blank until they came to the space allotted to the day before the one on which its owner had died.

'Done,' he had written. 'Done at last. Conscience clearer. Resigned. Expiation must follow. Shall I see Henry Bull?'

On the following page and right across the three days it represented, two words had been scribbled large.

'*Minute Fifteen.*'

Campion sat down. The strain had snapped. He felt flat and exhausted. If the fifteenth was not a date there was no hurry. As he sat gazing at the page, however, the three printed dates stood out in relief. Sixteenth? Seventeenth? Eighteenth? Which? None of them or all of them?

The insufferable burden of anxiety returned more heavily than before. Weaver, B.'s mission became more rational and therefore more serious. Fifteen itself was still a mystery. 'Minute Fifteen' might mean anything.

Miss Anscombe rose to her feet.

'Where is Annie?' she inquired, looking at Amanda.

'In the next room, waiting for you. Are you sure she can take you home all right?'

'My dear, don't let her hear you say that.' The old lady laughed as she spoke. 'Annie used to be my personal maid. Now I think she's my guardian. She delivered the message safely to you, did she, Mr Campion?'

'Eh? Oh yes, rather. Brilliantly. Was that your maid?' Campion was talking without thinking and he bundled his scattering thoughts together impatiently. 'I'm afraid she must have thought it a rather unconventional method of approach,' he said apologetically.

Miss Anscombe patted Amanda's hand.

'Not at all,' she said unexpectedly. 'These are unconventional times. We're not blind. It's no good being conventional in a world which is blowing up all round one. When the streets become shambles one has to raise one's skirts. Good-bye. I don't know if I've been helpful, but at least I've cleared my conscience without giving poor miserable Robert's mistakes over to the police.'

'Wait.' Campion was still clinging to the pocket diary. 'Who is Henry Bull?'

Both women stared at him. Miss Anscombe looked startled.

'Sir Henry is a Conservative and one of the Tey family,' she said. 'At the moment he's the Senior Master of Bridge and a Junior Lord of the Treasury.'

'Don't be silly; you know that,' said Amanda. 'Besides, we met him, didn't we, at your sister's wedding?'

XIV

Amanda came back into the room after seeing Miss Anscombe
and her maid out. She closed the door carefully behind her.

'I say, what's the matter with you?' she demanded.

He eyed her guiltily and got up to get away from her searching inquiry.

'I'm all right. When the wind is southerly I can tell a hawk
from a handsaw.'

The quotation escaped out of some shrouded cupboard in
his mind without any context, so that he heard the words as
though for the first time. They meant nothing to him now he
considered them and left him considerably startled.

'That's good,' said Amanda. 'The fancy dress was a mistake,'
she added, picking up the peaked cap. 'I told you to come clean.
She's that sort of old pet. I thought that would warn you.'

'Oh I see. I'm sorry. It never occurred to me to take the words
literally. I didn't realize the message came from you, you
see.'

'You . . . ?' She swung round and stared at him. He did not
understand her expression. She was astonished, but also, in
some indefinable way, hurt. 'But we've used that sort of
language between ourselves for years and years,' she said at
last.

'Oh, yes,' he agreed in horror as he saw the trap. 'Yes, we
have, haven't we? I forgot.'

He expected her to be angry with him. Any woman would
be. He was grateful that he had said it. Those intelligent young
eyes terrified him. He needed her beside him with an unbearable urgency quite out of character. He was not the sort of man
who ought ever to need the moral support of anyone else on
earth with this dreadful sick anxiety. Once she knew the truth
about him she'd stick to him with all that eager generosity
which was her mainspring. She'd be so kind, so sorry. Pity,
filthy humiliating weakening pity! Nauseating compassion!

His soul retched at it – the ultimate, concentrated essence of second-best.

His earlier determination to hold her at whatever cost shrank before that price. To have forced her into fidelity might have been admissable and even pleasurable, but to sneak it, to grovel round it, and prize it up this most repulsive of all ways, that was too much. He hadn't come to that yet.

He glanced across the room at her. She was sitting on the arm of a chair, looking half her age. Her short skirt showed her knees and her thin arms were folded on her chest. She grinned at him.

'You're up to something you don't want me to know about,' she said. 'That's all right. Don't fluff.'

'I'm not fluffing.' The protest sounded childish and he could have smacked her. She was so like that. They seemed to get on to schoolroom terms the moment they spoke together. He must have known her very well for a long time.

'Sorry,' said Amanda. 'To me you fluff. Miss Anscombe sounded as if she might have been being useful. Was she?'

'She was, very. I hope she keeps her mouth shut now. Aubrey suggested that you brought her along, did he?'

Campion was watching her very closely and he thought he saw her change colour.

'No,' she said. 'No, he didn't, as it happens. I rather edged her off Lee.'

'I see. You're going back there now, are you?'

'If you think I ought to.'

'My dear girl, that's your affair entirely.' Campion hoped he was not bickering.

To his consternation she got up and came over to him.

'Look here, Albert,' she said with unusual earnestness, 'I'm not asking for any explanation, of course. Our usual arrangement stands. You know exactly what you're doing and I'm only out to be useful, but just at the moment I'm probably rather slow. I'm not too good. I've had a bit of a shock, as a matter of fact. I'll tell you about it later, when I'm better. But at the moment it's making me a bit ingrowing and slow on the uptake and I don't see what you're up to at all. I don't know what to look for. I don't even know if I've done the right thing about Hutch.'

Hutch? Good heavens, of course! The Superintendent. Campion hoped that the sweat which had broken out on his face was not visible. The nightmare was riding him with a vengeance. It was bad enough to have one's previous life wiped clean off the slate of one's mind without developing this new propensity for forgetting any act of violence which came his way. First it had been Anscombe's murder and now it was his own attack on the unfortunate Superintendent.

'What did you do?' he inquired anxiously.

'Well, I convinced him that you were you, to start with. That took a bit of doing, but I got it into all their heads in the end. Then' – she coughed delicately – 'then I said you were never afraid to take the unconventional line if the urgency of the job demanded it.'

'How did they take that?'

'Not too well,' she admitted. 'You can't blame them, Albert. It was pretty drastic and high-hat, wasn't it? Very unlike you, too,' she added after a pause. 'You're not much like yourself at the moment. You'll find the police looking for you, by the way. They're not entirely satisfied and Hutch wants his car, for one thing.'

Campion held his breath. He could just remember that there must have been a car, but what had happened to it or to himself between the moment when he had knocked out the Superintendent and had subsequently walked into the paper shop he had no idea.

This was dreadful. Amanda must find him out at any minute now. Her trust was heartrending, too. He wished she would not treat him with the blind faith of the silly little sister who follows her brother up the elm tree.

'You knew where to find me yourself,' he remarked. 'How was that?'

Again that look of hurt bewilderment.

'That was our arrangement, wasn't it?' She did not speak of the car again and he guessed that this reticence must be part of their arrangement also. Evidently she was his lieutenant. She offered any information she found but their plan of campaign was entirely his own.

'I must see Henry Bull,' he said.

'Ye-es.' Her hesitation was fractional but it infuriated him. 'What else can I do?' he demanded. 'Stanislaus has disappeared and someone has got to explain this damned fifteen.'

She sat up stiffly, her eyes widening.

'But I thought you knew. I thought you'd been given all the hush-hush dope and that you and Oates were holding the entire baby between you, because nobody dare risk any sort of leakage. I didn't realize that you were in the dark at all. No wonder you're so jittery.'

He looked at her as she stood over him. His taut brown face was expressionless.

'Do you find me jittery?'

Amanda laughed. It was spontaneous amusement and her heart-shaped face was alive and sane and lovely.

'I find you theatrical, stinker,' she said. 'What's up?'

He took her hand and swung her arm to and fro. He had seen someone else do that. It had been Lee Aubrey. That was right; it had been that blighter Lee. He had done this, leaning against the doorpost, peering down.

'I can't look at you with great constipated cow's eyes,' Campion said suddenly. His wretchedness had assembled the words and they were out of his mouth before he could censor them.

Amanda drew her hand away. Then she boxed his ears.

It was a gesture rather than a blow, very light and very quick. There was no smile on her face now and no animation. Her fine bones made a stamp, a die of quality and she was as remote from him as if she had died.

He stumbled to his feet and stood looking at her wildly. At that moment every restraining consideration seemed utterly absurd. She was part of himself and she was lost. Her going would mean partial disintegration. He felt himself cracking hopelessly, shamefully, before her eyes.

The tap on the inner door came from another world. They both swung round to stare at the handle as it turned. Lugg came tiptoeing in, bouncing a little like a descending balloon.

'Watch out,' he said. 'They're on the doorstep.'

'Who?' It was Amanda who spoke. She seemed perfectly normal and at ease.

'The busies are downstairs. The Inspector is in the lounge and 'e's got two men just outside on the door. The proprietor 'ere doesn't want any fuss on 'is premises, thank you, and the Inspector's being obliging.' The fat man dominated the room and his little eyes were bright and excited under the jutting peak of his flat cap. 'The back doors aren't 'ealthy either,' he went on. 'I see the Lily 'imself down there, not to mention Nervy Williams and one or two more. You got a hornet's nest on your tail and no mistake. Anyone'd think you was a classic race meeting.'

'How did they find me here?' said Campion.

Lugg shrugged his shoulders. 'Ask me another. The police followed young Amanda, I should say, and the other little syndicate of blossoms must have a tip-off in the police somewhere. I merely strolled down after you to satisfy myself that everything was okay and I walked right into it. The police don't know me 'ere, so I came in through the lounge, 'ad a drink in the saloon, and nipped up the first staircase I could find as soon as I 'ad a chance. I've been all over the 'ouse. There's no one upstairs at the moment. I tell you what, there's a cat-walk over the roofs if you want it, but I'd think twice before I took it with your 'ead.'

Campion shot a glance at Amanda and turned the flat of his hand to Lugg. It was an entirely spontaneous gesture but miraculously the man seemed to understand in time.

' 'E's 'ad a 'eadache,' he said to the girl. 'Still, it's up to 'im.'

Amanda turned to Campion. 'What are you going to do?'

She was as natural and polite as if Lugg had interrupted nothing more important than a tea-party. Her poise was imperturbable and he knew that she must always have possessed it.

'I must see Bull,' he said. 'You'll go back to Bridge, won't you? Lugg can wait at the paper shop. I'll try the roof. I must get on. It's so urgent, you see. If fifteen isn't a date the whole thing may cook up at absolutely any moment. I've got to stop it. Whatever it is I've got to stop it.'

He saw that he was speaking with unusual violence, for they both looked at him under their eyelashes and there was an awkward pause when he finished.

'You'd better try it at once, then,' said Lugg practically. 'We don't want the busies coming up 'ere, do we?'

'Very well.' Campion had no idea what he proposed to attempt nor if he could make any serious physical effort without collapsing. It was obviously the next move, that was all.

His programme was unfolding before him like sealed orders and there was only the passionate anxiety raging behind the dark curtain in his mind to drive him on to follow it.

Lugg went over to the inner door and opened it.

'You wait a second while I make sure the coast's still clear,' he said over his shoulder.

Campion nodded and glanced at Amanda. She was looking at him and as he caught her eye she smiled with sudden frank generosity, her eyes dancing.

'The best of luck,' she said. 'You'll do it. How's the head?'

'Fine.'

'Honest? Oh well then, that's all right. I'd back you to get to hell and home again. *"Begone!" she stormed. "Across the raging tide!"*'

It was part of a couplet, of course, and he saw by her expression that she expected him to supply the missing line. It was doubtless some old joke they had shared since her childhood, something he knew so well that it should have come to his tongue without thinking. His mind remained obstinately blank. He could not remember ever having heard the melodramatic doggerel before. Amanda was waiting confidently, all her glorious natural friendliness ready to go back to him. He could snub and hurt her, or explain.

At that moment he saw his choice as clearly as if it had been presented to him in pictorial form, like one of the old morality pictures of the primrose path flanked with gin palaces on one side and the steep track amid the chasms on the other. It would be so easy to explain and so pleasant. Lugg was there to back him up and she was eager, too, forgiveness and intelligent understanding in every inch of her young body. Aubrey could be kicked out of her life as easily as if he'd been a hedgehog in the road. She would be so sorry, so abominably dutifully sorry . . .

He laughed. 'I've forgotten my cue. I'll always be able to get in touch with you at Bridge, shan't I?' he said.

The last thing he saw of her was the smile fading out of her eyes.

XV

'There you are. It's a straight drop to begin with and then you 'ave to start the fancy-work. Can you see anything at all?'

Lugg's whisper came gustily to Campion across the narrow corridor at the top of the old inn. The dark cul-de-sac in which they stood, bowing their heads to avoid the low ceiling, was warm and breathless and possessed a faint smell of dust and old wallpaper. Outside the narrow casement window the night was practically black, but the wet tiles showed occasional highlights under the far-away stars.

'I don't like you going off like this in the state your 'ead's in,' the fat man whispered, 'but I don't see what else you can do, do you? Besides, you can climb like a perishing cat, can't you?'

Campion sincerely hoped so, otherwise the project seemed suicidal.

Lugg touched his arm. 'I've brought this along,' he said, thrusting a package into his hand. 'It's some of that money out of the drawer. It never hurts to have plenty of cash on one. Then there's this little torch. It doesn't give no more light than a pin-'ead. Shade it with your 'and and nobody won't see it. Now listen, when you get to the ground make for the main road and turn down the hill. When you get to the bottom you'll see an archway on your right. There's a sort of alley through there. Take it and go up the steps at the end and there's the station right in front of you. You may 'ave to wait about a bit for a London train, but there's bound to be one for the mail even in these times. I'll sit tight until I 'ear from you.'

He broke off abruptly. Someone was moving very close to them. Heavy footsteps rang out blithely on old boards and someone's sleeve brushed against panelling which might have been directly behind them. Lugg opened the window.

'Out yer get,' he whispered. 'These old places either 'ave walls eight feet thick or a thin slice of canvas between two sheets of wallpaper. Button that old raincoat round yer neck. Pity you left the cap, but it can't be 'elped. Ready?'

Campion slipped through the narrow aperture and hung dangerously over the pit below.

To his relief, his muscles obeyed him miraculously. He was aware of them like a great webbing basket enclosing his bones. The discovery gave him an enormous sense of relief and then of excitement. Ever since he had left Amanda alone with the unanswerable line on her lips a recklessness quite different from anything he ever remembered experiencing before had taken possession of him. He felt so bitterly free, and so much alone, that the night itself seemed to have taken on a new quality. The darkness had become an element, like water or air, treacherous but stimulating. The soft moist wind on his skin was invigorating and his dizziness had gone, leaving him super-sensitive, as though every nerve in his body had become exposed.

Lugg's white face loomed close above him.

'Don't forget,' he whispered. 'Police in the front and the gentry all round the back. Good luck.'

Campion dropped. He landed very lightly on his toes and finger-tips. Good Lord, he could climb like a cat! His own skill astounded him, but he thrust the astonishment away from him in panic lest it should destroy this instinctive efficiency.

The little torch proved invaluable. It shed only a pin-point of light, too small to be detected immediately from the street below.

He edged his way carefully up the sloping pantiles, paused a second astride a gable, and then slid down noiselessly the other side. He went most cautiously, allowing himself to lie full length against the sharp slope and feeling his way with his feet.

He was hanging there, supporting himself with remarkably little effort, when he heard the voices. There were two of them, male, and apparently directly beneath him. He lay motionless, pressing himself into the protecting blackness of the tiles.

The two men were keeping very quiet themselves. No words were distinguishable but the murmur was furtive and secret. Presently one of them spat and, at a whisper from the other, laughed aloud. He cut it off short immediately, but the sound had not been attractive. Campion was not sure that he recognized it but he had a warning instinct that he ought to do so. He gathered that he must be at the back of the building, probably looking down on some sort of semi-enclosed yard.

He hung there for a considerable time, the strain on his arms growing slowly intolerable.

The two men stirred at last and he heard their light footsteps moving away in the darkness. He saw the glow of a cigarette slowly disappearing into the gloom. Once it paused and they seemed to be settling. Campion felt he must lose his grip and come hurtling down on to the cobbles, but the moment passed, the men went on, and soon all was quiet.

Finally Campion let himself down into the guttering and edged along it perilously until he came to a gable and had to climb again. This time he was more lucky. On the other side of the mountain of tiles he came down quietly on to a perfectly good flat roof. It belonged to an old coach-house, reconditioned as a garage perhaps, and it was set back a few feet from a narrow side road. His eyes were becoming more and more accustomed to the darkness, and here, with a comparatively wide expanse of sky above him, he could almost see.

There was no traffic in the road below him, but farther away to the right he could hear an occasional car engine revving as its driver changed gear. That must be the high road and the hill that Lugg had spoken of, of course.

He came quietly across the leads and paused with his hands on the low parapet. Beneath him was pitch darkness, but he could just see a gleam of wet pavement on the far side of the narrow road opposite. There was no movement, no sound, not a step on the stones.

He leant over the concrete ledge and flashed his torch. The little beam was so small that it shed scarcely any glow.

He flicked it off at once. He had seen what he wanted to. Garage, or coach-house, or whatever it was, the roof-high doors were ajar.

Lying on his stomach, with his thighs hooked over the parapet, he leant down and pulled one door wider. It was unexpectedly well hung and moved so easily that he almost over-balanced. He let it swing right back until it rested across the angle made by the building on which he lay and the blank wall of the next house. He waited.

There was not a breath from within, not a whisper, not a rustle.

Far away in the direction of the High Street a girl laughed foolishly as though someone had tickled her and afterwards shouted something which he could not catch, but here, close to him in the narrow alley, there was nothing, only silence and the soft damp kisses of the rainy wind.

He climbed on to the door and began to descend deftly by way of the old harness pegs. He made no sound at all and when his foot touched the paving-stone it was very gently, as if he had been coming down carpeted stairs.

He had just straightened himself when the door moved. It was swung back forcefully as the man who had been standing hidden behind it saw his opportunity and leapt for it. Campion side-stepped him with an instinctive swiftness nothing to do with his conscious thoughts. It was instinct, too, which made him thrust his foot out at the same moment that he struck blindly in the dark. He touched cloth and a hard shoulder beneath it, but the man went down over the outstretched foot and as he fell his cosh rattled in the gutter.

Campion ran and again he experienced a shock of delight in his own freedom of movement. All the unsteadiness of earlier in the day had vanished under the tremendous pressure of this new excitement. His illness had given place to a period of complete irresponsibility, coupled, of course, with the *idée fixe* which had never left him. Physically, he was in perfect training. He moved like a whippet, easily, gracefully, and so lightly that his feet scarcely sounded upon the tarmac.

The High Street was dark and empty, but as he turned down the hill the row started behind him. Shouts and heavy foot-steps echoed from the side-streets, and these were answered by others outside the front of the hotel. He put on more speed so that the falling ground sped from under him.

Someone behind blew a police whistle. He ducked through

the archway, just in time. It opened at his side like a huge mouth and he slid into it. The street was waking up behind him. He could hear cries and shouted inquiries and over his shoulder caught a glimpse of torches.

The lighting restrictions were on his side. His uncanny gift for finding his way in the dark, and above all his tremendous speed, were going to save him if he was lucky. He kept to the wall, found the stone steps, and emerged to find himself just across the road from a railway station. It was the only building in the town not quite in complete darkness and he found the entrance without difficulty. With remarkable presence of mind he took off his torn and dirty mackintosh and folded it over his arm as he walked in. He could hear a train panting in the station, but his ears were still strained to catch any ominous sound behind him. They would find him, of course. It was such an obvious place to come. The police, who never make the mistake of neglecting the obvious, would certainly look for him here, if the others didn't.

The booking clerk put every other consideration out of his head, however.

'Last train just going,' he said, slamming down the ticket and the change on the brass ledge.

Campion snatched it and fled. The collector at the top of the stairs did not wait to clip his ticket.

'Express right through. There she goes. There she goes,' he shouted obligingly as he dragged the other man through the gates. 'Might just do it. Run, sir.'

The train, a great dark centipede with dead eyes, was already chugging away from the platform, gathering speed at every gasping breath. Campion sprinted after it and just managed to swing himself on to the footboard of the last coach.

Ignoring the warning shouts behind him, he got the door of the final compartment open, and, as stale leather-scented air gushed out to meet him, he clambered into a first-class smoker. He had just slammed the door behind him, congratulated himself that there was no corridor, and had flung himself into a corner under one of the small blue reading lights with relief in his heart, when the train stopped with a jerk.

They had caught him. That was his first thought. The police had followed him and stopped the train. He was trapped, caught as surely as if hands were ready on his shoulder. He wondered if they would come up the line for him. If so, perhaps he had a chance if the farther door of the compartment was not locked. It was, of course. At the other window he made the unnerving discovery that the coach was still partly at the long platform. Moreover, there was no time to do anything. Flying feet and raised voices were bearing down upon him. He struggled with the door. At least he could make a dash for it. The darkness was on his side. Nothing else seemed to be helpful, however. The catch stuck and he was a moment wrenching it.

That delay defeated him. As the heavy door swung open a hurrying figure hurled itself in on top of him and as he caught a glimpse of it his arm, which had been upraised, dropped to his side.

'That's all right, that's all right. I'm quite all right. Very much obliged to you. Good night.'

The newcomer spoke over his shoulder to someone in the darkness.

'Good night, sir. No trouble at all. Good night,' an official voice answered deferentially and the guard's whistle sounded down the platform.

The train started with a jerk which unsteadied both men and Campion retired to his corner. It was another belated traveller; that was all. He was making a fool of himself. There was nothing to fear yet. He was still free. He leant back in his seat and closed his eyes. His body was chilled and clammy and he could feel his heart jolting painfully in his side.

The other man had settled himself diagonally opposite and was blowing gently in the semi-darkness. He was small and elderly and seemed taken up with his own near shave.

Campion dismissed him from his mind. There was plenty to think about. There had been no gun-play. That meant that somebody in charge of the crook element had issued very strict orders. In England gun-play invariably entails intensive police interest. It works like a charm. One shot produces forty policemen, endless inquiries, house-to-house visits, and more fuss than a football crowd can ever make over a foul. Someone was determined to get peace and quiet for his activities. Weaver, B.'s munificent offer proved that much, of course, but it was worth noticing.

Campion dug himself farther into the soft, old-fashioned upholstery and considered his chances. The train was an express. That should mean that he was safe until he got to a London terminus. There, of course, the Metropolitan Police would probably be waiting for him if the County Inspector knew his stuff, which seemed highly probable. Well, that could wait. He'd cross that bridge when he came to it. Meanwhile, here at last was a breather, time to think if his mind would work.

With the grim determination of necessity he settled down to make it function. Very carefully he reviewed all the concrete evidence which the last thirty hours had produced. All of it was unexpected and most of it apparently entirely unrelated. Behind it all was this desperate urgency, this passionate instinct for haste. If only he knew the essentials. He was trying to fit together a jigsaw puzzle without knowing what sort of picture the pieces were expected to make. A few of them married, though. Pyne and his Surveys Limited. The professional crooks and the method of Anscombe's murder. These three shapes made a corner, anyway.

Then there had been Miss Anscombe's painfully vivid picture of her brother's last few weeks of life. She had been so clear with her story of the alien, the suspected smuggling under the Nag, and the suggestion that Anscombe had made up his mind to atone in some way.

That picture should fit in somewhere, although at the moment he had no idea where.

Then there were the Masters themselves, the fleet of lorries, Anscombe's sudden decision to draw all his money in cash. Then there was the cash which Campion had brought in to Lugg, the other cash which Weaver, B. had offered, the parcel of cash which Anscombe had forgotten to bring in from the car. Fifteen. Minute Fifteen. The fact that it wasn't a date.

His head reeled and he bent forward and rested his forehead in his hands and his elbows on his knees. The train's wheels grumbled and vibrated soothingly beneath him. It was a pause at any rate, a moment of peace and security in a breathless race through nightmare streets with police and crook alike his pursuers. He felt almost calm, almost at ease.

The other man in the compartment stirred. Campion could just see him in the blue mist which hung over the carriage like dusty limelight. As the young man raised his head the stranger spoke, revealing a deep elderly voice, faintly suspicious as such voices often are.

'I've seen your face before,' he said accusingly. 'Where was that? Aren't you Albert Campion?'

XVI

Campion froze. Good God! Was the whole world after him? *Of course it was.* The recollection came like a scalding shower, shocking him back to reality. Of course it was. Hadn't he killed one policeman and assaulted another? Wasn't the whole countryside being scoured for him? He drew back in the shadows.

'No,' he said huskily. 'No. That's not my name. I don't think we've met.'

'Oh? No? Perhaps not. Perhaps not.' The voice sounded partially satisfied but its owner did not relax. Through the blue mist from the reading lamp Campion took careful stock of this new potential enemy. He was a neat little man, a character. His dark coat was sleek and unobtrusively expensive, but his hat was too large for him and his white hair was untidy beneath it. At the moment he was staring at Campion unwinkingly with unexpectedly shrewd eyes.

He had a small attaché case by his side and a walking-stick across his knees. He looked very English, very narrow, and conventional.

It was quite possible that they had met, of course, in the far-off lucid days thirty-six hours ago. Campion began to feel for a name which he might give if asked point-blank. He saw the danger of that just in time, fortunately. Suppose if out of the dark presses of his mind he fished up some famous name. The only one to occur to him at that moment was Dick Turpin. He had a strong feeling there was something against it, yet it had a vaguely attractive sound.

Fortunately the question did not come but neither did the stare waver. It remained transfixing him, paralysingly steady and confident, for what seemed the best part of an hour. He moved uneasily under it, leaning back in the leathery darkness to escape it, but it did not falter. It had almost demoralized him before he realized that the man was not seeing him but was looking through him into some introspective unknown.

This discovery was a relief, but all the same it was not easy to think of anything else with those intelligent eyes glittering straight at one in the blue gloom. In the end he was forced to speak in sheer self-defence. He was so anxious to be entirely natural that he tried out many openings in his mind and finally succeeded in being gauche.

'Worried?' he inquired baldly, adding at once, as the glitter faded and astonishment took its place, 'I mean, the – er – times are very disturbing, aren't they?'

The other man sat up. He was considerably flustered by the complete lack of ceremony. Campion could have kicked himself. Poor old boy. He was just a successful provincial business man chewing over the troubles of the day. There was nothing sinister about him, nothing to be frightened of. Surely his history as well as his character was written in his face. He looked tired, overworked, weighed down by the responsibilities of his job as the head of some firm or other. He was probably meticulously straight in his dealings, astute, too, in a narrow way, wealthy, and yet beset by problems. In fact, the great British public itself incarnate.

'Yes,' he said at last, having decided to forgive the intrusion. 'Not too easy, are they? I think we must face it that they're dangerous, damned dangerous.'

It was odd how he managed to convey such consternation by saying so little. Campion wondered if his business had been badly hit. He saw it as something to do with wool. A fine old firm, probably generations old.

His own mind was running feverishly on the subject. He wanted the man to talk, to babble on reassuringly about ordinary things; anything, the war, the weather, sport, A.R.P., anything to keep him as he was now, a normal comprehensible fellow human-being and not a pair of fixed introspective eyes in the shadows.

'What worries you most?' Campion demanded, knowing the question was infantile but panic-stricken lest he should escape again.

The old man blinked at him. 'Treachery,' he said.

Campion wondered if he had heard the word. It was so unexpected, so melodramatic. The stranger was looking at him again, too, and the blue light shone in his eyes.

'You find it in your business?' Campion inquired.

'I do.' The admission seemed to be wrenched out of the man. 'I do, after fifty years. Treachery on a vast scale everywhere I look. Sometimes I wonder if my own eyes are deceiving me, but no, it's there and it's got to be faced.'

He was silent and Campion took a liking to him. He looked such a dogged old chap, sitting there with his square hands gripping the stick across his knees.

There was a long pause and then the shrewd eyes rested on the younger man again.

'I could have sworn you were Albert Campion,' he said. 'It must be because I've been hearing about him tonight.'

It came back. All Campion's apprehension of the past few hours returned with interest. He held himself together with an effort and forced his mind to go slow. It was too dangerous to ask questions. The old boy was too sharp. Besides, he had recognized him. The old fellow was not certain, of course. That was the one saving grace. The only hope was to take his mind off the subject and to talk of something else.

Campion searched wildly for a likely opening. What would interest a wool merchant, if the wretched man *was* in wool? Sheep, perhaps? No, that was absurd. He was losing his grip on reality altogether. This was madness. Oh God, what was he going to say next?

The old man leant back in his seat and crossed his short legs.

'We've always fought our wars with money,' he remarked. 'I wonder if it's going to save us now?'

Money! Of course. Campion could have laughed aloud. Why hadn't he thought of it before? Everybody was interested in money. It was a universal subject.

'I don't know,' he said cautiously, choosing the safest lead. 'It's not to be confused with wealth, of course.'

'No,' said the old man briefly, 'no, it's not, but as it stands now, in its present position, it's a very important factor all the same.'

He went on to talk fluently on the aspect of the struggle which evidently interested him. He appeared to be quite sound, but Campion made no attempt to follow him. He heard the voice and that was enough. He was soothed and reassured and it gave him a moment to think. Soon, the train would come into the station. That was going to be a difficult moment. Detectives were almost certain to be there to meet it. They could hardly miss him, although they would be looking for a man alone and might with reasonable luck have only a telephoned description of him. If only there had been time he would have let them take him and have risked the inquiry. They could hardly hang him for murder in his present condition and almost anything would be preferable to this continuous hounding down. However, that was out of the question. He had a job to do and he must do it, at whatever cost.

Amanda came up in his mind and he thrust her out of it savagely.

'The unspeakable peril of forced inflation,' droned the voice on the other side of the compartment. 'The loss of faith in the country's essential soundness.'

Campion smiled at the man and nodded to him without hearing. How comfortingly ordinary he was. What a blessed piece of solid and familiar ground in this new world of quicksands and blackouts. The intelligent thing to do was to stick to him, of course. It would be dangerous in a way, but at least it would ensure that he did not go trotting off to confide his suspicions to the first bobby he saw on the station.

Campion glanced at the man, to see that he had just finished speaking and now rose to his feet purposefully.

What was this? Campion grew cold. Was he going to turn out to be an elderly Chief Inspector after all? Was it a last-minute arrest? Campion seemed to remember having heard of something of the sort long ago. His face must have given him away because the old man was looking at him curiously.

'We're just coming in,' he said. 'Can't you feel us slowing down?'

'Of course.' One crisis was over but another had arrived.

'Of course,' Campion repeated. 'I hadn't noticed. I was so interested.'

'Really? That's very gratifying.' The old man was opening the carriage door and he was laughing a little. 'I'm glad to hear that. Ah, thank you.' The final remark was addressed to someone outside on the platform. 'What's that?'

There was a muttering which Campion could not catch and then his travelling companion glanced over his shoulder.

'I'm afraid there's some trouble,' he remarked. 'The police are looking for someone on the train.'

'Oh?' Now that it had come Campion was himself again. His thin face became wooden and his voice entirely natural. 'What do they want us to do?'

Once again there was a murmur from the official in the darkness. The old man nodded briefly.

'Quite,' he said. 'Very sensible. They've shut off the main platform,' he continued, turning to Campion. 'This last coach is just outside the barrier. The fellow here suggests he takes our tickets for us and we go across the footway to the road. You'll want a cab, won't you?'

'Yes, please.'

'Right. Well then, this is where we part. Good morning to you. I enjoyed our chat. I'm afraid it was all about nothing.'

'Good morning, sir,' said Campion and followed him into the grey darkness.

It was incredible. He had no time to realize his escape. It was like one of those wild rides in a switchback in a funfair. A blank wall looms up in front of the car. Nearer it comes, nearer and nearer, and then when the crash is imminent, when the impact and noise of it is almost a reality, the track swings away, the car swerves sickeningly, the corner is turned, and the delirious journey continues.

He stumbled across the platform, which was littered with goods trolleys, milk churns, and mailbags. On his right, beyond a police-lined barrier, there was all the usual confusion of arrival. The detectives were waiting farther on at the ticket gate, no doubt. Meanwhile his own getaway was made absurdly easy. No one took the least notice of him. The railway official led the old man and Campion followed the pair of them. That was all there was to it.

He thought he saw exactly what must have happened. His travelling companion was obviously a constant passenger on this particular train. Probably he had used it every day for the past ten years or more. Railway servants get to know a man like that and if he is a good tipper will go to endless trouble on his behalf. He must have been in the habit of using the final coach and doubtless this was his regular porter who was waiting to meet him.

They came out at last on to a narrow road on the goods side of the station. The old man's car was waiting for him and he nodded to Campion as he climbed into it. A taxi crawled forward out of the darkness.

'Where to, sir?'

'The Treasury,' said Campion briefly and climbed inside.

The cab moved forward at once. There was no questioning, no delay, no pause at the station gates. He could hardly believe it. He had got away as neatly and smoothly as if he had been a ghost. It was an invigorating experience and he began to feel absurdly pleased with himself. The gods were on his side. He glanced out of the window and saw the chill grey outline of shabby old buildings, piled sandbags, and painted road-signs. The streets were practically deserted.

A sudden thought occurred to him and he rapped on the window. The taxi drew into the kerb and the driver turned to peer through the glass screen.

'Yes, sir?'

'What time is it?'

'Just on a quarter before five, sir.'

'In the morning?'

'Lumme! I 'ope so. Otherwise I've been drivin' back through Einstein ever since the pubs shut last night.'

Campion ignored the pleasantry. He was thinking. Even if he was half-way down the straight to Colney Hatch he yet had enough sense to realize that no Cabinet Minister is liable to be available at his office before five in the morning.

'You'd better take me to a hotel,' he said.

146

The driver, who was in a ferocious mood, shrugged his shoulders elaborately.

'Just as you say, sir. Got any particular place in mind?'

'No. Anywhere will do as long as it's open. I want to shave and get some breakfast.'

The cabby beamed. He was an elderly cockney, with the bright little eyes and thin rodent's face of his race.

'Well,' he said, 'since you're not paying your income-tax for the moment, I see, what about the Ritz?'

'I've got no luggage.'

' 'Strewth !' said the driver. 'I'd better take you 'ome and give you a nice brush-up myself. Sorry, sir, it's the morning air on an empty stomach. What about this place 'ere? You're outside it; that's in its favour.'

Campion looked at the gloomy façade across the pavement. A porter in shirt-sleeves was sweeping down the steps and at that moment a policeman sauntered over to speak to him.

'No.' Campion did not mean to sound so vehement. 'Somewhere more – more central.'

'Right you are, sir.' The cockney was looking at him very curiously. 'It would help me if you'd give me an idea. Can't you think of anywhere you'd like to go, sir?'

'The Cecil would do.' It was the first name to come into his mind and it was unfortunate.

'You're not by any chance Rip Van Winkle junior, are you, sir? The Cecil's been pulled down some little time now. Must be close on twenty years.'

'Oh well, take me anywhere. Anywhere where there's a lot of people.'

The policeman had given up chatting to the janitor and was looking their way. The driver cocked an eye at his face and an indescribably cunning expression flickered over his face.

'You want a nice railway-station hotel, that's what you want,' he said. 'Leave it to me.'

He drove off at a great rate and finally deposited Campion at a great terminus in Wyld Street, behind Charing Cross.

'You'll be safe and comfy 'ere,' he said as he undressed himself to get change for a pound note. 'Cosmopolitan, that's what it is. Lost in a crowd, that's what you'll be.' And he winked as he took the tip.

There was no mistaking his suggestion. As Campion saw him drive off his old panic returned. He had given himself away by funking the first policeman. Of course he had! These damned Londoners were too smart. They saw too much. Their experience of human nature was boundless. Probably even now the fellow was scuttling away to the nearest police station to take a list of wanted persons. That ruled his hotel out and he'd have to go somewhere else. Better not pick up another cab here, either.

He walked away and crossed Trafalgar Square, cutting down behind the National Gallery into the narrow streets beyond. The light was growing rapidly and the great friendly shabby old city was beginning to sit up and stretch itself like a tramp who has been asleep on a park bench.

He found a big tea-shop, finally, and went inside and bought himself some breakfast. The food restored him considerably. He was surprised to find how much he needed it and how much more intelligent he became after eating it. He began to see some things with painful clarity. If he was to get any help from Sir Henry Bull he must get it at once before any news from Bridge reached that distinguished gentleman. That was evident. The thing to do was to get hold of him at once, at his private house. If he turned out to be as worried as Oates had been then he should have the full story and the personal consequences could not be helped. The one vital consideration at the moment was to reach someone in real authority before the police held everything up by arresting him and letting the law take its majestic course.

There was a directory in the telephone booth at the entrance but the name was not in it, which was not extraordinary since public men do not often advertise their private numbers. Campion began to feel his disadvantage again. London confused him. The city had the same effect on him as Amanda had in the beginning. He knew that he knew it very well indeed. It smiled at him and comforted him. But its face was just outside his present powers of memory. Whole streets were gloriously familiar but they had no names for him and no definite associations. His only way of getting about was by taxi. The drivers knew the way if he did not.

It was confusing and it took a lot of time, but in the end he got what he wanted. He accepted his disability and set about circumnavigating it with a dogged patience which was characteristic of him. One cab took him to the nearest public library, where he consulted a battered *Who's Who*. The man was there all right. *BULL, the Rt Hon. Henry Pattison, Kt. created 1911, M.P. Honorary Member of the Universities of Oxford, St Andrews, Leeds. Senior Master of Bridge.*

Senior Master of Bridge. The words stared out of the tiny print at him, enlarging themselves before his eyes. What a fool! What a trebly mentally defective cretin! Of course. Miss Anscombe had told him what he already knew, that the Masters were holding their meeting on the fourteenth. The man must have been there in the very town he himself had fled from. Probably even now he was tucked up in Mr Peter Lett's best bed.

A sense of despair swept over him. He was beset, benighted, hag-ridden by his own horrible insufficiency. The gods were bouncing him on their great knees, saving him one minute, only to dash him within an inch of the abyss the next.

His eye travelled to the end of the paragraph, ignoring the impressive list of highlights in a useful career. The address was there, 52 Pytchley Square, W. He looked at it dubiously. It seemed scarcely worth while going there in the circumstances.

He decided to try it finally, because he could think of no alternative.

He reached the Square by taxi, which he dismissed as soon as he caught sight of the plane trees, continuing the journey on foot. The tall houses looked strangely virginal and unprotected without their iron trimmings. He could not understand what was missing at first, but when it came to him and he realized the reason for this nudity all the old fighting anger returned to his heart, coupled with the now familiar sense of impending disaster and the urge for haste. London's railings, her secret private little defences, were torn away to feed the big guns.

But what was this other danger which threatened her? What was this swift peril which drew so close and which he was floundering so desperately to defeat?

He saw the house across the corner. Very neat it was, and sober, with a polished number on the plum-coloured door and demure net curtains in the windows.

He was bearing down upon it when he saw the two men. One of them rose from the edge of the sandbin where he had been sitting under a tree in the Square and sauntered forward.

Police. Of course. All these public men's houses had police guards these days. Why should he have forgotten that?

He wondered if his description had already been circularized to every plain-clothes man in the country. He wished he were less conspicuous and less shabby from his roof climbing. The man was coming directly towards him. He was going to be stopped and questioned. He could see the fellow's face now clearly and he was grinning sheepishly, blast him. It was a 'fair cop', was it? What should he do? Run for it and have all London at his heels?

It was the little mock salute which stopped him, that and the man's obvious embarrassment.

'Sergeant Cook, sir,' said the stranger, his smile twisting wryly. 'You've forgotten me, I expect. Any news of the Guv'nor, sir?'

The sincerity of his anxiety outweighed everything else. It had a force of its own which was sufficient to kindle an answering spark from Campion's imprisoned mind.

'Oates?' he inquired. 'No, I haven't seen him.'

The man shrugged his shoulders expressively. 'I don't like it,' he said. 'I don't like it at all.'

They stood there for a moment in silence and Campion glanced up at number 52.

'I want to see Sir Henry Bull,' he said slowly, hardly trusting his voice. 'Can you fix it?'

Sergeant Cook gave him an astonished glance and Campion saw that he had made a mistake. Obviously his right move would have been to have walked up to the front door and given his name in the ordinary way. He set about covering his tracks.

'I want a word or two with him in private. I don't have to explain, do I?' he said.

He sounded pretty mysterious to himself but to his relief the Sergeant responded, although he glanced at him sharply under his lashes.

'I get you, sir. There's a side door on the left of the area there. It leads through to the yard at the back. Will you wait in that passage?'

Campion followed him and entered the side gate. He was waiting in the little alley inside when at last the man re-appeared. He came creeping in through the high latticed gate from the yard and beckoned.

'Okay,' he said with some satisfaction. 'Come round this way, will you, sir? Been tailed, sir?'

'I rather think so. Thank you. I – er – I shan't forget this, Sergeant.'

'That's all right, sir. This way.'

They passed through a warm little servants' hall, where a couple of maids eyed them inquisitively, ascended a back stair-case, crossed a flagged inner hall, and finally reached a white-panelled door.

'He's having a late breakfast,' whispered the Sergeant, 'but he's alone. Lady Bull has just left him.'

He knocked and listened.

'There you are, sir,' he added and opened the door.

Campion went into a small bright room which glowed with flowers and smelt pleasantly of coffee. A breakfast table was set in the window and a man in a dressing-gown sat at it with his back to the door. He turned at the sound of the latch and smiled affably at his visitor.

'Hallo, my boy,' he said. 'I half expected you.'

Campion said nothing. The world was reeling dangerously and he felt his scalp contract.

It was the old man he had met in the train coming up.

XVII

The eyes which had glittered so disconcertingly in the blue reading-light in the train were equally shrewd and uncomfortably penetrating at the breakfast table. Campion looked at them helplessly. This was disaster. This was defeat.

He was taken so completely off his balance that he could not trust himself to speak. His lean tight-skinned face was expressionless.

The old man indicated a chair on the other side of the table.

'Sit down,' he said. 'Have some coffee. Don't look at me like that. I know I've been very obtuse.'

Campion blinked. He began to feel impervious to surprise. He sat down obediently but did not dare to open his mouth.

Sir Henry Bull cleared his throat. He looked very uncomfortable.

'You've had a most nerve-racking experience, I don't doubt,' he said. 'Until we got into the terminus this morning I had no inkling of the extraordinary situation. You'll have to forgive me, my boy. You can't teach an old dog new tricks and I admit quite freely that I find it very difficult to get used to this – this transpontine world we suddenly seem to be living in.'

He was quite incomprehensible to Campion, who gave up trying to save himself. His astonishment showed in his face. Sir Henry misunderstood it and laughed briefly in his embarrassment.

'Even the word belongs to another era,' he said bitterly. ' "Transpontine". Over the bridge. Over Waterloo Bridge to the Vic and the Surrey, the homes of melodrama. Blood tubs, we used to call them. That's the world we're living in today. I can't get into tune with it as fast as perhaps I ought. Enemy soldiers disguised as nuns, carrying machine-guns and portable bicycles, descending by parachute. Armed secret societies. Microphones in the walls of railway carriages – it's all boy's halfpenny paper stuff to me still. I can't force my mind to be

152

on guard for its numberless ingenuities. I did no actual harm, I hope. The police got their man, no doubt.'

Campion snatched at his scattering wits and faced the situation. 'Microphones in the walls of railway carriages'? Was it possible that the old boy actually thought . . . ? He did obviously. Having once convinced himself that the world had gone mad, he was evidently prepared to see lunacy everywhere.

The question remained unanswered and the man repeated it. 'Did they take the fellow?'

'No,' said Campion. 'No. Not that it matters.'

'You don't think so? I'm very relieved to hear you say that.' Sir Henry had turned in his chair. He looked an old man, very tired and very anxious. 'I've been going over everything that passed and I realize I said nothing of value. Fortunately my training prevented me from being actually indiscreet. But I do realize I must have put you in a very awkward position. You see, when they stopped the train for me at Coachingford and I found you in my reserved carriage I immediately thought that you wanted a word with me in private. It never went through my head that you were there to look after me and that we might be overheard or overlooked. To be frank, I didn't understand your manner in the least, although it ought to have warned me. Then, when we arrived and the station people told me that the train was being searched, I saw the whole thing in a flash. This Fifth Column activity is incredible. They didn't get him, you say?'

'Not yet.'

'They will.' Sir Henry spoke with satisfaction. 'They're wonderful people. They're probably on his track at this moment.'

'More than probably,' said Campion absently. He could hardly assimilate the facts even now when they were presented to him on a plate, but he forced himself to accept them without question. There was so much to do and so little time.

Meanwhile, Sir Henry was so unused to making mistakes that he was still offering explanations in his own defence.

'I usually stay the night after a meeting of the Masters,' he said, 'but it was imperative that I got back early today, so Peter Lett phoned the station-master and reserved me a carriage.

Then we were held up on the road and I walked on to the platform to see the train starting. They held it for me but there was no time for explanations. I had no notion you were in the compartment until I saw you. I recognized you at once, of course, and then as I say I did not grasp the significance of the situation. I had been hearing from my fellow Masters that you were in the town and I simply thought you wanted a word with me. You see exactly how it happened, don't you?'

'I do,' said Campion. 'Exactly,' he added after a pause. Obviously the Masters had not heard of the assault on Hutch and so far the man in front of him knew nothing of the St Jude's Hospital episode. 'I do want to see you,' he went on hurriedly. 'I want to talk about Anscombe.'

'Anscombe?' Sir Henry frowned. 'Poor fellow,' he said. 'I heard about him as soon as I arrived, of course. What do you want to know?'

'Why did Anscombe die wondering if he ought not to come to you? Why did he convert every halfpenny he possessed into cash and then debate in his own mind if he ought not to come and see you?'

'Did he?' Sir Henry was surprised but not bewildered. 'He was a silly fellow. I've known him for years of course. He was too small a man altogether for his commitments. That's the weakness of these hereditary appointments. Old Anscombe ought to have been secretary of a cricket club, or a church-warden perhaps. I always understood that personal finances were his difficulty. He ought to have been perfectly all right, but his father played Old Harry with the Secretaryship. That income was mortgaged out of hand and the children were left very modestly provided for. Anscombe himself was even more improvident. Between ourselves, we financed him over and over again, but finally we had to put a stop to it. So he converted what little money he had into cash, did he? What was he going to do? Try to make a dash from the local creditors?'

Campion shook his head. 'His sister seems to have had a rather different idea,' he said. 'She suggests that he may have been going to make some sort of gesture. "In expiation" were the words she used.'

154

'To me? Really? What for?' Curiously enough, the suggestion did not seem to strike Sir Henry as entirely fantastic. 'I see you don't understand,' he said. 'The Secretaryship of the Masters isn't quite the important office it sounds. The Secretary is the – how shall I say? – well, the steward of the club and the general clerk of the domestic arrangements. His office is comparatively modern. His main job is to look after the premises. It would not astonish me to hear that Anscombe had done anything. He was a remarkably silly man, one of those theatrical, hysterical types. What did you discover he had done? Filched a pound or two from the petty funds?'

'No, I don't think so. Miss Anscombe wondered if he had allowed the caverns in the Nag to be used for contraband.'

'Really? I can't believe that. That would have been sacrilege. No, I don't think so. I fancy I know where that story comes from. I did hear something. What was it? Lett mentioned it. I think a great deal of wine was actually taken into the Nag some time before the war. It represented a sum of money which was due to us for the sale of our share of a Rhenish vineyard. The money could not be taken out of Germany so we received its equivalent in wine. I don't know the full facts. Our Bursar would tell you that. Anscombe would probably be responsible for the storage of the wine. That was the kind of thing he did attend to. He had nothing to do with the main function of the Brotherhood.'

'Which is?'

'The welfare of our country, young man.' It was an oddly dignified answer, completely unaffected.

Once again Campion took a sudden liking to this canny old man with his dogged stance and the streak of unself-conscious patriotism which showed in him every so often.

'Our principal business is the Institute,' Sir Henry added more specifically. 'That place is a great national possession.'

'National?'

The older man smiled with a deprecation which was very faint.

'The Masters of Bridge are the nation,' he said, unaware of

any naïveté. That is, they're typical of the best of it. Is there anything else?'

'Yes.' It was now or never and the ground was very uncertain. 'Tell me about Minute Fifteen.'

Once the question was out of his mouth the deepest misgivings seized him as he saw astonishment growing in the intelligent eyes.

'Minute Fifteen?' The man was not at ease. He seemed puzzled and slightly alarmed. 'I don't know what I can tell you that you don't know already,' he said at last. 'The whole world will know all about it tomorrow, or I sincerely hope so. As for the details of the publicity, I understand that you were one of the few men who had known about that from the outset. What do you want from me? The financial details of the actual loan? The Chancellor of the Exchequer will be explaining them on the radio tomorrow evening.'

'Why was the loan called Minute Fifteen?' he ventured.

'Ah, I see your difficulty. That *was* confusing.' Sir Henry seemed relieved. 'It wasn't. The Defence Loan had its own name, the Fifty Victory. Minute Fifteen simply covers the plan of its presentation. It was thought wisest to keep that anonymous since it was an innovation and secrecy was such an integral part of it, so it simply went under its own number on the agenda of the Cabinet meeting which approved it. However, this really isn't my pigeon at all. I can put you on to someone if you want details.'

'I don't.' Campion spoke desperately. 'I want to know its exact importance. I mean,' he added hastily, as a flash of bewilderment appeared in the older man's eyes, 'in regard to every aspect of the immediate situation. Has it appreciated or decreased?'

'My dear boy,' there was nothing but grimness in the old face now, 'its success is imperative. I wish I had never used those words before. They're stale and inadequate. We must have no hitch whatever in raising the money. We are edging along such a precipice now that I hardly dare watch, and I am no coward where money is concerned. Use your common-sense. Would we ever embark on a gigantic and drastic project like this, which virtually means that we are putting the British Empire on a company footing, with a personal invitation to every taxpayer to invest his all in it, if it wasn't absolutely vital? The forms which are going out tonight are, practically speaking, prospectuses. There is no other word for them. We're walking on the water. It's only the faith of the man in the street which is going to hold us from going under.'

Campion sat very still. It was coming. Behind the curtain hanging across his mind like an arras something of tremendous importance was trying to shine through. He could feel the emotion belonging to it. It was fear.

'Nothing must go wrong,' he said stupidly.

Sir Henry Bull pushed back his chair. He looked a dynamic figure, his white hair bristling and his long gown flowing round him.

'I said just now that I am never indiscreet,' he said. 'I am not. Both my training and my natural inclination are against it. But I am not made of wood. Now look here, Campion, I have heard whispers. Mind you, they have been little more than whispers, but they have come from most unexpected quarters and they are so terrible that I dare not even think of them. One of my informants named you as probably the only man who knew the full truth of the danger. I am not going to ask you for information, so you can take that blank expression off your face. I cannot and will not believe that the incredible story which I have heard has any reality, but, if it has, Campion, well then . . . the Dark Ages again, that's what it will mean.'

There was silence for a moment or so and then the old man leant on the table and looked full at his visitor.

'I think I can tell you what you're hesitating to ask,' he said. 'It is true that at the moment Britain depends practically entirely on her faith in herself and on her own internal stability. If that could be destroyed suddenly, by a single stroke, there would come confusion, exhaustion, and finally decay. At this particular point in history everything hangs on Britain's faith. Europe is conquered; the New World is not yet prepared. So, should this thing happen, it means that there will come once again the Dark Ages which followed Attila, and tomorrow civilization is a thousand years away. It *could* happen; that is the lesson of this generation. World barbarism is still possible. The Beast is not dead. It has not even slept. All these years it has been lying there watching with lidless eyes. To a man of my age that is the most awful discovery that could ever have been made. That is what you want to know, isn't it?'

The younger man did not speak and his host, with a little twist of the lips which was alarming because his face was not one used to weakness, demanded abruptly: 'How bad is it?' Campion felt cold. His fingers were numbed and there was a chill in the small of his back. His determination to make a clean breast of his own disability, should Sir Henry seem as alarmed as Oates had been, faded before the question in those anxious eyes.

It was the same story. Everyone was turning to himself for assurance. He dared not reveal the dreadful emptiness of his mind. Somehow he must struggle on, blind and half-witted though he was. There was to be no outside help. He was quite alone.

'I don't know,' he said slowly. 'I don't know. These prospectuses, or whatever they are, for Minute Fifteen; they go out tonight, do they?'

'Yes. I can't understand why you didn't realize that. It hasn't been possible to keep the thing a complete secret. Quite a number of important committees, including the Masters of Bridge, who are going to take up large portions of the loan, have had to be prepared for it. I was talking to the Masters on the subject myself last night. Then the Post Offices had to be warned that they will be expected to deal with the enormous traffic, while the local tax authorities have had to put the thing out. So a tremendous number of people know something about it. Only taxpayers will be approached, of course, but that's half the country. It must not fail, Campion. Nothing must happen to make it fail or to . . .' He shook his head. 'That eventuality won't bear considering,' he said.

Campion nodded. He was thinking fast. More corners of the jigsaw were forming, although the whole picture was still obscure. Meanwhile the great missing portion was assuming an incredible shape. He wondered how he could persuade Sir Henry to be more specific. It was not going to be easy. The old man was very quick and already he had been puzzled several times by little exhibitions of ignorance.

Campion thought he knew the man. He was a realist, a believer of facts. A gambler, perhaps, but only in form, and that meant that once he discovered his visitor's mental condition he would never take a chance. Campion saw himself pushed into hospital again and not one word of anything he had to say believed or even considered until the doctors pronounced him lucid. The urgency of the situation would not make any difference to Sir Henry. Campion's disability would simply go down on the debit side.

He was interrupted by the arrival of the secretary, who came in with a word of apology and murmured to Sir Henry for some time in a deferential flow.

'Really?' The old man was surprised. 'Where is he? In the house?'

'In the study, Sir Henry.'

'Oh, I see. Yes, well, I shall have to give him a minute or two. You might warn him I'm overworked, vital information or not. I'll come down.'

As the secretary went out he turned to Campion.

'I'm afraid I must see this fellow,' he said. 'He's a curious product, part genius, part crank, and one of the most influential men in the country in his own peculiar way. One moment he's doing untold service and the next he's trying to advance a hare-brained scheme for running the country. The trouble is one never knows which tack he's on until one's seen him. He's breathing mystery and disaster, Cuthbertson says. Don't go. I haven't finished with you yet. I shan't be more than five minutes.'

He went out. The gentle latch did not quite slip home and the door swung open an inch or two behind him, so that Campion heard his voice as he entered the room across the hall.

'Hullo, Aubrey. What's this "awful warning", my dear boy?'

Aubrey. Campion's hand closed over the door knob. Aubrey. Miss Anscombe. His own attack on Hutch. There was a complete line there. Aubrey had been going to see Miss Anscombe. She must have given him an account of her interview with himself and Amanda. Aubrey would be far too superior to go to the police direct. It would be so like him to attempt to stop the mischief at the head and to warn his distinguished Governor that a lunatic was at large.

There was nothing for it but flight again. It was the only way and this time he'd *got* to get away with it.

He stepped out into the hall and went straight from the house the way he had come. The maids eyed him as he passed them silently, but he nodded to them and walked by with the same odd singleness of purpose which had been his salvation before.

He came quietly out of a side gate, glanced sharply at the detective on the opposite side of the road, and, keeping well in so that he should not be seen from the windows of the house he had left, strode on down the side of the Square.

He was shaking with suppressed excitement. All the facts he had stumbled on in the last thirty-six hours were blazingly vivid in his mind. Minute Fifteen, representing the greatest war loan ever launched, was about to be presented at a time of trembling national emergency personally and privately to every taxpayer by post. That was the pivot. That was fact number one. All round it, gyrating like swing-boats round a tower, were the others. He went over them in his mind. The cases of wine in the Masters' store-rooms. The story of a foreign contraband before the war. The murder of Anscombe just before he 'made expiation', obviously done by professional thugs probably employed by Pyne. The fleet of lorries under the Nag. The small array of well-paid crooks gathered together under Pyne's Surveys Limited. The activities in the Institute. There was something there he could not remember. What was it? Something he had seen with his own eyes and forgotten. The attempt of the Enemy to buy him off when they thought him a crook like themselves, and their subsequent decision to kill or capture him when they discovered who he was.

It was all there in his hand. He held it without knowing what it was. In his blindness he had discovered his objective. In his miserable ignorance he could not identify it.

He must get back to Bridge. That was the all-important factor. It must be now nearly eleven. He had, he suspected, until the provincial post went at about six in the evening, but he had to get back to Bridge and to do that he had to get across the City to the terminus.

Still he had a chance. For the first time he felt he had a chance.

He found a taxi and made the station in twenty minutes. Luck was with him and he discovered a Coachingford train actually waiting at the platform. He entered it in a state as near jubilation as he ever remembered. Amanda was the only dark spot on his horizon and he refused to think of her.

All through the journey he made his plans. It was going to be a near thing and abominably risky, and to get into the Nag by daylight would take some doing when every man's hand was against him. All the same, it had to be done and he had great faith in himself.

When at last the train carried him into the station at Coachingford he was already in his mind hurrying up the Nag's Pykle looking for the narrow passage by the side of the shop which should have sold love philtres. He was so engrossed with his project that he did not see the two plain-clothes men standing behind the ticket collector and did not realize their intention until their hands fell on his shoulders and he heard the strangely familiar form of arrest.

XVIII

Campion sat in a cell at the Waterhouse Street Police Station at Coachingford and prayed. He was a damned fool. He knew that. If only he had at least gone quietly and had given himself a chance. If only he hadn't lost his head in the station booking-office as they were taking him through. He saw himself now behaving like a lunatic, raving, expostulating, saying all the wrong things, citing all the wrong names.

That final attempt to make a dash for it just outside the present building! That had been a mistake, probably the worst of the lot. He was battered and dishevelled now and in the last condition in the world to inspire confidence in anyone, even to the extent of getting a message through to Lugg or Yeo.

They were leaving him here to cool his heels while they made out the charge. At any moment now they would come for him and take him out of this cold, disinfected tomb and march him into a big smelly charge-room, warm with breath and sweat. That was going to be his only chance. God knew what the charges against him were. As far as he knew, they might contain practically everything on the calendar. However, that aspect was trifling. Moreover, it belonged to another world. What was important was the time. Somehow or other he'd got to get out and get down to Bridge immediately.

An obvious idea which had occurred to him coming down in the train was torturing him. Very likely he had not got until the evening. More than likely the lorries had to spread their loads all over the country and were even now setting out on their journeys. England was such a little place. It would take so short a time to fan the poison out all over her lovely petite body.

He had given up worrying about the mystery. The actual facts of the Enemy's attack were still entirely beyond him. Even the identity of the Enemy himself had escaped him. All he knew were those things which were set out under his nose;

the lorries, the date of the launching of the Minute Fifteen loan, the work at the Institute, and the wine cases in the Nag.

He must get out. Oh God, dear God, he must get out!

He was sweating when they came for him. The larger plain-clothes man, the one whose eye he had closed, was not present. The other one, the ratty specimen with the little moustache, gave him a wide berth and left the work to the old turnkey and the enormous young constable who would not normally have accompanied them.

Campion went quietly, meekly. He was so restrained that he felt they must notice that he was shaking and see that his hands were clenched to keep them down. They were all very gentle and so nervy that he guessed that they suspected him of mania. Very likely. God, what a situation! He would be in a strait-jacket with ice on his head when the blow fell, when the Enemy succeeded, when the knife slipped into her little green heart.

He was deferential to the Charge Sergeant. The man was a fool. He saw his great square head with the unnaturally grey face on one side of it nodding over the top of the high desk and was panic-stricken. He could hear the asinine jokes and heavy admonitions before they left the big mouth under the water-fall moustache. Yes, here they came. Here was the Charge Book. Here was the pronouncement.

'Wait,' he said, and was hurt to find that even his own voice was going against him. It sounded strangled and hysterical. 'Get into touch with Lady Amanda Fitton at the Principal's House at the Bridge Institute.'

He saw they were surprised by something. It had not been the name, but the address had touched them. He seized the pause and hurried on.

'Also get hold of Yeo, of Scotland Yard. Find him. Tell him I'm here.'

That made them laugh. Their great grins merged into one huge idiot face, like a mask of comedy on the ceiling of a theatre.

'All in good time, my lad,' said the Charge Sergeant. 'You shall have the Queen to see you if you don't hurry it. Mean-while if you could wait a minute I'll just charge you, if you

163

don't mind. We don't want to do anything against the book, do we?'

The clock with the face as big as a tea-tray leered over the Sergeant's shoulder. One o'clock. There was no time for anything. He must get to the Nag at once, within the half-hour. The big hand moved while he looked at it.

'Send for Hutch,' he implored in panic.

Hutch was at least intelligent. Angry and suspicious he probably was, but at least his mind worked. Perhaps he could be got to see the hideous urgency of the occasion.

'Here, that'll do, that'll do.' The Charge Sergeant was scandalized. 'Superintendent Hutch has quite enough to do without bothering himself about you. If he wants to see you he'll come in his own time. Now then, Albert Campion. You are charged in that you did feloniously utter counterfeit banknotes to the value of one pound at the railway station booking office at . . .'

Campion ceased to hear. He went deaf and blind. A great avalanche of fury at their incompetence descended over him, sweeping away every shred of his control. Good God, they couldn't even charge him with something he'd done! They were going to hold him in this gimcrack police station on some drivelling mistaken or invented charge while the minutes rushed by. The door was open behind him and he did the fatal thing.

As he sprang for the rectangle of light the plain-clothes man seized him. Campion slung him off, pitching him half across the room. The turnkey shouted and the young constable raised a great fist, while a slow silly smile of surprised delight spread over his face. Campion took the blow just under the ear. The force of it lifted him off his feet and sent him sprawling across the boards towards the forms built in all round the room. The rounded edge of polished wood met his left temple with a crack which echoed round the building. He fell into complete darkness and lay still.

*

Albert Campion came to himself in the cell. He gathered where he was at once and sat up on the hard couch, smiling ruefully. A clock striking two somewhere out in the town surprised him and he raised his eyebrows. To the best of his knowledge it must have been round about six in the evening when he had encountered the toughs down at the quayside. It was now daylight, so that if he had been out for round about twenty hours he must have taken a pretty severe blow. How extraordinarily like these country police to bring him into a cell and leave him to die while they found out who he was! So far they must have been singularly unsuccessful, the damned fools, and, while he was on that subject, where was Oates?

For the first time he felt a twinge of anxiety. Oates had certainly been with him. He remembered his own amused exasperation when the shambling figure, really astonishingly unfamiliar in the dirty flannels and threadbare greatcoat, had appeared at his elbow as he stepped out of Lugg's paper shop. Poor old Oates! He had been badly rattled. The thing was getting him down, as well it might of course, but it had been shocking to see him losing his grip and to hear his voice go husky as he admitted: 'I wrote you last night, but I couldn't stick it. I simply couldn't sit up there and wait. I just walked out to see you. For God's sake, Campion, have you got a line?'

Well, he had, and he'd said so and they'd gone on together. The fight had been pretty sensational. Campion felt his head cautiously. Yes, there it was. A very nasty spongy little spot, by jiminy. There must have been five or six in the gang, all pro's and all using coshes, which had been fortunate. Had it been razors he might well have awakened to hear a harp quintet instead of the mouth-organ which some misguided amateur was playing in the street outside.

All the same, it had not been exactly a walk among the apple-blossoms. The money had drawn the gangsters, as he had hoped it would, and he had recognized them. He went over them in his mind. The Lily had been there, and the elder Weaver, and Williams, and the Glasshouse Johns, all C.R.O. boys as he suspected.

Who were the others? He could not remember at the moment.

He didn't feel too intelligent. He felt exhausted and some-how – yes, that was it, chastened. How off! He might have had some deep emotional experience rather than a bang on the head. He longed for a newspaper. He hadn't seen the news from the Front for seventeen hours. Anything might have happened. There was this business, too. The whole thing might have suddenly broken and what had been left of the ordered world be in chaos while he was sitting here.

He laughed at himself softly. He was getting jittery, like poor old Oates. It was having so much at stake, of course. Still, there was plenty of time. There would be no move until Minute Fifteen was about to be launched and that was several days away.

The clock struck the quarter and he admired its chimes. Some of these old towns had lovely chimes. Lovely corners, too. Bridge was a remarkably lovely place if only one could forget the calendars, the picture postcards, the ornamental biscuit-tins which made it hackneyed. Seen for the first time, Bridge must be staggering. Amanda was at Bridge and in a month they'd be married. A dear kid, Amanda. So young. Too young for him? Sometimes he was very much afraid so. His fine thin mouth twisted regretfully. One got so beastly self-sufficient as one grew older and there was the girl to think of. He'd hate to imprison her, to suppress her in any way.

A definite twinge, physical and yet bringing with it a sense of shame, stabbed his heart over. At the same time he saw Amanda in his mind's eye as clearly as if she stood before him. She was looking at him with a sort of stricken astonishment and reciting the first line of that silly old tag they had found together in the *Gentleman's Magazine* for 1860. '*Begone!*' she stormed. '*Across the raging tide.*'

The hallucination was so vivid, the pain in his side so acute, and the sense of self-disgust so strong that it brought him to his feet. He was ill. This blow on the head had affected him seriously. Good Lord! Nothing like that must happen now. Things were a damned sight too serious. Of course they were, because no one *knew*. He and Oates were the only pair on earth who knew the full strength – and it was stupendous when you saw it in the round. It was criminally dangerous; he'd argued that from the beginning. Besides, where was Oates?

He went over to the judas-window in the cell door and peered through it into the empty passage outside. Not a soul, of course. He sighed and, putting his fingers to his mouth, gave a very reliable imitation of a police whistle. Five minutes' intensive effort produced the desired result.

The turnkey, puce in the face with fury, put his head in at the farther door.

'Shop,' said Campion pleasantly. 'Can I see the manager?'

'You'll be lucky if you see fresh air again, my lad. We've had to send Detective-Sergeant Doran to hospital.'

(Hospital? Why should the word send a thrill of terror through him? He was ill, dangerously ill. He'd have to go and see old Todd of Wimpole Street, when he got back. Where had the old man evacuated himself to?)

'I'm sorry for Doran,' he said aloud. 'I can't say I recognize the name. Still, I sympathize with your domestic worries. And in the meantime, do you think you could make an effort to do a little business? This isn't the Central Coachingford Station, is it?'

The turnkey came farther into the passage, looking like a mystified bullpup.

'You've changed your tune, ain't you?' he demanded.

'I'm no longer unconscious, if that's what you mean,' said Campion with gentle dignity. 'And while we're on that subject, as a Metropolitan man I don't like to criticize your County arrangements, but, just to soothe my curiosity do tell me, when you bring in a concussion case do you usually leave it for the best part of a day and a night without medical attention?'

The turnkey gaped at him, his small eyes bewildered.

'You're crackers and you're impudent,' he said. 'That's what you are. You won't get anywhere by putting it on either. Shouting for a doctor now, are you? You'll be lucky if you see a magistrate the way you're going on.'

Campion, whose face was pressed against the narrow slit in the door, frowned reprovingly.

'Just clear your mind,' he said. 'Save a little time by using the brain with which I see a kind Government has issued you. Which of the five Coachingford police stations is this one?'

'Waterhouse Street. You know that as well as I do, or ought to, after the way you tore the road up coming here.'

'Really? It's that sort of concussion, is it? Bits of bone sticking in the grey matter. My hat, you don't look after your professional guests, do you? Have you left me here since last night biting buttons off the furniture?'

'Being difficult won't pay,' said the turnkey and turned away in disgust.

'Let us hope Superintendent Rose will accept your diagnosis,' Campion murmured, reflecting that it was better to mention the regular police Superintendent rather than the C.I.D. man. What was his name? Hutch, was it?

'Superintendent Rose?' The name appeared to have certain magic properties. The turnkey was hesitating but at the last moment some new consideration appeared to make up his mind for him. 'Superintendent Rose doesn't bother himself with snide-panners who beat up plain-clothes men. Besides, you've only been in an hour and a half. What d'you think this is – a quick-lunch counter?' he said and went out, locking the door behind him.

Campion was astounded. He had always found County Police particularly intelligent. This type of crass idiocy was new on him. The clock outside chimed another quarter hour and he cursed it. It had lost its charm and was now irritating. The whole thing was really damnably unfortunate. Besides, he'd got work to do. There was that date with the C.I.D Super to go over the Nag, and he wanted to have a look at the Institute.

He had discovered the main game, he was sure of that. He had told Oates so, definitely. He lay down on the hard bed and began to rearrange his mind. He seemed to have the afternoon before him. Oates – and where was he, by the way? – had the wind-up. That was very unlike him and argued that he must have had the importance of the thing pretty hot and strong from the Cabinet itself.

Well then, to return to business. When Oates had borrowed him from Headquarters and had first come out with this staggering tale of thousands of counterfeit notes, so perfect that 'one has to boil them down to detect them', he had said that he thought the scheme was on a colossal scale and might actually be aiming at some sort of sudden unofficial inflation, which would of course pitch the country's whole economy into hell, destroy public confidence, pull down the Government, and, if issued at the right moment, bring about the moral collapse of the nation. Since Britain, as usual, seemed to have nothing absolutely ready save her morals, the danger had seemed terrifying.

As he lay looking at the little barred window high in the wall, Campion reflected that so far he had been inclined to doubt the possibility of the scheme being so enormous. Oates had shown him the notes which had been found in two or three industrial towns. They had certainly been cracking good forgeries and could have been manufactured only in the official printing houses of an enemy power. Moreover, and the ingenuity of that move still took his breath away, they had been artificially dirtied most ingeniously.

Oates had put various picked men on to the job in different towns. All of them had drawn a blank save the man at Coachingford. He had reported the presence of some sort of crook organization, either in the town or at Bridge. Poor chap, he hadn't got much farther. They'd fished him out of the estuary with a broken neck. It had been professional work, very neat and nasty, done with a lead pipe as like as not.

Campion stirred uncomfortably. There was something curious about that killing, something personal and near at hand. What was it? There was something on his mind that kept escaping him. It was probably nothing important but he found it irritating.

That damned clock again. That was a quarter to three, he supposed. He dismissed his irritation and went on dreamily with his reminiscences. Well, Oates had borrowed him and sent him to Coachingford. Amanda had got them both an invitation to stay at Bridge with Lee Aubrey, who was brilliant, he supposed. Everybody said so. Personally he suspected these academic dreamers. Still, let that pass. He had instated old

Lugg in the town with a stock of the counterfeit and some old clothes. Then he had spent half a day at Bridge making arrangements, had come into Coachingford, changed into a tramp's outfit and had gone off reconnoitring.

That had been an experience he would never forget. All the subversive element in the town was in a ferment. 'Blokes were giving away cash – great wads of it.' All the riff-raff of the place had been turned into a great greedy bulging-eyed secret society, getting rich quick as quids were handed to them behind doors, in doss houses, over greasy coffee-tables.

This had been a discovery, but it had been followed by another one. He had discovered that a whisper was going round to the effect that the great day was coming on the sixteenth. That was going to be milk-and-honey day, the day when it was going to be everybody's duty to spend and the wherewithal was going to be miraculously provided.

That had been a peculiarly uncomfortable discovery because the sixteenth was to be a red-letter day in other, more orthodox financial circles. On the sixteenth the Minute Fifteen Defence Loan was to be presented to the public. There was no doubt about it, the whole affair was alarming. If it was by any staggering chance as bad as Oates thought it was then it was hair-raising.

Leaning back on the bench Campion reflected on his subsequent actions. For a long time it had been impossible to locate any of these munificent agents and he had finally decided to take the bull by the horns and appear himself as one of them. That had drawn the flock. The whole bunch had turned up together, as he had known they would. Both he and Oates had been able to get a good look at them. They had made quite an impressive gathering and it had occurred to him then that it had taken someone with a real flair for organization to get that crew together.

Then there had been the fight and the police had come up. He remembered very little of the action save the sticky paving-stones of the quay and the awful mud-coloured water, thick with scum and rubbish.

Since the police had no idea who he and Oates were, either,

they had been extraordinarily lucky to get away alive. That was why it had been so criminally dangerous for Oates to have come down and taken part himself. Suppose they had both been put out, then what might have happened? Of course, if Oates's theory of engineered inflation had anything in it at all he was justified in trusting as few people as possible, since any whisper of such a disaster might very easily start a scare nearly as bad as the thing itself. Good God, it was a horrible idea!

Campion pushed his hands through his hair and shivered. All the same, now he looked at it in cold blood he still maintained that the enormous scale of the plan as Oates saw it must be impossible because of the difficulties of distribution.

As long as the Enemy stuck to his present method of doling the money out by hand to the vagrant population the whole affair could be dealt with by the police. But a decisive blow of the kind Oates envisaged would demand instantaneous distribution of the stuff all over the country. Campion did not see how it could be done without the co-operation of the public. After all, the public had got to be induced first to take and then to spend the cash. It just was not possible. It is notoriously difficult to give away money by cash in the street. Generations of ordered living had taught the ordinary citizen that there is something very fishy and dangerous about banknotes which are not paid for in blood and sweat. No, the thing as Oates foresaw it could not happen, not on that scale, thank God.

And yet . . . yet . . .

He got up and walked irritably up and down the cell. This knock on the head was serious. It was having an extraordinary effect on him. The clock chiming another quarter sent an unexpected and unwarranted thrill of pure despair through him. Why was that? What the hell was the matter with him? There was a burden on his shoulders. Self-disgust leant on his arms. His feet were heavy with grief. Misery and the utter wretchedness of failure clung to him. This was terrible. This meant he was a . . . what was it? Manic depressive? Something like that. Perhaps he ought to try and sleep it off. After all, he must not go sick now. Today must be the fourteenth, by jove. And the sixteenth was the zero-hour. However, since he had located the actual men engaged the round-up should not take long. Fortunately the police had a few new powers under the Emergency Laws. They could finish this thing off quickly and release him to his work again. Perhaps there would be time to get married in the interim, if only . . . If only what?

Once again there was that physical tug at his heart, again that overwhelming sense of self-disgust, and again a definite picture in his mind of Amanda herself, hurt and puzzled, waiting for the other lines of a doggerel couplet. It was mania all right, obviously. Some variety of mental kink, probably irritatingly well known. The sooner he got himself out of here and put himself into the hands of a reliable doctor the better. All very well to be gallantly negligent about a sore thumb or a lump on the skull, but mental trouble was a different caper altogether.

It wasn't going to be very easy to get out either, with this peculiarly obtuse specimen on the door. He must have been taken in completely by the vagrant's outfit; that and the money, of course. Those two taken together would be a difficult pill for any honest copper to swallow.

He glanced ruefully at his clothes and made a discovery which took him completely off his balance.

He was not wearing the suit in which he had had the quayside fight.

He stared into the cloth of his trouser knees and wrenched at the inside pocket of his jacket to find the tailor's label. It was his suit all right. He recognized it and knew too that it should have been hanging up in a wardrobe in his bedroom in Lee Aubrey's house in Bridge. Moreover, it was a new suit according to the date on the label, yet as he looked at it now he saw that it was dirty and crumpled and showed signs of having had hard wear for some little time.

The jolt to his nervous system was tremendous, the mental equivalent of a gigantic thump between the shoulder-blades. Then a frightful misgiving crept up close to him and laid its cold cheek on his heart. He had been here some time. How . . . long?

Out in the town the clock struck again, announcing that yet another quarter of an hour had passed.

XIX

He saw Amanda through the judas-window. She came walking into the passage with the turnkey, completely un-selfconscious and comfortably serene.

'Hullo,' she said cheerfully as she caught sight of half his face through the slit. 'They phoned your message to me, but they won't let me bail you out.'

'What message?' The question was in his mouth but he did not put it. His eyes had narrowed and his thin face wore a startled expression. The instant he had seen Amanda it had come to him that something revolutionary, he was not at all sure that it was not evolutionary, must have taken place within him. He had grown old, or seen a great light, or else his blundering feet were on the ground at last. He thought he knew what it was all right. The symptoms were unmistakable. That sense of exasperated shame, that desire to kick himself or to cover his eyes with his great burning ears, all these indicated that his self-confidence had received a dangerous blow. A great weakness must have been uncovered. His misgivings increased and he remained staring at the girl through the judas-slit, with his eyes fixed and his forehead wrinkled.

Presently he realized what it was that he found so puzzling. He had known Amanda since she had been a child and yet now there was something new about her. He found out what it was. He was seeing her through some sort of mental curtain. His subconscious mind reached out for this infuriating barrier and drew it slowly aside like a wet page.

The complete picture lay before him.

He saw it all in a single dreadful moment of revelation. The whole kaleidoscopic history of the last thirty-six hours, painted with pitiless clarity and minute detail, unfolded before him in all its stark gravity; a mad, uncomic strip with himself wandering blindfold through it like a lost soul.

Then, as his two minds and personalities merged at last, as

the new Campion's witless discoveries fitted over the old Campion's certain knowledge, the three-dimensional truth suddenly sprang out in blazing colours. He stood petrified. Good God Almighty! He knew now what the contraband was in those cases which the wretched Anscombe had been bribed to accept as honest Rhine wine! It could only be a counterfeit, the artificially dirtied indetectable counterfeit itself. Millions and millions of pounds' worth of lies and disruption. Anscombe had been murdered because he was preparing to salve his conscience and to confess to the contents of those packing-cases. Probably he intended to hand over his own small fortune in cash to the Treasury by way of a gesture after his confession.

Then there were the lorries. They were for the distribution, obviously. How this was going to be done, and what the magic password was which would make the sober, suspicious British public accept and spend this dynamite, was still a mystery. But the time, the hour of striking, was not. Anscombe had given that away by mentioning Minute Fifteen. Today *was* the fifteenth, and they were not going to wait until tomorrow. The hour was now. Perhaps this very minute. It had all come back to him. He knew where he was. He knew what he had got to do.

The danger was stultifying. His body winced inside. A year, six months, even three months ago such a gigantic project would have been fantastic, but tonight, in this beleaguered England, with all the tides of a new and diabolically astute barbary lapping at her feet, the plan was a sound weapon and it was poised squarely at her heart.

Panic possessed him and all but choked him. The time was almost gone and he was piteously helpless. He pressed his face to the judas-window.

'Amanda!'

'Yes?' She smiled at him quickly, reassuringly.

Campion took careful hold of himself and strove to compress and clarify the message he had to give her. Time had become as precious as a little drop of water in the bottom of a pannikin in the desert.

The clock chiming across the street was pure medieval torture.

174

'Look, my darling,' he said, aware of the state of affairs between them, aware of his loss and its magnitude and thrusting it out of his mind because of the racing minutes and the disaster ahead, 'I've got to get out of here immediately. Listen, Amanda, there was some sort of scrap on the quayside before I got into that hospital. One or two people may have got beaten up in it, but that's not the point . . .'

' 'Ere, what are you saying?' The turnkey was very excited. 'I'll 'ave to ask you to repeat that.'

Amanda ignored the interruption. She leant forward to catch anything Campion might have to tell her.

'Oates was with me then,' he said distinctly.

He saw her brown eyes widen and a flicker pass over her face.

'Where is he?' he went on desperately. 'I've got to get out, Amanda. I've got to get out and go down to the Nag immediately.'

'Yes, I see,' she said briefly. She turned on her heel at once and the turnkey had to hurry to keep up with her. She went so quickly that her going might have been desertion. The turnkey certainly put it down as that.

He came back a moment or so later, carrying a police memorandum. He was inclined to be amused by Amanda's exit, but very soon the description of the wanted person took up all his time and intelligence. He was a type mercifully rare in the Force, but every great organization has its minor blunders. He sat on the long bench which ran down the corridor wall opposite the cell and spelt out the points line by line. At every fresh item he got up and came over to peer at his victim through the slit. He was studiously deaf to every remark addressed to him and frequently returned to the beginning of his task, having forgotten how far he had got in it.

Campion began to suffer the tortures of the damned. The war, with all its noisy horror as he knew it in the battle zones, was very close to him. He could see and hear it over Britain, not merely as air raids but as invasion, and then, as well as these, he saw the whole country suddenly hit in the wind by an entirely unexpected blow. The magnificent jingle from the end of King John came into his mind: *'Come the four corners of the world in arms and we shall shock them. Naught shall make us rue if England to itself do rest but true.'* 'But true'; there was the talisman, there the strength, and there the danger. 'But true'. But confident of her own solidarity. 'But true' . . .

Oh, God, let him get out! O sweet sanity! O ultimate honesty and the final triumph of the best! O faith in good as a force and an entity, let him get out in time!

The turnkey began to read the description again with cross-reference.

'Yeller 'air . . . yeller 'air. Six foot two inches . . . well, just about. Very likely. 'Ere I say you in there, 'ow tall are you?'

'Yes, yes, that's a description of me.' Campion's voice was shaking with his effort to control it. 'I admit that. Don't worry about that any more. Now look here, this is serious. This is a million times more important and more urgent than any air raid siren. Either fetch me the most senior officer in the building or let me use the telephone at once. This is vital. Do you understand? It's so vital and so urgent that if you don't do it it won't much matter if you've discovered grounds for an arrest on that bit of paper or not. If you don't bring me someone in authority immediately I don't think you'll wake up in the same world tomorrow morning.'

'Threats, eh?' said the turnkey with idiot satisfaction. 'I'll 'ave to report all that. You want to be very careful what you say, my lad. This may not be the East Coast, but even so you can't be too careful these days. Fifth Column, that's what we're looking out for all the time.'

'Listen.' Campion's hands were sticky on the door of the cell. 'I want to make a complete statement. I'm entitled to have a detective-sergeant take it down.'

'In good time. In good time you shall have one of His Majesty's judges listening to you,' said the turnkey without stirring. 'In half a minute I'll take your statement myself.'

This was a form of torture new to Campion. The Ordeal by Fool might well go down in the calendar, he felt. He swung away from the judas-window and walked down the cell. His agony of exasperation was so acute that it was physical, catching him in the throat and diaphragm, pressing on them until he could scarcely breathe. He sat down on the bunk and stared at the stone floor. His mind began to work over the situation feverishly. There was the plan itself. That was simple and terrible. There was only one last secret there: how was this devilishly convincing counterfeit to be distributed in sufficient quantities and in sufficiently short time to do the work of destruction? It was just possible that this snag had not been entirely overcome. If so, there was just a chance of salvation still. Yet it was madness to hope for a mistake or a weakness in the Enemy. That was absurd. That was criminal.

The clock chimed again. Each note beat through him in shivering pain. Outside in the passage the turnkey had risen and was peering at him through the judas-slit.

'Slim build . . .' he was muttering. 'Slim build.'

Campion's mind scurried on, tearing at the knots with nervy, unsteady fingers. His head still hurt him considerably and he felt weak and physically unreliable, but there was still a great reserve of raging nervous energy boiling within him. Everything was startlingly clear. What he did know stood out in bright colours. What he did not know was defined and impenetrably black.

The whole scheme must have been Enemy Alien in the beginning; so much was obvious. The neatness and ingenuity of the arrangements all pointed to the same diabolically competent organization.

He went back to the judas-window and peered out at the policeman. As his eyes rested on that square, well-padded head, with its bald spot and fringe of oiled grey hair, it came to him with an overwhelming sense of finality that there was absolutely nothing he could say or do which would be of the slightest use.

Now that he had the whole picture in his mind he could see his own mistakes standing out like enemy flags on a map. That dash for freedom after they charged him, that had been suicidal. He knew from long experience of the police and their ways that nothing he did after that would make one ha'porth of difference. He knew what they were doing. They were letting him cool off. The more noise he made, the more he argued, the longer they would leave him. It was maddening, like being held at bay by one's own dog.

He had closed his eyes while he swallowed the inevitable and he stood now with his hands resting high up on the inside of the door and his blank face held to the judas-slit. There was no sound. Nothing concrete disturbed him, yet presently his eyes flickered open eagerly and he stood watching without moving.

The turnkey was sitting on the bench with his head raised and a foolish, startled expression on his face. His eyes were fixed on the farther door, the one which led to the corridor and the charge room, and he too was listening intently.

Campion realized that there was a judas-window in the farther door also and someone was watching the pair of them through it. It was a moment of intense excitement. Hope leapt up in him and he forced himself to hold his tongue. After what seemed an age of indecision the turnkey blundered to his feet and went to unlock the door.

Campion's fingernails cut into his hands and his mouth was dry. So much depended on this silly little question. So much. An Empire? Perhaps a civilization. All depending on who came into a prison corridor.

His first despairing impression was that the man was a stranger. He stooped to pass through the doorway and he was wearing a scarf wrapped round the lower part of his face. As he lifted his head, however, Campion knew him. It was Hutch.

The scarf took Campion off his guard. He knew quite well what it must be protecting but he had not expected it. He had not only never meant to hit so hard, but in his present three-dimensional world the whole notion of doing such a thing at all savoured of madness.

It was the clock again which pulled him together. Its fifteen-minute chimes must have been a torture to any prisoner at any time, but to Campion they had become a scourge.

'Hutch,' he said softly.

The man came over to the door and looked in through the window. He did not speak and his blue eyes were very bleak.

Campion took a deep breath.

'I must have a word with you,' he said quietly. 'I know there's a hell of a lot to explain. I've been walking around punch-drunk for the best part of two days. However, you shall have chapter and verse for everything in an hour or so. But just at the moment there's something that's got to be done. We've got to go to Bridge. We've got to get to the Nag at once. My dear fellow, you needn't let me out of your sight.'

Still Hutch did not reply, nor did he alter his expression. Desperation made Campion very quiet and almost conversational.

'I can give you any bona fides you need,' he said. 'My S.S. number is twenty-seven. I've been lent to Chief Constable of the C.I.D. Mr Stanislaus Oates. The work we're engaged on concerns Folio 6B and Minute Fifteen, but it's so damnably urgent now that I must insist . . .'

Hutch stepped back from the judas-window.

'For God's sake, man!' Campion's cry came from his soul and to his relief he heard the lock. The door swung wide and he stepped out to confront the Superintendent, who was still regarding him with a curious expression on the half of his face which showed above his muffler.

Campion opened his mouth to speak, but got no further. Hutch had turned to the wall and was scribbling a line or two on the back of an envelope taken from his pocket. The message was enlightening.

'Just located Oates. Has been St Jude's Hospital unconscious since Tues. night. Has been under police guard in error. Was thought to have killed copper in street fight on quay. Police here b. fools. Oates just come round and Doc says thinks out of danger.'

Understanding came to Campion. Of course! That explained it at last. The policeman and the nurse and that incredible conversation he had overheard from his bed in the huge deserted ward. They could never have been talking about himself. They must have been discussing poor old Oates, who was probably lying in a little private room leading off the main ward. Now he had his wits about him that much was obvious. When a police constable watches a man in bed he watches him from a chair at the foot of that bed and does not stand about in a passage. Yet it had all seemed very convincing at the time.

Hutch was still scribbling.

'Lady A found him. Sent for me. You can leave here when you like. We'll square this lot. Understand it's urgent. She's outside with the car.'

'Is she?' Campion leapt to the door. 'You'll want twenty or thirty armed men,' he said over his shoulder. 'Bring them to the Nag at once. It's desperate. What's the time?'

'4.50.' Hutch wrote the figures and Campion had to step back to look at them.

'What's the matter with you?' he demanded as the oddity of the proceeding suddenly occurred to him.

Hutch gave him a slow sidelong glance and his hand began to move again.

'You've cracked my ruddy jaw, blast you,' he wrote. 'Get on with it. I'm following.'

XX

Campion stepped out of the comparative calm of the police station into a world of exuberant speed. A tremendous wind had sprung up over the town, and low-lying clouds, like shoals of enormous blue-black sharks, swam across a brilliant sky. There was rain coming and the air felt damp and soft and exciting. Everywhere, from the scraps of waste-paper cart-wheeling down the road to the flying patches of alternate sun and shadow which flickered over house-tops and pavements, there was an impression of desperate urgency, of superhuman efforts to be quick.

The car was at the kerb with the engine running and, as he appeared, the door swung open to meet him. Amanda slid out of the driving seat and handed over the wheel.

'That's good,' she said with characteristic understatement. 'I say, God bless Hutch. That man hasn't a grudge in his make-up, Albert. Rather a mercy in the circumstances, of course. He came at once when I phoned him from the hospital and Oates did the rest.'

Campion climbed into the car and slammed the door.

'You found Oates pretty quickly,' he remarked as he let in the clutch.

'Well, naturally.' She was astonished. 'You told me where he was. Why didn't you part up with the information before?'

'I hadn't got it.'

'I thought you said he was with you in a fight before you went into hospital yourself? You were all right, you see, but he was knocked out completely. No one recognized him, as of course they wouldn't, and it was assumed he'd killed the copper.' She shot a dubious glance at him from under her eye-lashes. 'Anyway, he's conscious and he's recovering,' she added, 'but he's practically out of his mind with worry. They were having to hold him down in the bed when I came away. He told me over and over again to impress it on you that every

181

moment mattered. Turn here. We've got to go down to the paper shop.'

'What for?'

'A message from Lugg,' she said calmly. 'I got him to go over to the Nag at once. I went straight to him when I left you. We didn't know what you wanted done there, so he's just going to scout round and phone the paper shop if there's anything to report.'

Campion looked at her out of the corner of his eye. She was sitting placidly beside him with her slender brown hands folded in her lap. She might have been a self-possessed sixteen-year-old going to a race meeting. Her heart-shaped face was serene and her brown eyes clear and level. There was no telling what was going on in her mind. He must have taken her for granted for years now. The reflection sprang up in his head and shook him off his guard.

'That was remarkably bright of you,' he said, and knew as soon as he had spoken that it was not so. Amanda always was bright. There was nothing remarkable about it. Amanda was God's own gift to anyone in a hole and always had been. He seemed to have become too used to it. However, she was entertained by the compliment.

'Praise is always welcome,' she observed, grinning at him. 'Nothing fulsome, of course. I say, it's pretty serious, isn't it?'

He nodded. 'Not so hot. Time's short. That's the shop, isn't it, over there?'

'Yes. You wait. I'll get the message if there is one. Keep the bus running.'

She was out before he reached the kerb and he watched her disappear into the dark entrance between the empty newsboards. As he sat waiting the familiar chime of the fifteen-minute clock reached him from across the house-tops. Fifteen minutes: Minute Fifteen. It was a ridiculous little coincidence but, once it had occurred to him, he could not get it out of his mind.

Fif-teen min-utes. Min-ute Fif-teen. Hur-ry hur-ry. Ding-dong. Ding-dong. Late. Late. Late. Late. Late.

He counted the strokes. Five of them. Too late,

He *was* too late.

The sudden and startling reflection came like another revelation. He felt as if he had just opened his eyes to find that he was staring down into a well. Good God, he was not going to pull it off! Hutch and his men could never get there in the time. The secretly unthinkable was actually going to occur. They were going to lose. The police, including himself, were licked. The ultimate disaster was going to come off.

'I say, don't look so terrified. It's bad for morale,' said Amanda seriously. She had come back without him seeing her and now settled down beside him. 'This is where we travel faster than light,' she announced. 'Lugg did phone, ten minutes ago. It was a message for you and the shopkeeper had the presence of mind to take it down verbatim. I'll read it to you while you concentrate on the road. He says "The hornet's nest is round the back of the hill on the old coast road. I expect you know that but they are. A railing over the entrance to the hill cave has been took down and I see several hundred jams inside." Is "jams" right?'

Campion nodded. 'Rhyming-slang. Jam-jar equals car. Go on.'

Amanda continued obligingly, the message gaining in piquancy from her clear, well-bred young voice.

' "All our friends are there. Not half they are not and some more. There is strong signs of a move any minute now. The local rozzers have an idea that it is all some kind of Government work, but it cannot be with all that gang on board or I am barmy. Have hid myself in garden of empty house bottom of coast road right side of hill. If you want to catch them, which I take it is what you are after, you will have to put your skates on. I am about as good as a bucket of nothing here alone." '

Amanda folded the sheet and thrust it in her jacket pocket.

'Of course he is, poor old tortoise,' she said. 'Coming from him, that's by way of being an S O S, isn't it?'

'I'm afraid so.' Campion was taking the last of the town at speed. He had had some wild journeys on this road to Bridge, which was so anonymous and difficult without its signposts, but this evening, with the yellow sun streaming behind him and the dark flying shapes overhead, it had an entirely new quality. For the first time for what seemed a lifetime he was in full possession of all his senses and the condition seemed to have its disadvantages.

For one thing he was acutely aware that Amanda was beside him. Her share in his recent nightmare was very vivid in his mind. He remembered, too, exactly how he had reacted to it. In his lonely and terrified ignorance she had emerged as a necessity, a lifeline, heaven-sent and indispensable. Now, with the full recollection of a long and sophisticated bachelor life behind him, and the most gigantic disaster of all time looming just ahead, he was startled to find that she remained just that; static and unalterable, like the sun or the earth.

The recollection of her confidences concerning Lee Aubrey made him feel physically sick. He had been in love, he remembered, many times. This was not much like it. To say that he was in love with Amanda seemed futile and rather cheap. To lose her . . . His mind shied at the idea and his body felt cold.

'Hurry,' she said at his side. 'Hurry and we'll do it.'

He shook his head. 'Sorry, old lady,' he said heavily, 'but to be honest I'm terribly afraid we're sunk.'

'What?' She sat bolt upright in the seat beside him, her back stiff and her eyes scandalized. 'But I say, Albert,' she said, 'you *must* pull it off. Oates made it so clear. He said everything depended on you. You can't say you're afraid we're sunk. You've got to stop it somehow. Everyone's relying on you. You can't fail and go on living.'

Campion frowned and a faint colour spread over his face.

'Oh, stow the heroics,' he said unpardonably, because he was wretched. 'Some things are impossible, and for poor old Lugg and me to stop three hundred crook-driven lorries without police assistance is one of them. I can't even appeal to the local Bridge police because the chances are that as soon as they see me they'll pounce on me and stuff me in jug again. It's all very well to be an optimist, my beautiful, but one doesn't want to be a dear little nut, does one?'

'Nonsense,' said Amanda, unperturbed and without resentment. 'All it means is that there are times when one has to do a miracle. This is one of those. You think one up.'

Campion did not answer. The request seemed to him to be unreasonable. He allowed himself to think of Amanda for a moment or two. This attitude of hers was typical. She never had and never would get it into her dear head that anything was impossible. Her optimism was childlike and unbounded, her faith in himself embarrassing. At the moment she was exasperating. Things could hardly be worse. Time was certain to beat him. If he was honest with himself, he saw no way round it.

Unless . . .

An idea slid into his mind complete.

He sat gripping the wheel while the suggestion turned over and over in his head. It was wild and probably suicidal, but it did contain one very slender thread of hope.

'Are those gates where the sentry stands the only entrance to the Institute?' he inquired.

Amanda cocked an eye at him. 'None of those sentries would ever stop *us*,' she said, catching his thought. 'There's only three of them. They take it in turns and they've all seen us about with Aubrey.'

It was like her not to ask any questions. As usual, her only concern was to further the project whatever it might turn out to be.

Campion took hold of himself. Losing Amanda was going to be like losing an eye. Life would be a little less than half itself without her.

Meanwhile, however, the car was speeding down the narrow roads. The wind roared behind it and overhead the dark blue clouds streaked out across the sky like dirty finger trails. It was a wild ride, leading directly towards almost certain catastrophe. The rain in the air, the urgency of the wind, the tremendous drama of the skyscape, were all a fitting part of the great central situation. A spiteful energy rose up in Campion and he trod hard on the accelerator. If he was to go down it might as well be scrapping.

He drove straight to the Institute and, leaving the car outside the gates, went in past the sentry on foot. It was a ticklish moment but it went by successfully, Amanda creating a heaven-sent diversion by attempting to turn the car in a space six inches wider than its length. He left her graciously accepting both advice and assistance.

Five minutes later he came back, walking very fast. He was a little white round the cheekbones and he carried himself very carefully, but the new recklessness was still there and when she relinquished the wheel to him he took it eagerly.

He drove into the town with unusual caution and stopped at the top of the Pykle, the hill looming up over them dirty and grey in the evening light.

'You take the car,' he said urgently. 'Go and find old Lugg and tell him from me to get Hutch to block the coast road both ways as soon as he comes, at the same time avoiding the actual entrance to the hill. No single lorry must get out. When both barricades are up they can play Annie Laurie or something else appropriate on a police whistle, but not before. The one thing that really matters is that no lorry gets by.'

'Right.' She nodded and took the wheel again. 'They probably won't get here in time,' she said, catching his eye. 'You've got a scheme in case of that, I take it?'

He grinned. His head was very sore and the prospects were about as bad as they could be.

'I've only got a lucky bean plus a profound and lovely faith in myself,' he said.

She echoed his expression, her eyes as affectionately derisive as his own.

'Then I'll pray,' she said cheerfully. 'Good-bye. See you at dinner or in the Elysian Fields.'

Campion hurried. Keeping one hand in his coat pocket, he swung down the narrow passage beside the little old-fashioned shop under the Nag where Hutch had taken him. It was not an easy journey to repeat in daylight, especially when any delay was certain to be disastrous and one was not at all sure one had not dreamt one's directions in the first place.

He found the store-room door standing wide and walked straight in, nodding briefly to the startled boy who stood weighing dried fruit in the back of the building. The fatal thing, he realized, would be to lose his way. One moment's hesitation and he betrayed himself instantly.

He strode on, hoping devoutly for the best, and plunged down a dusty aisle lined with tea chests and bulging sacks of cereals. He heard the boy moving behind him, then a new step on the boards and a lot of whispering. He was going to be stopped. Now, at the eleventh hour, he was going to be held up, caught like a mouse, in a damned grocer's shop.

There was a bundle of long, old-fashioned soft brooms hanging from a hook in the ceiling and he snatched one of them. The door leading into the Masters' domain was unlocked, as before, and when he went through it he took the broom with him and wedged it between the door panel and the angle of the opposite wainscot. It was not a very effective barrier, but it would certainly hold the door against the most determined shoulder for a minute or two, and it seemed most unlikely that any longer period was going to matter very much.

Once inside in the dark a new difficulty presented itself. He had no torch. Everything in his pockets except his cigarettes had been taken from him at the police station and was probably hanging up now in a little official bag outside the cell door.

He began to climb in the dark, praying against giddiness and keeping one hand tightly clasped over the thing in his coat pocket. He was desperate with exasperation at his own slowness. Every moment counted. Every minute which galloped by might be the one which made all the difference between success and failure. His journey across the Council Chamber turned out to be a crawl through hell. Once he cannoned into the table, the hard wooden edge missing the burden in his pocket by inches, and all the time the seconds were racing by.

He found the farther door after what promised to be complete defeat, by observing a minute sliver of light showing just beneath it. He got it open, to discover that the corridor within was lit by a hurricane lantern standing at the entrance to the first of the Masters' store-rooms. Although Campion was profoundly relieved to see it from one point of view, it presented another danger. He had no desire to run into anyone before he reached the Nag's Trough.

He went on, still with the same cautious haste which demanded every ounce of nervous discipline he possessed. His eyelids were sticky and his muscles hard and bunched against his bones.

There were lanterns in every vantage place and the damp stone had dried round them, indicating that they had been burning for some time. A great change had come over the Masters' store-rooms. The packing-cases were empty and the great caverns in confusion, as if an army had been at work there. There was so much debris about, so many dark corners and unexplained machines, that he hardly dared move, convinced that at any moment a living figure must detach itself from the chaos and bar his way.

He pushed on, feeling like a hurrying snail with all the world depending on his speed. The iron ladders required very cautious negotiation in the half-dark and he had his precious coat pocket to take care of during the descent.

He came down into the last narrow passage without being seen. Here the fumes of gasoline were almost suffocating and the throb of revving engines made the very heart of the hill vibrate.

He edged on towards the right-angled bend which would bring him out on to the ledge overlooking the whole Trough. At least some of the trucks were still there, although by the sound they were on the point of moving. The police could never have arrived in time, and even had they done so there could hardly have been enough of them. No one, not even Hutch in war-time, could conjure up such a large army of police at five minutes' notice.

He turned the right-angled bend cautiously and looked out into the Nag's Trough. It made an amazing picture. The only light in the high cavern came from the masked headlamps of the vehicles themselves, so that the lorries and vans looked like great black humped insects trembling on a lampshade. There appeared to Campion's horrified eyes to be thousands of them, all loaded to capacity with bursting sacks.

He kept flat against the dark wall of rock and edged farther along, so that he could get a glimpse of the entrance round the protecting screen of the natural rock partition.

When at last he was able to get an uninterrupted view his heart jolted violently. There was sacking curtain hanging over the single exit of the coast road, and the foremost truck was stationary a good twenty feet away from it. If he could do anything he was still in time.

The whole place was alive with people but voices were kept down and the roar of engines predominated. It was a ghostly inferno of a scene. He knew the trucks and vans must all be loaded up with financial dynamite, freight far more dangerous than ammunition. It was the counterfeit all right, that much was obvious, but inasmuch as its form of presentation and distribution was still undiscovered it remained a secret weapon, its degree of danger known only to the Enemy.

Campion strained his eyes through the gloom. Exhaust fumes were rising all round him and he was beginning to feel their effects. Was that Pyne in the far corner over by the sacking curtains? He thought it was. The man was calmly checking trucks over on a time-sheet as if he had been running a goods yard.

The fumes were growing worse up in the roof. Campion felt himself swaying and he put out his arms to steady himself. The sudden movement must have caught the attention of someone in the crowd below, for a shout went up and immediately the wide beam of a powerful torch began to rake the ledge on which he stood.

Campion made up his mind. He had no idea what the effect of his solitary 'lucky bean' might be. From the beginning it had only been a forlorn hope, but now the time had come to take the risk.

As the torch beam came nearer he drew the little steel egg from his coat pocket and pulled out the pin. It had been really disgracefully easy to steal it from Butcher's workshop. That had simply been a question of walking in and lifting it from its rack in the cupboard. The whole proceeding could not have taken more than five minutes.

The phoenix egg nestled wickedly in the palm of his hand. Below him the trucks trembled and steamed. The torch beam was within a yard of him. He threw up his arm and stood spread-eagled against the wall.

'I hope you're praying,' he said grimly to Amanda wherever she might be, 'because this is our first attempt at a miracle and it's got to come off.'

The egg sailed through the air to the goal he had chosen for it, low down on the left-hand side of the entrance to the Trough. At the same moment the torch beam got him and he dropped forward on his face as a bullet spat at him.

The next moment the world pancaked. It was no ordinary explosion. Campion's immediate thought was that Butcher was another of those damned maniacs with a passion for under-statement.

There was very little noise, but it was as though some gigantic animal had placed its lips to the entrance to the Trough and had sucked in very sharply, only to blow out again immediately afterwards. There was a rumble and the exit to the coast road disappeared under several tons of earth and limestone sliding down from the Nag. The roar of fire followed as a score of petrol tanks exploded and the whole of the upper half of the cavern became a mass of flying paper.

Campion scrambled to his knees. Blood was trickling into his mouth and his body felt as if it had been through a clothes wringer, but he was alive and, as far as he knew, unwounded save for the bullet graze across his face.

Below him, in the bowl of the Trough, there was a sea of blazing petrol and paper and the fumes of smouldering sacks. Millions of envelopes covered the place like a fall of brown snow. Injured men swore and died under their lorries, while others fought each other in their attempts to clamber on to the ledge. But the ladders which were normally used for this purpose had been smashed to matchwood and the bare sides of the rock provided no foothold.

Campion gathered up a handful of the letters which were still fluttering down over him as the hot air winnowed them up from the bonfire below, and, using every ounce of strength left in his body, he crawled painfully towards the mouth of the passage.

Hutch and his handful of men found him at the foot of the first iron ladder as they came swarming in through the Masters' store-rooms to investigate the explosion, which had shaken the town. The sergeant and the constables went on at once to do what they could for the temporary staff of Surveys Limited trapped in the horrors of the Trough, but the Superintendent sat down by Campion on the stones and they looked at the envelopes together.

There is something unspeakably shocking about a very simple idea which, as well as being elementary, is also diabolical.

Both Campion and Hutch were highly sophisticated members of a generation which has had to learn to steel itself against ever being astonished by anything unpleasant, but there was a streak of frank bewilderment in both their expressions as they glanced at each other across the handful of envelopes.

The plan by which false inflation was to have been induced overnight in the most civilized island in the world was an exquisitely simple one. Each of the envelopes was of the familiar Government colour and pattern. *On His Majesty's Service* was printed across the front of each in the standard ink and type, as was also the black frank-mark, the familiar crown in the circle. Each envelope was, in fact, exactly the same as any of those others which were being circulated officially in millions on behalf of Minute Fifteen.

By the light of the Superintendent's torch Campion opened one of the packets. It was addressed to a Mr P. Carter, 2 Lysander Cottages, Netherland Road, Bury-under Lyne, and it contained seven of the spurious and artificially dirtied bank-notes, as well as a buff-coloured printed slip, the text of which was masterly in its uncomplicated wickedness.

'The Ministry of Labour, Whitehall, London, S.W. SRG. 25039.

Dear Sir/Madam,

'The enclosed sum of £7 os od. has been awarded to you on the War Bonus Claims Committee's recommendation,

'This money is paid to you under the arrears of renumeration for Persons of Incomes Below Tax Level Board (O. in C. AQ430028), as has been announced in the public press and elsewhere.

'Note. You will help your country if you do not hoard this money but translate it into good immediately.

'R. W. Smith,
'Compt.'

The second envelope was directed to a Mr Wild, or Wilder, of 13 Pond Street, Manchester, 4. It contained a copy of the same slip and four of the counterfeit notes.

The third should have gone to a Mrs Edith somebody of Handel Buildings, Lead Road, Northampton, and contained, beside the familiar slip, nine pounds in spurious notes.

The addresses explained the scheme to the two men and they shivered. It was very obvious. Someone had simply got hold of the registers belonging to the various social service schemes functioning in the poorer districts of the industrial towns. These would contain between them the names of most of the permanently unemployed, those who had ever received help from State or local bodies, and all those thousand-and-one poorer folk whose names and addresses had ever been tabulated.

Campion held his breath. It all pointed directly to Pyne again. Lists of addresses of that kind would be just the thing in which Surveys Limited would have specialized. More than probably millions of addresses like these constituted the firm's main stock-in-trade. Many of them would be out of date, of course. The main bulk was bound to be damagingly correct.

The central idea lay revealed in all its destructiveness. Vast numbers of needy folk in all the poorer parts of the country were suddenly to be presented with a handful of money and instructions to spend it. The evil genius of the proposal lay in the fact that the windfall was to appear to come directly from the one authority from whom the recipients would accept money not only without question, but also with the dangerous assumption that it was in some inexplicable fashion their right to receive it.

As soon as Campion saw the scheme in its simple entirety he realized the overwhelming fact that in such circumstances the only thing any Government could hope to do was to admit the notes as legal tender and accept the consequences, however terrible they might turn out to be. It would be quite impossible to take the money back.

The practical arrangements had been a miracle of efficiency. The money had been inserted in the envelopes by a machine. The trucks were obviously due to spread out all over the country, posting their 'Government mail' at main post offices all over the West of England. By synchronizing the plan with the launching of Minute Fifteen at a time when the authorities were prepared for an enormous influx of official letters, the G.P.O. was to be neatly tricked into rendering vital assistance and ensuring that the secret blow would fall at the same moment in every part of the land. The earlier, clumsier method of distributing the money must have been in the nature of a try-out to test the actual currency itself.

Campion wiped his face, which was still bleeding slightly. He felt sick with relief. Hutch leant close to him and his eyes were questioning. Campion guessed what he was asking and as suddenly knew the answer also. The whole vivid procession had brought them directly to Pyne, and Pyne was not convincing. The principal thing about him, the thing that overshadowed everything else, was that he was first and foremost an ordinary commercially-minded business man. There was no passion in him, no fanaticism, no emotional driving force. As a full-blown enemy agent he seemed unlikely; as a Quisling he was frankly absurd. From first to last he had behaved like a business man undertaking a delicate job for a client, and in that case who was his principal? Who was employing Pyne? Who was it who had carried this half-prepared plan of the enemy's through to within an ace of success? Who had discovered the presence of the counterfeit and had then, either with or without direct contact with the enemy country, put the whole diabolical scheme into existence? That was the question.

The answer seemed to be contained in another. Who had the facilities for acquiring and accommodating a large army of local volunteer labour to address 'Government envelopes'? Who would have had access to sufficient petrol, real or synthetic, to propel so many lorries?

Sir Henry Bull's description of Lee Aubrey came back very vividly to Campion.

'He's a curious product, part genius, part crank. One moment he's doing untold service and the next he's trying to advance a hare-brained scheme for running the country.'

XXI

Campion leant against the wall in Lee Aubrey's gracious, comfortable study and considered the scene before him. It was one of those lucid, almost contemplative moments which sometimes arrive in the very heart of a crisis. Just for a moment he saw the whole history of the plan and its defeat in the round, as if it had been a play and this present moment the final scene.

The picture in front of him might easily have been on a stage. It was so brightly lit, so tense, so painfully dramatic. The room was very quiet. The two constables on the door stood stiffly. The distinguished company, with Oates himself in the middle looking like a grey corpse which had begun to fidget, was anxious and constrained. Sir Henry Bull, who had just arrived from London and was now surrounded by most of his fellow Masters, was glancing at the documents over which Hutch's Chief Inspector and an M.I.5 man were presiding.

The cupboard beneath the high bookcase stood open. So did every drawer in the room, as the squad of trained men methodically packed and docketed the papers they were taking away.

Lee Aubrey himself stood on the hearth-rug with a plain-clothes man on either side of him. He looked astonished and faintly irritated, but there was no trace of alarm in his big-boned face and he was certainly far less gauche than usual.

It was the importance of the men which made the scene unique in Campion's experience. There was a note almost of domestic tragedy about the situation. It was like the disowning of the eldest son, the disgrace in the regiment, the expulsion from the school.

The Masters of Bridge were angry and horrified but also deeply hurt and ashamed. Even the police were not triumphant.

'The evidence against that fellow Pyne, who was killed, is of course conclusive,' said Oates to Sir Henry. He spoke softly but included in his glance the thin, scandalized man who was Aubrey's solicitor and had only just arrived.

Sir Henry nodded grimly without speaking.

'I think there is no doubt that he must have been the moving spirit,' the solicitor was venturing timidly when Aubrey interrupted from the hearth-rug.

'My dear chap, don't be an ass,' he said. 'I employed Pyne because, not only was he obviously the right man for the job, but he had the right kind of organization at his fingertips. He was doing his work very efficiently until he was stopped.'

'Take care.' Oates turned on the man sharply, his haggard face unusually grim. In the background a detective-sergeant had begun to scribble in his notebook unobtrusively.

Aubrey's colour darkened and he threw out his long arms in an awkward gesture.

'My dear good people, this is all too absurd,' he said, his deep pleasant voice flexible and persuasive as ever. 'I'm perfectly willing to reserve my defence as you all advise so magnificently, but there's no point in making a mystery of the thing where none exists. It's quite *clear* what I've been doing. For heaven's sake see those fellows at my desk handle the green folders with care, because they contain the one vital scheme of government for this benighted country at the present time. I had to be unorthodox in my methods of forcing the Government to take it up, I admit that, but it was a case of necessity.'

'Good God, Aubrey, do you realize what you're saying?' Sir Henry's face was as white as his hair.

'Yes, Bull, of course I do.' The Principal of the Bridge Institute was at his most gently superior. 'A great deal of the blame is yours. You made a very dangerous mistake last year when you failed to understand the importance of the financial scheme I put up to you then. All these Social Credit fellows, and Keynes and the rest, they have glimmerings of the idea, but they're none of them sufficiently drastic or far-reaching. My plan would have put the economic life of the country on an entirely new basis. Since I could not get a government to see reason by argument I realized I had to put them in a position in which they would be only too glad to listen to me. I had to smash their existing economy and create a chaos in which they would automatically turn to the one man who could save them. That's perfectly clear. There's nothing difficult to understand about that.'

He was leaning against the mantelpiece now, lecturing academically from what he clearly felt to be an infinite height of intellectual superiority.

'Poor Campion here, who probably believes he's done his duty,' he continued, 'in reality he has betrayed his country and probably civilization by his interference. I had the whole little ingenuity completely in hand. It wasn't out of control. I knew Feiberg quite well. I met him in Frankfurt years ago. Quite an interesting mind. Extraordinarily meticulous over detail. I knew he was a Nazi agent when he turned up here, and in fact I think I probably suggested to him that the store-rooms in the Nag would be an excellent place for his counterfeit. I may have mentioned too that the Masters were taking their money from the Rhenish vineyards in wine instead of cash and pointed out that such a shipment would give him a perfect opportunity to get his stuff into the country without query. I certainly put him on to Anscombe. I knew that man would be reasonable if properly approached. There's nothing to get excited about in that. I allowed it to happen because I knew it was perfectly safe. Last August I knew we had nothing to fear, because no foreign power on earth could have got the plan into operation once we were at war. I knew it was coming and Feiberg did not. He did not believe we should fight so soon. I saw that the money arrived and when war came I arranged for Feiberg to be interned. That left me with a weapon in my own hand if I needed it. I did not use it until I really was convinced that there was no other way. Then I saw that something had to be done, to be done quickly, and my plan was the only solution. So I found the man Pyne, who chose his own assistants, and through him I arranged to engineer the greatest crash in history, so that in picking up the pieces I could restore a decent order at last. You're following me, of course?'

They were. The whole room was hanging on his words with sick fascination. The old solicitor was in tears. He was an honest man with a wide reputation. He sat down abruptly in a corner and wiped his face again and again.

'God bless my soul,' he was ejaculating in a soft regular monotone. 'God bless my soul. Good Lord. God bless my soul.'

Oates leant forward in his chair. He looked a very sick man and was out strictly against doctor's orders.

'You had the envelopes addressed at the Institute by voluntary labour?' he said. 'That enormous undertaking was organized by a woman, wasn't it?'

'Mrs Ericson?' A flicker of kindly regret passed over Aubrey's face. 'Yes, she did all that for me and did it very well. She hadn't the faintest idea why I needed them, of course. She's one of those intense people who are simply very gratified in having a job to do at all. She made a religion of being discreet in the matter, as I knew she would. Pyne and his fellows, on the other hand, were arranging a private pool to clean up a packet on the crashing markets. That shows the different temperament. The mere fact that they did not think I knew, and they imagined they were being disloyal to me, satisfied the criminal streak which I recognized in them at once and made it safe for me to use them. They're both examples of what I mean by choosing the right people for the right job. It's a gift and an art. My whole scheme of government is based, virtually speaking, on just that main essential.'

Sir Henry passed a stubby hand through his hair. His lips were grey. He looked very tired.

'You have not explained the part you were to play in this new government of yours,' he said.

Aubrey turned on him. He seemed taller and leaner than ever, but there was a fire in his pale eyes.

'I should have to have exactly the same power in the country as I have here at the Bridge Institute, of course,' he said. 'That surely is obvious. When there is so much of passionate importance to be done quickly and ruthlessly then the man in charge must assume full responsibility.'

As his voice ceased there was such a breathless, such an electric silence in the room, that the undertones of the pronouncement hung in the air. To Campion it was the most ghastly moment of them all. The man was brilliant, able and in his own limited sphere doubtless extremely useful, yet as he stood there, smiling faintly at them, his mistaken belief in his own superiority cut him off from reality as completely as if he were living in a coloured glass jar.

He was utterly unaware of the enormity of his sin. He believed implicitly that he alone was capable of directing the Empire and had been fully prepared to destroy the whole structure of its economic life in order to get into command.

The men who had trusted and admired him remained looking at him and the same thought was in all their eyes: 'This is not even the stuff dictators are made of, but this is the kind of madness which is often not found out until it is too late.'

Campion pulled himself away from the wall and edged his way out. He had had so much emotional strain in the last three days that this final and objective example was too much for him. He felt physically ill. The house was alive with police. In the drawing-room across the hall a woman was crying wearily, her sobs sounding above the steady rumble of the interrogating officer. He guessed she was Mrs Ericson.

He pushed on through the plain-clothes men, the influential friends, the M.I.5 personnel and the Home Office experts and went out of the front door. It was another clear bright night with visibility nearly as good as day. The constable on duty on the door saluted him with such spontaneous deference that he knew he was already a nine-days' wonder in the West Country police force. He strode on across the grass, drawing the clean night air deep into his lungs and enjoying the moist wind on his skin.

Presently Amanda joined him. She materialized at his side as he passed under the shadow of the house and they walked on for some time without speaking. Campion had been thinking of her steadily for some hours. Ever since the answer to Hutch's unspoken question had come to him so decisively in the Masters' store-rooms, her reaction to the affair had haunted him. The present situation was irretrievable as well as being so miserably awkward that, had she been anybody else in the world, the only possible thing to have done would have been to hurry back to one's job immediately and concentrate on other things with one's eyes, ears, and heart shut. Since she was

Amanda, however, and not just an ordinary woman with whom one happened to be in love, that was not possible. She did not seem anxious to talk herself, but there was no constraint in her manner. She had taken his arm, as usual, and seemed content to wander and speculate much as he was doing.

They walked on for so long that his thought had time to settle and crystallize and become almost impersonal.

'I tell you one thing,' he said suddenly. 'Even if he hadn't turned out to be this particular kind of lunatic you would never have married him.'

'No,' she agreed frankly. 'No, I wouldn't.'

He looked down at her and caught her grinning to herself. It was an unexpected reaction and he wondered if the light was playing tricks.

'Are you laughing?' he demanded.

'Only at me,' said Amanda with typical if devastating honesty. 'Go on.'

He looked ahead of them at the great silhouettes which the trees made against the moonlit sky. There was something on Campion's mind and he intended to say it, not because it might comfort her – if she was human and female it would probably infuriate her – but because she was Amanda and her education was important. She ought to know it and it might help some day.

'In spite of his brilliance and his staggering conceit, which throws his whole vision out of focus, that chap is a type,' he began abruptly. 'Did you ever notice that woman Mrs Ericson?'

He thought he heard Amanda catch her breath. Then she chuckled. There was no other word for that murmur of mingled amusement and relief.

'Of course I did,' she said. 'I'm terrifically relieved you saw it too. I mean if you're trying to explain that Lee has a habit of making extravagant passes at people and conveying that he's hopelessly in love with them, so that they'll respond and he'll have the flattering experience of declining their affections with sweet sympathetic understanding, I know about it. I don't think he works it out like that, of course, but it just keeps happening to him and one side of his mind finds it a delightful surprise to him every time while the other side attends to the machinery for making it come off. I was the complete mug. I was awfully surprised.'

How like her. Not 'I was wounded.' Not 'I was furious.' Not 'I was wretchedly degraded.' Just 'I was awfully surprised.'

'When did all this happen?' he inquired.

'Just before I brought old Miss Anscombe to see you at that pub. I was going to tell you, because I was rather full of it, and – oh you know how one is – rather sore and embarrassed. But it didn't seem to be quite the time for intimate revelations. You were a bit peculiar yourself, if you remember.'

Peculiar! He did remember. He remembered her face, too, hurt and bewildered as the idiotic couplet hung unfinished between them. Another thought occurred to him and he turned to her in consternation.

'You had to come back here. I sent you back.'

'Yes, I know,' she said, 'but it had to be done. Besides, it rubbed the whole thing in until I really did understand it. He enjoyed it so. I did get the whole thing clear and I *was* here when they phoned from Coachingford Police Station, so it was worth while.'

Campion put an arm round her and held the small circle of her shoulder-bone. For the first time in his life he felt completely adult. His hesitancy, his qualms, his intellectual doubts seemed suddenly the stuff of his childhood.

'Let's get married early tomorrow,' he said. 'I've only got thirty-six hours' leave. A message came through tonight. I ought to have this conk on my head looked at too. It's time we got married.'

'Yes,' said Amanda, who never bothered with illusions. 'It's time we got married.'

They went back to the house to get hold of Oates, who could probably fix any licensing difficulty. Just before they reached the door Amanda turned to Campion.

'I'm sorry I boxed your ears,' she said, 'but you flicked me on the raw. You weren't quite like yourself, either, you know.'

'My good girl, I was nuts,' he began and hesitated. It was no good. He just did not want to tell her the full extent of his recent disability. The dreadful revelation of his helplessness and his need for her was still a vividly remembered pain.

Amanda waited a moment and finally laughed.

'Get it right this time, then,' she commanded. ' "*Begone!*" *she stormed. "Across the raging tide!"* '

Campion grinned as the delightful cockney rhyme returned to him. He pulled her towards him.

' "*Dear Jove! Why did I go?*" ' he quoted accurately, and kissed her as he finished with triumphant satisfaction the ecstatic Victorian anti-climax, so apt and so absurd, ' "*I should have stiyed!*" '